THE BASTARD PRINCE

Dragonspeaker Chronicles Book 1

PATTY JANSEN

GET FREE EBOOKS

CHAPTER 1

FOR SOME PEOPLE, a fiftieth birthday was a cause for celebration. A life well lived, a caring family, children and grandchildren aplenty, and golden years during which one was treated with respect.

For Nellie, her fiftieth birthday was none of those things.

She got up early because there was work to be done. She dressed well, if inelegantly, putting on many layers of clothes because it was cold in her little room on the ground floor of the palace where the servants lived and worked. It was only slightly warmer in the kitchen, but on a busy day like today, people would walk in and out through the back door to deliver supplies for the banquet. When it was windy, which was most of the time, the gusts came right off the Saar delta, and that was a big chunk of water where the wind picked up biting cold air and cloying humidity.

She pulled the blankets and sheets of her bed straight and put the Book of Verses back in the drawer of her tiny bedside table where she had forgotten to return it after prayer last night. She shut the door to her clothes cupboard and turned down the wick to the oil light until the flame went out.

Phooey, it was pitch dark in here.

In the corridor that ran from the servant rooms to the kitchen, it already smelled of pudding and sweet cakes, even if the Regent Bernard's banquet in honour of the sixteenth birthday of his son was still more than two days away.

Her coat hung on the hook outside the door to her room. She took it off, stuck her arms in the sleeves and tied up the belt in front.

In the kitchen, a woman yelled, "It was supposed to be here yesterday! What are you doing? What are we going to feed two hundred people if you can't get it here on time?"

Nellie cringed.

An upcoming banquet brought out Dora the cook's legendary temper.

She treated each menu-related mishap as an assault on her reputation and yelled twice as much as usual at the kitchen workers.

Mountains of work waited for anyone who dared enter the kitchen. *Get more firewood; pluck those chickens; scrape those carrots.* Nellie knew it all too well. It was hard, thankless work, and with each season that passed it grew more tiring, but it kept Nellie warm and out of the poorhouse.

Before she joined the madhouse, though, she had an even less enviable task to perform, and she needed to hurry.

She stuck her hand in her pocket. Her fingers met the thick paper of the envelope, which she'd put there when she could no longer stand looking at it sitting on her bedside table.

On the front, in curly letters, it said, *Miss Cornelia Dreessen.*

Nellie snorted every time she saw that. Nobody in

their right mind called her Cornelia. Except perhaps the shepherd, when he needed to address her formally in church—which wouldn't happen until the day she died and then the only people who would hear it were the very few who cared to come to her funeral. The name belonged on a headstone.

The letter came from the office of the solicitor who had worked for her father when he was still alive and working for the church, and had been written by her father's old solicitor. The letter inside the envelope—which had been delivered by a mail boy when she was working in the kitchen a few days back—had only told her a day and time that the man wanted to see her. Nothing about the reason.

It worried her. What did this man want?

She walked through the dark hallway.

A biting cold wind lashed her face when she let herself out onto the steps. Fuzzy grey clouds chased each other over the choppy surface of the Saar delta. A seagull floated in the sky, not even needing to flap its wings to stay in the air. A sole fishing boat made its way across, sails billowing and sprays of water blowing over the bow.

Bastian, who collected the scraps from the kitchens, fed them to the pigs and chickens and took the animals to the slaughterhouse, was just arriving at the yard with his cart. The wind blew all his grizzled hair to one side.

He greeted Nellie with a wave of his hand.

Nellie pulled up her shawl, walked down the steps and left through the side gate. It led to a narrow alley that ran past the side of the palace—and the laundry door—to the forecourt and past the stables that were neatly swept for the impending arrival of banquet guests from out of town.

At the marketplace, farmers sold the last of the autumn's harvest from a few rows of cloth-covered stalls. A cheese vendor stood watch over droplet-laced cheeses, hands deep inside his pockets and stamping his feet.

It was a worry to see, this early in winter, that the wares were already sparse and poor in quality. The apple season had been poor, and a hailstorm in early autumn had damaged the fruit. A couple of chickens for sale resembled wet rags huddled together on their perch.

With all the bands of rogues roaming the countryside, the only produce that came into town was that from the farms surrounding the city.

There were no more Estlander sausages, those hard and salty ones full of spices. The seller of pickled peppers and dried fruit from warmer climates had stopped coming months ago, because he couldn't get enough produce, and even if he did, it was too expensive for most citizens to buy.

Dora still made the Regent's cakes with juicy raisins, but Nellie hated to think what he paid for them.

Nellie passed the stately houses of the merchants and other well-to-do people in town, many of whom would come to the palace tonight. She walked past the big church where the doors were still closed. Once this horrid meeting was over and the day's work done, she would go to church, but she preferred to attend the smaller church near the harbour. It was a nicer place, and she liked the shepherd there.

She went through the main street that led to the harbour front, to her destination: the office of the old man who used to be her father's solicitor and whom she hadn't seen for many years.

She did not have enough possessions to justify using a solicitor. Even when her father still lived, this man had never spoken to her.

"Maybe you're inheriting money," Dora had said when Nellie told her about the letter a few days ago.

But Nellie had already considered that and discounted the possibility. Her father died six years ago, and he had never been rich. He worked for the Church of the Triune as an accountant. She was certain that all matters to do with money, including those of the church, had been dealt with soon after his death. Her mother died a few years later, but she had lived with her sister and that side of the family were even less well-off. They'd never owned a house and possessed no more furniture than what Nellie had given to her aunt in return for looking after her mother in the final years of her life.

"You worry too much," Bastian had said about the matter, while eating his soup at the kitchen table.

"I don't know what you don't want me to worry about," Nellie said. "This letter scares me. I don't understand what this man wants from someone like me. I have nothing to give him and know no one with influence or money."

"There be only one way to find out," he said in his typical pragmatic manner.

And true to his word, Bastian never worried. He came to pick up the scraps, and he'd feed them to the pigs or chickens. Day in, day out, whatever the weather, whoever sat on the throne, people in the palace would always eat food and there would always be scraps. His job was as dull as it was reliable.

Nellie tried so very hard to take his advice not to worry about the letter, but she couldn't.

Once she'd been a maid to the queen; she'd worn fine dresses and she'd eaten beautiful food. Then, one day, it was all gone. Things could change so quickly.

She had already lost so much, and couldn't stand the thought of losing even more.

And during that walk through the city, she worried about *everything*. She worried about her position in the palace; she worried about the upkeep of her parents' graves she had fallen behind on—because money was tight. They would not repossess graves, would they?

She even worried about her little bedside table with the Book of Verses, both of which had belonged to Queen Johanna. Nellie had taken them to her room when she saw that that boor of a man—the Regent, a distant cousin of the King's, newly instated by the church—would put these beautiful things in the dark and damp storage room where they would get dusty and mouldy and no one would appreciate them. Nellie had waxed and dusted that table for years. She thought it would be fair for her to use it because no one else would.

And the book . . . Nellie knew every single word in that book. She knew it by heart because it was the book that Mistress Johanna—before she became queen—had used to teach her to read. She had wanted Nellie to learn, because the Queen said women should, even if Nellie's father said they shouldn't.

The book reminded her of happy afternoons they spent learning, because Nellie wanted to know what the Triune said in His book that the shepherds preached and interpreted in their own way.

The little table and the book were the only things that Nellie still had from those happy days, and she did *not* want a junior office clerk half her age to tell her that an audit of the palace stores had shown that some items were missing and should be returned to the mouldy cellar where they belonged.

Because why else would this solicitor be so keen to see her?

He wanted something because that was the only thing that jolted these men into action: when they thought there was money to be made. When they thought a common *old woman* had something they liked, and that they didn't think she should have.

You couldn't stand up against men like that, because they always won, and not only would they take what they wanted, but make you pay a fine. Nellie had no money.

And so, with each step that brought her closer to the office, her knees grew weaker.

She walked along the harbour front.

A low riverboat had just moored, and a man with a horse and cart was waiting for the first of the cargo to be carried down the gangplank.

The ship was one of those that belonged to the Guentherite order of monks. A couple of young men—and the monks were always young, because they were often the sons of noble families who were sent to the order to be taught humility and hard work—were rolling barrels of wine across the deck.

The supplies for the banquet.

The window of the solicitor's street-level office was still dark. For a moment, Nellie feared she was too early or that she'd misunderstood the date, but then she spotted a small light in the depths of the shop.

Nellie opened the door. The bell rang loudly in the stuffy silence. She entered a narrow, rather bare hallway. A sign on a door to the left said *reception,* so she let herself into the large and messy ground floor office. A young man looked up from his desk.

He raised his eyebrows.

"I was told to come and see Master Oudebrandt," Nellie said, her jaw stiff from nerves. She showed him the letter.

She tried very hard to speak in a matter-of-fact tone, but her heart thudded against her ribs. Her voice sounded high to her ears—childish, even.

He took the letter from her, gave it a quick look and said, "Certainly, madam. Please wait here."

He rose and left the room. His footsteps clacked

through the hall and then went thud-thud-thud up the stairs. The sound of voices drifted through the ceiling, followed by more thud-thud-thuds and clack-clack-clacks and then the young man returned.

"You can go upstairs. First door on the left."

Nellie went back into the cold hall and climbed the stairs. The steps were steep, the wood creaked, and it was terribly dark in here.

A thin strip of golden light spilled out of a door that stood ajar on the upstairs landing. She knocked.

"Come in," said a gravelly male voice.

Nellie went in.

A fire in the hearth appeared to be the source of the golden light. The room's window looked out over the north side of the harbour. It would get little light even in the middle of summer. The half-drawn curtains made the room even darker.

Everything in the office was dark. The walls were dark green, the shelves were made of dark-stained wood, the curtains made from dark brown brocade fabric. A huge imposing desk that seemed out of proportion to the size of the room took up much of the space.

It, too, was made from dark wood.

The air was heavy with pipe smoke.

Nellie had never seen the man behind the desk. He was perhaps in his thirties, with a short reddish beard that reminded her somewhat of poor King Roald.

His eyes, clear and blue, regarded her with curiosity.

Nellie felt like sinking through the ground. She wanted to go back to the kitchen where she trusted the people.

"Yes?" His voice was dry, neither friendly nor unfriendly.

Nellie showed him the letter. "I received this from your office. It says to come here."

He took the letter from her, a frown on his face, but

after a glance, his face cleared up. "Oh, my colleague sent you this, but I can handle it. Wait here." He got up from the desk and left the room.

All alone in that creepy dark office with its dark wallpaper and dark curtains, Nellie looked around. The shelf behind the desk spilled over with books about law, big fat leather-bound tomes with gold lettering on the spine.

Men's voices drifted through the wall. A moment later, the man came back. He carried something that he put on the desk: a small flat box made of polished wood with a brass fastening. Nellie recognised it as the box that held her father's leather-bound notebook.

On rest day afternoons he would sit in the living room smoking his pipe with this book on the table before him. He would call it his book of thoughts and would write in it with a pen he dipped in an inkpot. She could still hear the scratching as he made curly letters on the paper.

No matter how much Nellie asked, he would never show her what he wrote. Her mother would tell her not to ask, because her father's writings were men's thoughts, and not for her to understand. Nellie would ask why her mother wasn't curious, and her mother would say that some things one was better off not knowing.

The man handed the box to her. Nellie took it.

The lid was waxy and dusty under her fingertips. It felt all wrong for her to have it. Any moment now, her father would come in and say, "Give that to me, young lady."

Her heart was racing.

"Where does this come from?" Her voice sounded nervous to her ears.

The bearded man said, "There is a story connected to this item. When your father died, lacking a son, his academic effects went to his brother."

Because women shouldn't be taught to read. Nellie found it hard to suppress her annoyance. Why should her uncle Norbert have cared about her father's books? The two brothers couldn't be more different, and couldn't possibly think less of each other.

"Your uncle sold your father's books, having no interest in them, but this box was never touched. When your uncle died, and this box came into our possession, being your family's solicitor firm, we were at a loss what to do with it, because the first page states that the content of the book is important; but it also contains a specific written instruction that no woman may read it until she has acquired the maturity of fifty years of age."

"Did he say why?" This sounded like something her father would do: always making up rules. Nellie was not allowed to wear stockings until she was six—she had to wear short dresses until she wouldn't crawl on the floor anymore. She could not come into the front parlour until she was ten, when she could sit still for more than fifteen minutes. After this time, she could no longer play in the street because she was done with children's things, but she had to help her mother in the kitchen.

The house had been full of rules.

"I'm sorry, madam, we're a solicitors firm and neither dispute nor investigate our clients' wishes. We act on them with as much integrity as possible. We've kept this item for you in our office for the past two years so we could hand it to you on your birthday, as per your father's instructions."

"And what if I hadn't lived to this age?"

But as she asked the question, Nellie knew this had been the point of her father's words. He had not expected her to live healthily until the age of fifty, so that whatever was in the book would be useless to her, because she would have been too old and frail to act on it.

Then Nellie had a further thought: her father didn't

even know that mistress Johanna had taught her to read and write.

He had said many times he didn't think girls should learn. After all, when would they use those skills?

So, he had made up rules to ensure that she would never get the book.

She clutched the box to her chest, the blood roaring in her ears. Something rattled inside, so the box contained more than just the book.

"Is that all?" she asked. It cost her a lot of effort to keep her voice straight.

No, she should not get angry. Her father was *dead*. She shouldn't let him taunt her from beyond the grave. That was *not* worth it.

"Yes, that's all." The man gave her a penetrating look.

Nellie was shaking too much to contemplate what his expression might mean. Was it pity for the poor simple dumb kitchen maid who wouldn't understand the great importance of the thing she'd just received?

Nellie said a hasty goodbye, because the sun was coming over the roofs of the houses on the other side of the harbour, and she needed to be back at the palace. She had her job to go to. Real work, for which she was paid, even if it wasn't much.

Real work, like her father had never done, because he used to get paid by the church out of the donations of the citizens.

She didn't care about her father's secrets.

CHAPTER 2

NELLIE STUMBLED down the staircase. She was so angry that her knees felt weak. She had no idea how she managed not to fall down those steep and creaky steps.

The narrow passage didn't allow for much light to come in, and the air was cold, stuffy with tobacco smoke. She wanted to get out of this place and go back to work.

All the fear she'd had about this meeting had been a waste of time. His book of thoughts! Her father always made a huge fuss over the smallest things.

Once, when she was little, her mother had sent her to the shops for a pound of sugar. It was very busy at the grocery store, and she had to wait amongst all those adults, who smiled at her and then pushed in front of her anyway.

It had taken so terribly long before her turn came.

When she got home, her father told her he hadn't given her permission to stop along the way and play. Then he demanded the change. She could still see her hand as she put the grubby coins on the table.

His face became a mask of anger. "That's half a cent. Where is the last quarter penny? Have you lost it again?"

Nellie searched her pockets, but she already knew she would not find the missing coin in there. She had been given the change and had clutched it as if it were the biggest treasure, because it was *money* and money was *important*. "This was what they gave me."

"And you didn't check it before you left the shop?" His voice sounded like the clap of a hammer.

Her ears glowed. No, she had not. Because she hadn't thought she should. Or she had forgotten, because now she thought about it, she knew her father would have wanted her to check *because you can never trust people when money is involved.*

He dragged her back to the shop. In front of the customers, he made a big speech that just because Nellie was an innocent child, it didn't mean they could get away with stealing *his* money. He said it should never happen again and that, because he was the bookkeeper for the Church, there would be *consequences*.

Yes, over a quarter of a cent.

Nellie's ears still went red whenever she thought about it. She had never felt more embarrassed in her life. Especially because the poor boy behind the counter, the grocer's son, admitted that he'd made a mistake and because he was crying by the time her father dragged her out of the shop, and his mother was calling her father "miser" She had not dared ask what it meant and had only later learned the meaning.

Nellie was no longer that little girl.

Once, in times better than these, she had served the queen and lived upstairs in the palace, with her own room. She didn't need to know the pompous musings and opinions her father had kept from her. Those were best left where they belonged: in the past. She liked to remember the *good* things about him, even if right now, she was so angry that she couldn't remember any of those.

A moist and cold squally wind lashed the quayside, making deck covers flap and rigging rattle. She turned her face into the breeze, clamping the box with the hated book in her hands. She crossed the walkway to the bollards that held the ropes restraining the sailing ships in their positions.

A space between two tall ships would do just fine. She'd fling the book into the harbour. It would become soaked within moments, her father's precious ink would run and no one could ever read his pompous, hateful words.

She swung her arm back to fling the book into the water—

—And stopped.

What if, just if, it contained important things? Not just important things from her father's point of view, but *really* important things?

About the church. About the royal family.

But surely he would have made sure that if those things were that important, someone knew about them before his death? He had not died suddenly and there would have been plenty of time to warn someone.

But what if these things made him *afraid* to speak out?

She tried, and failed, to picture her father afraid of anything. He would say whatever came to his mind to whomever he pleased—except perhaps to the king.

No, definitely, he would not speak his mind to the king. But the king had been dead four years when her father died.

And except to any of the shepherds.

No, he would also never speak ill against any of the shepherds. More than the king, the church ruled his life. If he had any secrets relating to the church, he would never risk upsetting Shepherd Wilfridus by revealing them.

She hesitated, the book heavy in her hands. An insane

desire to throw it as far away as possible consumed part of her.

Her father had been rigid, fond of rules and all too quick to apply them to his family with an iron fist, but she refused to believe he was a bad man.

No, he was not. He believed in the Book of Verses. In fact, he would read them out every day before dinnertime. He would read the Verses as they were written, without the embellishments and interpretations added by the shepherds.

He believed in utter honesty and would never, ever lie to anybody about anything.

Maybe she should have a look at the book tonight. She could always throw it in the hearth later. The fire in the kitchen was always roaring hot. It would love a thick musty book full of lovely paper.

She let the box sink into her carry bag, where it felt like a stone dragging her down. She had hoped . . . she didn't know. Nellie ought to be old and wise enough to know that life never gave her any lucky breaks, that happiness always passed her by.

But she could have used a little bit of money. Her lack of a husband or family doomed her to work until she no longer could, and then die of starvation or illness brought on by poor nutrition in the poor house.

Money would help a great deal, even just a little bit of it.

Failing that, just to have a proper birthday would be nice. A moment shared between friends—all of whom worked in the palace kitchens—around a table with some tea and sweets. Just a little token of appreciation.

But none of them knew it was her birthday—and whose fault was that? She had told no one.

Fifty was so *old*. Many people never lived to her age, and many who did were worn out. They relied on their families, looked after grandchildren. They put their feet up in well-earned retirement.

But Nellie would get none of that because she was just a maid, because her father had never liked her and would give money to the church before giving it to his own daughter, and because she was just perpetually unlucky. She had never gotten married and her parents had no other children.

And now she had better stop feeling sorry for herself and get going, because nothing ever happened by complaining about it, she used to say to beautiful Princess Celine with the golden curls.

Nellie hurried through the moisture-laced streets back to the palace.

Saardam looked so grey these days. All the hope, the colour and the life had been sucked out. The weather was grey, the offerings at the markets were poor, many shops were closed and houses had not been painted for years. In other parts, houses stood empty, because people had left or because they had failed to keep up with the rent and joined the growing horde of the city's destitute.

All because the ships failed to come into the harbour. Sea captains went elsewhere with their exotic products, due to hordes of rogues making the inland rivers unsafe; and the river captains rarely came down, since so few wares were available for trade.

The palace guards stood forlorn in their guard boxes, staring into the greyness. They knew Nellie and nodded to her as she slipped into the only enclave in the city where life still looked relatively normal.

All was quiet in the courtyard, waiting for the many guests for tomorrow's banquet.

The courtyard lay neatly raked and the stable roof had received a new cover of straw. The steps had been swept to within an inch of their lives and the stable boys hung around in their crisp uniforms, doing nothing while they waited for the horses and coaches to arrive from those guests who lived out of town.

Nellie went down the side entrance, through a low door and down a few steps into the servant's quarters.

She stopped off in her room to hang up her coat.

A soft cry caught her attention: a little black and white kitten, hiding in an alcove. It couldn't be more than a few weeks old.

"Poor thing." Nellie crouched.

She'd fed the creature some milk, yesterday, because it was as thin as a bag of bones, too small to hunt mice and probably without a mother. Now it saw her as a source of food. Typical. She always collected all manner of strays—people and animals.

The kitten didn't let itself be touched, but scooted into the darkness of Nellie's room. Oh, well, it would be safe there and might scare mice, even if it was much too small to catch them.

She'd get it some milk later.

Poor thing.

She took her father's box from her carry bag and shoved it into the back of the small cupboard that held her clean work clothes and linen. She'd look at it tonight. The thought of the unpleasant memories she might awaken filled her with dread, but the sooner she did this, the sooner she could get rid of the hateful thing and forget about it again.

She put on her apron and did up the strings while walking down the corridor into the kitchen—

Several voices called out, "Happy Birthday!"

What?

Nellie stopped in the doorway.

There they all were, around the table: the people, who —for all their warts and foibles—were her family now:

Dora the cantankerous cook, Wim, the elderly and often confused taster, Lily and Corrie, who worked for Dora, and a couple of the young kids who came in if they were needed.

In the middle of the table stood a plate of fresh apple turnovers, still steaming hot.

For a moment, Nellie couldn't say anything.

"You thought we forgot, is that right?" Dora said.

"Well, I hadn't told anyone." Her voice felt choked up.

"No, because you're such a grump. But someone told us. Also that you're turning fifty, and you didn't think we'd let that go by without mention."

"Someone?" Who would have known?

"One of the guards."

"The guards?" She knew none of them well. They were neatly dressed dapper men who stood by the gate and who wore leather belts with *swords* and who would kill intruders. How could any of them know about her birthday? "But I don't know any—"

Dora laughed. "I think people know you better than you think they do."

Well, clearly, but a guard? "Who was this?"

"Oh, one of the older ones. I don't know his name. I'm glad he told us, though." She gestured at the plate. "Come on, have some, before they get cold, and before upstairs complains we're not doing anything. Don't tell me that dry prune of a *solicitor* person gave you any food."

"No, he didn't."

Nellie sat down, and then had to explain to everybody about the book, which brought many questions, such as why her father would go through such efforts to make sure she never read it.

"I bet he kept it from her because he didn't want to burden her with his secrets," said Wim.

Dora scoffed. "Oh, come on, what sort of secrets

would he have that a woman can't handle? This is all about showing how much of a dick he is, frankly—no, don't say anything, Nellie. I've heard enough about your youth to know he was a dick."

"I would just prefer if you used less crude language. He was my father. He did a lot of things right. He looked after my mother and me and we never wanted for anything at home. I won't have people speak of him in crude words."

"Hmph. I'm a cook. Crude words are what I do best. I stuff pig guts, I cook ram's balls. I cut up all the bits you never knew an animal had by looking at the outside. If you can't do crude, you can't work in a kitchen. I make no excuses. Your father was a dick, and I've heard enough to think he was a dick to you and your mother even more than he was a dick to the rest of town. Only he was a *kind* dick, and that's the worst type: the ones who fool you with praising words while taking away your pride. If he didn't want you to know about his thoughts, then he was a dick."

"He may have wanted to protect us. We were the closest family he had." Save Uncle Norbert, who she didn't think had been a bad man either.

"Maybe, maybe, but my money is on the dick side of things. Because if he really wanted no one to know about his stuff, then why write it down in the first place? Why not burn the book before his death? He didn't die suddenly; he would have had plenty of time to do it."

A chilling truth hung in Dora's words, much as Nellie didn't like to acknowledge it, because it *upset* her.

Nellie had never witnessed her father chastise her mother, but his actions made it clear he was disappointed that she couldn't give him any more children, specifically male children.

Her mother had fallen pregnant when Nellie was fifteen and already lived with Mistress Johanna. The twin boys were born too early. They were small and sickly and never stood a chance when disease ripped through the city a few years later. They were not even five years old. It had broken her mother's heart.

"What about your uncle?" Corrie asked. "What did he say about it?"

"I don't think he ever opened the box and wouldn't have read the book even if he had. My uncle and my father didn't get along at all—"

Dora interrupted. "A dick, as I said. Norbert was a fine man."

"Can you shut up?" Corrie said. "You wouldn't like it if we spoke about your family like that."

"Go ahead. I learned all of my foul language while listening to people describe my parents. Heretics, devil-worshipers, whoring bitch—I've heard it all. What do you think they told us kids when all the fuss was going on after the death of the royal family? We were devil's brood and whore spawn, all because our father was a gifted baker who made no bones about the fact that he put his magic into his bread."

"But your family cared about you and taught you well."

"That, they did."

There was an uneasy silence, in which Nellie sipped from her tea. Yes, Dora came from a family of cooks who were open supporters of artisan magic. And since the death ten years ago of the royal family through the crown princess' wayward magic, the Regent and the church had been on a rampage to eliminate magic, no matter what the type.

The two young girls, sisters Els and Maartje, watched with wide eyes. They had come to work in the kitchen only recently, after Nellie had spotted the eldest, Els with the thick blond hair, coming out of a sailor's tavern, and knowing what women did in there, was determined that anyone that young and innocent shouldn't have to do *that*.

"This is not about you, Dora," Wim said. "We know what you think. Nellie asked what to do with the book."

"Especially because her father thought she couldn't read it," said Maartje, eyes wide.

"But I *can* read it," Nellie said.

Dora spread her hands. "Then why is this a question? You should read it, because that's what books are for, right? You should read it, and decide if it's worth the fuss."

"Probably not," Nellie said.

"Fine. Then we'll have a bonfire here tomorrow. With a bit of luck, the Regent's wine will have arrived by then—"

"It has," Nellie said, remembering the barge from the Guentherite order she had seen moored at the quay.

Dora smiled. "Good. Then we can celebrate with a bit of pretasting with our friend here." She clapped her hand on Wim's back. The Regent employed him to certify that none of the food that went upstairs contained any poison or other ingredients that would have ill consequences for the noble guests. "We'll celebrate, have a party."

She pushed herself up from the table, having solved everyone's problems in one clear swoop. Dora was like that, as decisive and outspoken as Nellie was timid.

Sometimes, Nellie envied Dora.

"But now, I need you to start on the pastry dough. I need the ducks cut up and gutted for the soup. I need you to slice the leek, and I need you to bring in some firewood and core the apples."

While they sat at the table eating and drinking tea, a boy had brought two dozen ducks with their feet tied together and feathers still attached. They needed to be plucked and cleaned and hung out overnight.

There were carrots to be scraped and cut into cubes, puddings to be made, a whole crate of apples to be turned into applesauce, bread to be baked—the list was endless.

CHAPTER 3

NELLIE STARTED making applesauce.

Around mid-morning, a cart came to the back door, delivering barrels of wine, sausages, cheeses, dried fruit and pickles from the ship of the Guentherite order that she had seen in the harbour.

A bit after midday, the kitchen workers "helped" Wim sample the wine, sausages and dried nuts to make sure they weren't poisoned—they weren't. The order's farms were on church property. Monks grew this food, although Nellie hated to think how much the palace would have spent on it, because they would have had to pay market prices for this.

The sausages were wonderful and made her pleasantly full. She was not used to drinking wine either. For most of the afternoon, while she helped to pluck, chop, peel and stir, she felt wonderfully warm and comfortable. She was grateful that in the chaos following the death of the royal family, she had been able to keep a job at the palace.

Her father's musings about the church or about life in general were unimportant.

Nellie worked hard all day, and even managed to forget about the book.

But eventually the work was done. The workers drank tea at the big table in the kitchen, surrounded by dough set to rise on the end closest to the fire, beans covered in water in a pan, carrots and cabbages cut up and ready to cook, chickens marinating in bowls, raisins soaking in brandy, pots of applesauce, jars of cherries and much more. It smelled heavenly.

Only when she came back to her little room was she reminded of the book.

She was tired. Her hands ached. She wanted to go to sleep.

But she knew that Dora and the others would ask her about it tomorrow and the prospect of seeing the book burn was attractive, so she shut the door, lit the oil lamp on the little table and took the box from the shelf.

At that moment, the kitten came out and she remembered that she had intended to bring some milk, so she went back to the kitchen to scoop some creamy liquid from the big vat with the wet cloth over the top. Now that people had left, mice and other vermin skittered around in the dark spaces under the benches and in the pantry.

In her room, she put the bowl on the floor, almost tripping over the kitten circling her legs. The contents were gone quickly.

She opened the box.

There were indeed other things inside besides the book. Her father's old pipe, and a leather pouch with the monocle he used when reading. The old-fashioned pen made of a wood handle and a goose feather that looked a bit worse for wear. There was also a tobacco box which contained nibs for the pen, a tamper for the pipe and an elaborate metal key.

Most of those things—except the key—brought back

memories of her father, like the scent of tobacco that clung to the pipe.

Nellie took out the book and sat on the bed. But she was about to open it when the kitten mewled and looked up at her, licking the last milk from its mouth. It tried to climb up on the bed, but once its claws had found purchase on the bedspread, it didn't have the strength to keep climbing. It just hung on the bedspread, mewling.

Nellie lifted the poor little thing on top of the bed. The kitten curled up against her legs.

She opened the book. On the thick and smooth title page, her father had written, *To those who are willing to see the truth* in beautiful capital letters such as he had learned to use in his work with the church. He had embellished the first letters of each word with finely drawn figures: a row of monks, a shepherd facing the light through a window in the sky, a woman bowing to a shepherd.

Underneath, he had written his name, *Cornelius Augustus Dreessen*.

Just this page was an artwork.

For all that he enjoyed writing so much, it pained her that he had never seen the value in teaching her to read and write. Sadly, it was still true that far more girls than boys never learned. Those who could write could do tasks that people respected. They were the teachers, the shepherds, the councillors and the people who worked in libraries and offices. Those who could read could make sure that shop owners didn't cheat on them. Those who could do neither were doomed to keep doing dull and monotonous jobs like working in the kitchens. Women. That picture of the woman bowing to the shepherd said it all, as far as her father was concerned.

She turned the page.

Here was the declaration that the solicitor referred to, a loosely inserted card in the book:

After my death, my books and scholarly possessions are to go to my brother, little use as he will have for them. I hope that in his old age, he wisens up and learns to appreciate knowledge by people wiser than him, but I know that this is a long shot.

By all means, none of the women in my family are to inherit my books and other items of knowledge, because they will appreciate them even less than my brother. If you must, pass my books onto a female member of my family only after they have reached the age of fifty and have perhaps acquired the maturity to understand the gravity of the issues I have investigated, but only if you are left with no other option.

Nellie heard Dora's voice echo in her head. *A dick.*

It was probably equally telling that the solicitor had left that note addressed to him in the book.

Why should she even bother reading this?

Her father's musings and dissertations started with the words, *There are many who claim to have seen the light, who fail the most basic understanding of the teachings of the Holy Triune.*

It went on to explain many things Nellie had heard before about the moral ambiguity within the church and royal family.

In her father's words:

How could the royal family support a church that decreed magic was evil while harbouring citizens with magic at the same time? Saardam was built as a safe haven against magic from the east and it was the task of the church to safeguard it. Old king Nicholaos had understood that, while similarly trying to engage a necromancer to resurrect his daughter after she died.

There is no logic or morality to any of these people. The royal family has been destroyed—twice now—because they kept dallying with magic. The church is the only proper guardian of the city.

Nellie suspected that her father would have loved to assume the revered mantle of shepherd, but his parents had been practical people and had sent him to learn accounting. Besides, the Church of the Triune had been quite a new development in his youth and many of the older folk—which would have included her grandparents —were quite hesitant to accept it. They had all grown up with the Belaman Church, that institution of beautiful rich buildings, golden statues and ages of tradition.

They had viewed this new church, which preached simplicity and values—and sermons—that people could understand, as an upstart.

By the time the Church of the Triune became more accepted, her father had been married, and married men couldn't become shepherds. Another reason why he might have treated his wife and only daughter with so much disdain.

Nellie leafed through the book. It was all the same stuff she had heard so often when she was young. Every single word on those hateful pages brought up memories of her miserable youth spent justifying herself to her father and seeing in his face just how inadequate he thought she was. A whole book full of it.

Nellie had thought she'd have finished with this nonsense after he died, after she'd helped her mother pack up his clothes and donate them to the poor house.

Her eyes pricked. She didn't want to read any of this anymore.

She stopped reading the pages and flicked through them instead, determined to at least look at every one before getting out of bed, walking to the kitchen and tossing this wretched thing into the fire.

And then some text caught her eye.

They are hiding the dragon in the dungeons of the church.

What?

Nellie stopped midway through turning another page. There it was. She had not misread.

The Church is undertaking activities in our name that it shouldn't get involved with. As a trusted assistant of the Church, I have always been aware of the purchases made by the leadership in the name of the community. I see how much the Church spends on new buildings, on supporting their deacons, on food they give to the poor. But there have been some much less fortunate purchases. I can no longer fail to speak out about a development that has always concerned me. In the the early days, when I was a much younger man, the Shepherd Romulus, in his old age, ordered a book to be purchased from Burovia. It was a very rare book, and word had gotten out of its availability through the death of a recluse noble who was said to have one of the few surviving copies. The Belaman Church, our great rival who once considered us under their protection, has large libraries of religious study texts, and I strongly supported the building up of such library. However, the work in question, the rare and deeply secret Arts Of The Arcane, can scarcely be called a purchase in the public interest, since many of its secrets are so evil that they can never be revealed to common students and thus cease to have relevance to such. Moreover, by their secret nature, these arts are vile purporters of magic such as we hope to banish from this land.

When I raised objections to the purchase of this very costly book, the shepherd told me that in order to understand one's enemies, one must study them. The shepherd knew well enough how to spot the use of common or artisan magic. But while common magic is not condoned, it is also, generally speaking, pretty harmless when practiced by innocent individuals. There may be some mischief when someone eavesdrops on conversations through the magic of wood or on the wind, but this type of common magic is passive. It should not be encouraged, but little harm can be done with it.

It was the Shepherd's conviction that in order to detect the much more evil art of ghost-whispering or the dark arts of the conjuring of fire constructs, or—heaven forbid—necromancy, we needed to know the signs that could lead us to such, because the practitioners of these arts are well aware of the vile nature of their practices and don't ply them in open daylight.

That was the reason I was given for the purchase of the book. I saw the sense in it and accepted it. Knowledge is good, even if it can occasionally be knowledge of something truly vile.

The book was purchased and arrived in a great wooden case. It sat in the crypt of the church for a long time before the shepherd took it into the room with restricted books. Naught was spoken of it, and I almost forgot about it.

But when Shepherd Wilfridus was ordained as Shepherd Romulus' replacement, the Church went through a period of renewed interest in the dark arts, and continued purchases of these unspeakable materials. I asked the shepherd if it was necessary to continue this activity, and was told that by locking up all evil magic materials in the church, the use of magic could be stopped.

In the wake of the terrible tragedy that befell the royal family—a tragedy wholly of their own making because they allowed the princess to stay in the palace even though she displayed classic signs of possessing evil magic—the church successfully argued that all magicians should leave the city.

As a result, the spies from the Belaman Church left the city, as well as the eastern traders, who we all knew had magic, but who were smart enough to hide it.

Nellie remembered those dramatic days all too well. Of

course, in hindsight a lot of people said that the royal family should have done something sooner about the burgeoning magical talent of the young princess, but no one, not even the shepherd, would have thought that a six-year-old girl could kill her entire family as well as a good number of the court attendants.

Nellie had not been in the room—if she had, she would not be alive—but she remembered the panic. How no one knew what was going on. How guards were running everywhere. How they were told to hide downstairs in the servants quarters.

And how, after two long days, the guards laid out rows of bodies in the ballroom and Shepherd Wilfridus had made that speech to the citizens that the city would be forever cleansed of magic.

After the terrible events, it was a comfortable opinion to cling to. It almost seemed to make sense.

She read on.

In the aftermath of the deaths, when those afflicted with magic were fleeing the city in the wake of the anger that had broken out amongst the people, the shepherd hastened the purchase of dark magical materials, at great cost.

The church managed to take possession of a fabled item, the existence of which had only previously been rumoured: an eastern dragon box complete with its occupant. Those unfamiliar with the eastern dragons can bless themselves. They are powerful magical creatures who answer only to the magician owner of the box. They are bigger than a full-grown bull; they have wings of gold with which they can fly wherever they please, and they do the owner's bidding at the snap of a finger.

The church conducted a study into this creature, which they found to be exceptionally strong and autonomous, unlike the fire demons which can only appear at the command of their masters. The people from the Church discovered this to their detriment. In the time they experimented with the dragon, it burned down the wooden furnishings of the crypt room twice, and almost killed two deacons. When freed from the box, the dragon unleashes a fury such as can only be conjured through evil magic. It cannot be extinguished, and cannot be commanded. Nor does closing the box cease its activities. And, once released, the dragon does not easily return to captivity. It is a wonder that no one was killed through the foolish exploits of the Church in relation to this creature.

Despite having seen the danger, the shepherd keeps this dreadful thing in the crypts. In the past years, I've asked many times why, and have never received a reply. I've told him to dispose of it, but I'm told that one doesn't easily dispose of a dragon. I've asked for it to be sent back to the eastern lands where it belongs, but I'm told it can only be returned to its owner. I've asked who this owner is but no one seems to want to say anything about it.

But I have a theory.

King Nicholas' son King Roald was an idiot. Everyone knew it and no one dared say the word, so I will say it out loud: he was an idiot.

He seemed to neither know nor care that the two children under his roof were were not his. The young boy Bruno was obviously not his, because he had the face of his eastern trader father, but the crown princess wasn't his daughter either.

Both were children of powerful magicians who wanted to increase their influence in Saardam. The eastern trader Li Fai did this through giving his little son a dragon box, hoping that the dragon would escape and do the father's bidding. It is this box that is now in possession of the church.

Now the young prince is dead and the creature in the

box is getting angry. Every time someone goes down in the crypts, there is a chance that it will break free and wreak havoc over the city. But more than that: I fear that someone in the church, someone with good intentions but misguided ideas, might unwittingly unleash its power. On top of that, I know that certain members of the church do not have good intentions. They seek to use these evil arts against those they perceive as their enemies, even if those people may be defenceless against this type of magic, because these people will stop at nothing to gain power. Those who read this will know who these people are. They must be stopped. They must be stopped before the question of the Regency of Saardam becomes an issue and before Regent Bernard demands to be crowned king, because the church as it stands will never consent, and because once the Regent demands to be crowned king, all our lives will be in danger.

Nellie stared at the final words, tearing herself loose from the fear on the pages to the soft purring of the kitten on her bed.

In all the years that she had known her father, Nellie had never heard him speak words like these. Whenever someone predicted ill conditions, he would shrug it off. Doomsayers, as he called them, would see that life was good and fair if only they saw the light in the Triune and His teachings.

Back in the days before he died and was already quite frail, her father had seemed unusually taciturn—not unexpected for a man who knows he's near the end of his life. But there had been one occasion that he had even refused to see Shepherd Wilfridus, who had made a special effort of coming to the house.

He'd been too tired, he said.

Nellie had not thought any more of it, but in light of what she had just read, a chill crept over her back. Her father had believed that the church was the main force for good in Saardam. Her father might have been shaken in his belief.

Those who read this will know who these people are.

No, she didn't. But the book suggested that problems started when Shepherd Wilfridus took over.

Her father didn't like Shepherd Wilfridus. Nellie didn't like him very much either. He was a stiff, pompous man who shouted a lot in his sermons, mostly about the sins of the people, saying that, if they did nothing, evil would rule the world. It was very tiresome. But he would never allow evil to flourish in the church.

Once our Regent gets sick of waiting for a suitable time to be crowned king, the trouble will start. This decision needs to be made and approved by the church and the church has become quite happy with being the effective ruler of Saardam. They don't want the Regent on the throne. They will find reasons not to put him there. I fear that if the Regent is well-liked by that time—and why would he ask for the throne if he was not well-liked?—then some elements in the church will do whatever is in their power to stop him. I fear they will not hesitate to use dark arts.

The text in the book went on to describe exactly where this dragon could be found in the crypt under the church in the marketplace. There was even a clumsy map to show which chamber.

And with that, Nellie had come to the last page of the book. She closed it and sat with it on her knees.

It was late, but some people were evidently still up because people were talking down the hallway, or maybe the bakers had already come into the kitchen.

A deep black fear took hold of her.

She had half hoped that her father's book would contain nothing of importance. But a dragon was important. Especially one that was angry and might do harm to innocent people. Especially if the church already knew about it and had been sheltering this creature for the past ten years.

The question was: what could she do about it? The dragon—presuming it was still in the crypt—could only be commanded by the owner, and the prince was dead. The prince's father, the eastern trader Li Fai, was gone.

It sounded like a dangerous situation, and what good was it to put it in the hands of a kitchen maid?

CHAPTER 4

"SO," DORA SAID. She was pounding a cloth bag containing dry bread onto the table to make crumbs she needed for the duck stuffing. A line of plucked and marinated ducks lay before her on the table. "What did it say, this big secret book of your father's?"

Nellie sighed and sat down at the table, clutching her tea and facing her plate with bread and cheese.

During the long night, she had spent much time looking at the ceiling in the dark, wondering what she would answer to these inevitable questions.

"The book told me I didn't want to remember the bad things about him."

"What I said. He's a dick."

"He was not a bad man in his heart."

"Pfaugh." Dora hit the bag on the table a few times. Dust wafted through the pores in the fabric. "No one is perfect. Not even our parents."

"I wanted to remember the good things about him. He looked after us. He taught me what's right and wrong."

"But?"

Nellie met Dora's eyes. They were blue, and some said

they were hard and cold, and that Dora was a careless woman. Nellie thought that was because Dora, as an older woman, had nothing to lose, so she said whatever she thought, and not everyone liked that.

"Well," she said, and she blew the steam off her tea. No, she *really* didn't like saying bad things about people in public, not even when those people were dead. "My father had strong ideas about what's right and wrong."

"Don't they all, these church men? They think they know what's best for everyone, but most of them do not understand our messy real lives. Sometimes the best thing to do, and the thing the church tells you to do, are not the same. I mean—these Church shepherds can't marry, so what do they know about having families?"

And Dora's family was a messy subject no one spoke much about. Not her abusive husband whom she had left, who might have been involved in a robbery where someone was killed, not her daughter who had also fled an abusive husband, and who lived with her, with a two-year-old child.

"This is not about that."

"Oh?" Dora's eyebrows rose. There was flour in one. "What's it about, then?"

"My father worked for the church and he saw a lot of things that the church spent money on. He didn't agree with some of their . . . purchases."

"Like what? Did they contribute to the Regent's banquets and wine?"

"This is from before the Regent."

"Oh, there would have been many things to disagree with when old King Nicholaos sat on the throne. Like how he hired necromancers."

"It is also not about those."

"What is is about, then?"

Nellie licked her lips. "He says the church bought

secret books of dark magic from Burovia, books that described the ways of the dark arts. He says he was told that the church needed to learn what the dark arts were in order to stamp them out, but he feels the church was all too happy to learn about the dark arts with the view of using them."

"Well, the enemy uses magic, why not inform yourself? Seems sensible."

"While at the same time they were telling the citizens that magic is evil?"

Dora shrugged. "I never understood that part." Her cheeks were red. "Magic is not evil. Not most at least. It's how you use it."

"Necromancy and ghost-whispering is evil. Fire demons are evil."

Dora nodded, but gave no further comment. The subject of magic was never an easy one because you never knew who listened.

So Nellie said, "He also said the church was hiding a dragon."

Dora looked straight at her. "You're kidding. A dragon? One of those huge ones that spits fire like *'aaaggghhhhh'?*" She made a hissing noise while holding her crumb-covered hands in front of her like claws.

"That's what he said."

"Did you mean one of these dragons that lives in a box and comes out to do the master's bidding?"

"I don't know any other dragon."

"But those were only owned by the eastern traders."

"Yes, those."

"I thought the eastern traders had all left the city."

"Evidently, they did not to take their dragons with them."

It felt like a flippant response. But Nellie felt very much out of her depth talking about the subject of dragons. In all the years the eastern traders had lived in Saardam, they had never displayed the dragons they had. The dragons were real, though, because Nellie had seen one once.

Dora snorted. "What does the church want to use a dragon for? Where did they get it?" Like you could just buy dragons at the markets.

Nellie shrugged. She wasn't sure that Dora was taking her seriously after her earlier comments about her father. "The book doesn't give me any information about that. I'm not sure if my father knew, only that he was asked to sign the transfer of money. And that he didn't agree with that. He said the church collected magical artefacts in the crypts in case they needed to unleash magic to defeat magic. He didn't think they were honest about this. He said they were keeping the dragon for their own aims."

"And what would those aims be?"

"The Triune only knows. The book said gaining power." Nellie lowered her voice. "He said there would be trouble if the Regent wanted to be declared king."

Dora threw her head back and laughed. "This's hardly news, is it? If the church had wanted a new royal family, they would have crowned the man king already. Ten years in, and we're still waiting. Is it going to happen? No!"

"But who is the rightful heir to the throne? The Church was going to sort it out."

"Someone boring, fat and rich. They will sort it out. I don't care as long as they eat. Come on, Nellie." She put a hand on Nellie's shoulder. "You worry too much. This book is just a thing full of empty words. A dragon! What are you supposed to do about this dragon? Just walk into the crypts and ask to see it? If you bring me that book, I will throw it in the fire for you when we 'test' another cask of the Regent's wine. That book just fills your head with nonsense."

"You're probably right."

Nellie finished her tea and set down her cup. Time to start working.

The stairs across the hallway came out in the foyer just outside the doors to the ballroom.

Preparations were in full swing.

The room was normally fairly empty, as it was also where the king would see formal guests. Normally, it just held the dais with the throne and a few ornate chairs on either side. They needed many more chairs and tables. Some of those chairs were stacked against the walls, others were in the garden room.

The tables stood in a storeroom. They needed to be brought into the hall.

Lines of boys and young men were carrying in tables from the storage rooms, placing them in rows so that the kitchen hands could cover the tables with white table-cloths and put out the palace's beautiful gold-rimmed tableware.

So many guests were coming that Nellie had asked her helpers to collect plates from storage.

A sixteenth birthday was a significant event. Casper would now be of marriageable age, and the Regentship of Saardam had propelled the family into a position of importance. Many of the nobles and royal families from surrounding nations were expected to attend, and some would only be here to explore the possibility of marriage between their daughters and Casper.

All these people would stay in the palace and eat in the main dining room, entertained by the Regent and his family. Over the past ten years, the Regent's parties had become somewhat of a legend so it was not something that anyone with an invitation wanted to miss.

The guest list had been a point of contention. Did one

invite the rulers of the surrounding nations, even if you were not friendly with them?

The Regent had said no, his wife, Madame Sabine, had said the boy should meet eligible women from all surrounding countries, and eventually, Shepherd Wilfridus had to be called in to approve the guest list.

All these people would need somewhere to sleep, and the guest rooms had to be prepared.

Not all the guests were happy to have their rooms near some other guests.

Others had strange requirements, like the Regent's advisor Lord Verdonck, who always insisted on a room where he could open the window, because fresh air was *good for the humours.*

It was the Regent's housekeeper's task to sort this out. The poor woman had spread out a few chalkboards on a table in the hall, each with names written on them. Whenever Nellie walked in or out carrying boxes with tableware or freshly washed serviettes, she would stand there shaking her head. Nellie was glad she only had to make sure the tables were set and everything looked pretty.

Word went that Regent Bernard was holding a meeting in his office—which was upstairs—with a few of the guests who had arrived early. He asked for "a few pretty girls" to bring snacks, so Dora filled a big plate with pastries and made tea in a pretty teapot with flowers, which were carried upstairs by Els and Maartje, two of Nellie's young assistants.

The guests from out of town started arriving.

Whenever Nellie walked through the foyer and looked into the palace forecourt, some other elaborate coach had come in through the gates. The guards and courtiers would congregate at the door to welcome the guests and take them to whatever rooms were ready, wherever the housekeeper had decreed that they would sleep.

Soon, the guests started to explore the guest rooms, asking for extra pillows or blankets or for food. This put Dora in a foul mood, because was busy preparing for the banquet.

Nellie ran up and down the stairs with trays of food more times than she cared to count.

The guests met up with each other. They occupied the hall and other spaces where the servants still worked. Neither the Regent nor Madame Sabine came out to entertain their guests—the Regent was supposedly still in the meeting—although Nellie spotted Casper and his younger brother Frederick strutting about in their new suits looking like peacocks.

Nellie knew the Regent had engaged the modiste Mistress Yvette, who had made Casper a bright blue suit. It consisted of a pair of blue velvet trousers, a velvet jacket and a long-sleeved shirt with a ruffled collar. He wore gold-buckled boots with high heels and had tied his straw-blond hair in a ponytail. Two strands on either side of his head had been treated with a curling iron.

He had decided he was an adult now, and dressed as one.

A lot of the noble guests had brought adolescent children, either theirs or their family's, who all gathered around the birthday boy in the palace foyer.

Casper ordered the servants around, too, in a haughty voice, telling them to bring items for the ever-growing group of well-dressed young people who were, frankly, getting in the way of the servants and kitchen staff entering the hall or getting work done.

The group included Casper's fourteen year old brother Frederick, dressed in red velvet, but still with his curls loose about his head, as well as Hestia, the blond-haired, big-bosomed daughter of Baroness Viktoriya and at least twenty years old; Duke Sylvan's daughter Odilia, dark-haired and thin, with deep-set eyes like her father; and King Leopold's grandsons Max and Patrice, both of whom looked disturbingly like Casper. They were cousins, but they were not that close.

While the adults moved off into their own rooms, the youngsters loitered in the foyer, getting ever louder in their laughter and demands.

Nellie gathered her own young helpers in the kitchen, a handful of pale and tired faces. The kids were all from common worker families and Nellie had collected them in her group because some misfortune had befallen their families.

Johan's mother had died a few years ago, and Els and Maartje came from a very large family with far too many children to feed. Their father had broken a leg while working at the docks and now walked with a crutch, which meant he couldn't work anymore. The older children had gone to work, but there was never enough money.

The problem with Els was—and this was why Nellie had called them all together—that she had a mouth too big for her position. The upstairs housekeeper had already beaten her twice in the last year for "having a big mouth" toward the Regent's guests.

The combination of Els and the group of noble youngsters upstairs was a disaster waiting to happen.

Els stood with her arms crossed over her chest, leaning against a kitchen bench. Wisps of her flaxen blond hair came out from under her bonnet; her cheeks were bright red and her eyes blue and feisty. She was only fourteen, but she looked at least four years older. She was big and sturdy, and had a healthy bosom on her.

Nellie said, "I know that there will be a lot of bad behaviour in the next couple of days. A lot of very bad behaviour. All the noble guests have brought their sons and daughters with them. Many of these youngsters have

never been to a banquet, and they are likely to go slightly
. . . overboard. I want none of you to get involved with the
trouble they get themselves into. They will demand ridiculous things from you—and you will smile. They might even
demand rude things from you—and you will walk away. If
any of them promise you anything at all, don't believe
them. These are kids, and they don't know what they're
saying. They're drunk with power and money. Do not trust
them. Remember that you work for the palace, and not for
them. Ignore them."

Els said nothing, but Nellie gave her a stern look that
said, *I want no trouble from you, young lady*.

"Have you seen what some of them are wearing,
though?" said Maartje.

"Yeah," Johan said, and he laughed. "That light blue
suit looks ridiculous."

"I was thinking about Baroness Hestia's dress," Maartje
said.

"Oh yeah. When she bends over, you can almost see
her tits."

"Johan!" Nellie said. "I will not have you use any sailor's
language in the palace."

"Are you lot finished holding a meeting out there?"
Dora called. "I need someone to bring in more firewood."

Of course, there was more work to be done.

For now, however, the group of young nobles—and
there were almost twenty—appeared to be happy just to
stand in the foyer and make silly comments about the
attire of the guests walking through the hall.

This, of course, led to complaints by those guests.

The Regent's meeting had included the mayor and his
daughter, who was also sixteen. The girl objected to being
called *dumpy* and an argument broke out between the
mayor and the palace staff about moving the group of
youngsters along to a less prominent position where they

wouldn't bother and insult people. The Regent came down the stairs when Nellie was walking through the foyer and made a show of jokingly berating his son for saying these things. But he added that the girl *was* dumpy.

The poor girl ran off crying and she and the mayor left in protest. He had, he said, come here to welcome the distinguished guests but would not stand for being insulted by a spoilt brat.

"No," Casper said. "You have come here for one purpose: the chance to foist your daughter on me. I don't want her."

He held a glass of wine. Nellie had lost count of how many he had drunk that afternoon. His cheeks were red, and his voice sounded a bit funny.

All the noble sons and daughters surrounded him, most from more respected families and many of them much older than he.

The Baroness Hestia laughed raucously when the girl and her father strode out of the foyer. Her cheeks were red, too, and the pink dress kept slipping off one of her shoulders. She stood next to Casper, encouraging him by laughing at everything he said.

"Well, I know that I'm not supposed to say anything while upstairs," Els said when she met Nellie in the kitchen, "but *I* think she looks like a whore and she behaves like a whore, so someone should call her a whore."

"Don't be surprised that even nobles like whores, especially when they're dressed up in ridiculous outfits," Dora said. "And the men are so dumb about it, too, like their gazes are so transfixed on a pair of tits that they fail to notice other stuff. When a man is with a whore, either the woman steals something, or she spies on him. Beware of whores, young Els. They're smart women and they usually leave the room with more than the agreed payment."

"Be careful talking about such things," Nellie said.

"Next thing Baroness Hestia will send people down here to punish us because we said she's a whore."

"What they don't hear us say, they don't know. And she *does* look like a whore."

Nellie agreed. And she also knew that women of loose morals often stole things. And, having visited Florisheim, Hestia's home, Nellie knew Hestia was not here to look at the scenery and that, as heiress of the Barony of Gelre, a noble woman's only way to influence politics was through the man's bedroom, as long as she didn't marry, because the moment she agreed to do that, she was no longer worth more than a pretty piece of fluff on the man's arm.

Hestia was here to do damage. They would have to keep a close eye on her.

Nellie worked in the ballroom, setting plates on the tables, feeling the anger stew inside her each time she heard the Baroness squeal with laughter. *Whore, whore.* She couldn't bring herself to say the word out loud, but that's what Hestia was: a whore in a garish and expensive dress.

Nellie was working in the hall when a man said, "Don't you youngsters think you should save some wine for tomorrow?"

Nellie recognised the voice, but only remembered who it belonged to when she came back to the foyer: Lord Verdonck.

The Regent's advisor was a man who stood tall for his age, even if his face bore wrinkles and his hair was almost white. He dressed more elegantly than many, in muted colours, without the hideous but fashionable ruffles.

He held a considerable estate outside the city, where he derived his wealth from his fertile farms. In the chaos that often reigned in Saardam, he was a sensible voice. As Regent's advisor, he made frequent visits to the palace, and was one of the few people who could silence a room full of nobles.

"No, youngsters, don't look at me like that. The big banquet is tomorrow and you want to be presentable. You also want to avoid insulting so many people that someone will stick a knife in your back. There will be a lot of knives in the dining room."

"Ha, ha, he thinks he's funny," Hestia said.

"I'm deadly serious, young lady, and I think you're drunk and you had better take off to your rooms and stop insulting our host's guests. You may think you're so brave now, but wait until your family hears of all the damage you're doing to their reputation, and no, young lady, that does not stop with who sits at the table with whom, but who buys stuff from whom, too. If the people you insulted stopped buying your family's wine and sausages, how would you explain that to your family?"

Lord Verdonck might be old, but he had a formidable voice that Nellie could still hear while going down the stairs to the kitchen. The next time she came into the foyer, the group with Casper and Frederick and that terrible Baroness Hestia was gone.

Good.

She hoped those kids would learn a lesson and have more respect for their elders.

CHAPTER 5

THE GUESTS AND the Regent devoted most of the afternoon to business meetings. The kitchen had to serve meals in a few different rooms.

Regent Bernard had ensconced himself at the head of the table in the official palace dining room with about twenty minor nobles. These dinners were for everyone who wanted to speak with him but was judged insufficiently important to get a private audience.

The Regent loved his food and piled many things on his plate while most of the guests were much more modest.

Nellie hadn't seen it but, on one such occasion, he had chastised a guest for "eating too much" and had told the poor man, "You've already gotten your money's worth out of your visit. Now bugger off."

The guests were usually local nobles, although one time when Nellie came in, a man was stuttering in a heavily accented voice.

The Regent burst out, "My younger son is fourteen. What makes you think we want to marry him off already?"

The man in question grew red in the face and scurried out of the room. Everybody laughed.

Nellie, as servant and thus invisible in this gathering, collected plates and poured glasses of water. She listened. She knew more about these men than they knew about each other.

The noble women had gathered nextdoor. In the conspicuous absence of the Regent's consort, Hestia's mother, Baroness Viktoriya, acted as host for the meeting.

Compared to the men's gathering, it seemed more civilised.

Baroness Viktoryia said she was sad that her husband couldn't come, but he'd been injured fighting a bear.

That brought gasps from around the table. Women asked how common bears were in Florisheim—very, apparently—and how lucky she must be to have such a strong husband. The Baroness said her husband single-handedly defended his horses against the bear and then rode back to town with a broken leg.

Having met Baron Uti, Nellie suspected that every word was true, and the only reason he wasn't here was that he didn't think the Regent was important enough to build a relationship with. Which was also why, although all the dukes and kings from surrounding countries had been invited, only a few minor nobles had turned up for a look-see.

King Leopold's cousin twice removed, from a simple estate in Burovia, just did not command that level of attention. He was only Regent, living on borrowed time until the church figured out who would be king, never mind they'd been deciding that for the last ten years.

In the next room, several men were discussing business. This meeting, led by the Regent's advisor Lord Verdonck, was livelier than the other two. The men around the table were merchants and business owners.

Master Pieters, who did the ordering for the palace, was also there.

This room was full of talk about grain and wine and cheese.

Nellie had to dodge books and contracts being signed on the table.

When she finished there, it was back to the kitchen to get the soup.

In the Regent's room, his grilling of minor nobles continued. The mayor of a nearby village wanted permission to charge tolls to all who passed through their town.

"Many of them have stopped coming altogether with the rogues about, and those that visit don't even stay in our town anymore."

The Regent laughed so loudly that his belly shook. "Good man, you think if you charge tolls, more will come?"

"No, but it will fill our coffers."

"If you charge tolls, nobody will come. Look at all these men." He waved a sausage-fingered, beringed hand at the gathering.

Most of the nobles were well dressed, but some of their jackets were scuffed or missing a button, or the lace had a small tear, or their wigs bore signs of discolouration. None were half as tall and round-waisted as the Regent.

"None of you like spending money. That's why you're here. Free food! Let's see if we can get the palace to pay for something. It bores me. Has anyone in this room come to ask me something that I'm not expected to pay for?"

A young man said, "Yes. I want your permission to build a church in New Harbour."

Several people gasped. New Harbour was where the very poor lived. Recently settled, with streets made from dirt and houses with tiny gardens where people grew their own food, the area was also the home of some warehouses, the hospice and the poor house.

Nellie could almost hear the Regent's next question, *Why do you think those people deserve a church?* But she had given out all the soup and her trolley was full of plates and leftovers, so she decided it was wise to leave the room.

The dirty plates went into the scullery, where Els and Maartje were hard at work, and the scraps into a bucket for the pigs.

Anything that looked still appetising, she collected into a large bowl she stashed away on a shelf in the corner of the pantry.

Then it was back upstairs with the next load of soup.

The women had progressed to talking about why Madame Sabine was not there. The suggested reasons included the suggestions that she must be pregnant, that she was ill, that she thought she was too good for them, or that her husband had hit her and she was ashamed to show her face.

"She has always been strange," a local noblewoman said. "Coming from Lurezia, one would expect her to dress well and have a flair for style, but no. I've even heard that she rides through town after dark wearing men's trousers."

Several women gasped at that statement.

That was also true. Madame Sabine had a majestic white horse that she loved to ride and she proclaimed to have little time for the ways in which women were supposed to sit.

"She pretends to be from a rich family, but she has no refinement or taste at all," a woman said.

"Her family *is* very rich," said another noblewoman.

"How so? She's clearly not of noble blood. I don't think she's related to the royal family at all."

"Oh no, she isn't. Her father is a military commander."

That drew exclamations of disgust.

Nellie was glad to be out of that room. If she were Madame Sabine, she wouldn't be happy to spend any more time than necessary with these gossiping women either.

Madame Sabine rarely showed herself in public.

Nellie went back to the kitchen with more empty plates, more leftovers and some untouched bread rolls , and then on with the next course to the business meeting.

Lord Verdonck appeared to have finished with the negotiations, and the men were talking and laughing, discussing their various travels and which music performances were worth seeing. The air in the room was thick with pipe smoke.

Nellie was just about to go back to the kitchen when the door burst open and a man in a dark robe came in. Deacon Fredericus, of the main church. Nellie had spotted him in the hallways with Shepherd Wilfridus, and assumed that both had come to discuss something with the Regent or to bless the food for the upcoming banquet. The two men often visited the palace and often came together.

She hadn't known that either of them were still here.

The men in the room fell quiet.

The Deacon looked around, as if searching for someone. Not finding this person, he walked to the table.

"I heard you have cut back on your orders of wine from the monastery," he said, looking at Master Pieters.

That gentleman replied, "Well, your grape vines appear to be affected by blight. Some of the ladies complained that the wine was sour, and we received some excellent samples from the estate of Duke Aroden." His voice sounded prim.

"Our monastery's wine is *not* sour."

"No? I will give you a bottle of the latest batch and you can test it for yourself. Good money we paid for it, too. I'm thinking you sold your best drop to others who paid more, and we got the second choice."

"None of our wine is sour."

"See? There you go. You admitted to giving us second-rate quality. Who got the best batch, which we were promised and paid for? Who was it?"

Lord Verdonck rose from the table and inserted himself between the two men. "Calm down. I'm sure we can sort this out like gentlemen. The monastery is free to sell its best wine to those who will pay most for it, and the palace is free to order wine anywhere it likes."

The Deacon whirled around. "Will you keep out of it, filthy heathen! Of course you would tell the palace to buy from thieves and unbelievers."

Lord Verdonck snorted. "I fail to see why the divine has anything to do with the production and quality of wine. For all I know, the Triune disapproves of drunkards; so what? Does the monastery enrich itself over the backs of people who love to do the very thing the divine doesn't approve of? How ironic."

"Shut up. You have no idea what you're talking about!"

"Clearly, I do not. Then again, I don't have the same intimate knowledge of the church as you. Tell me what the church does to help the people who drink too much of *your* wine?"

The deacon looked at him, his nostrils flaring. "Filthy heathen. The shepherd will hear of this."

"He's welcome. I'm sure you won't be telling him anything he doesn't already know."

The deacon whirled around and strode out of the room.

The closing of the door was followed by an intense silence in which Nellie very quietly set two plates on top of one another, and still the resulting "clink" sounded like a thunderclap.

Then Master Pieters said, "Ronald, much as I appreciate your support, I'm not sure that taking up a position so vehemently opposed to the church is wise."

"The church knows what I think. That has never been a secret. I have an issue with being called a nonbeliever. At my house, the Triune we worship is a kind deity, which has passion for the needy. True, the poor are not poor without reason, but for some, the only reason is bad luck. The Book of Verses says we should look after everyone, including the common people, because that is the cornerstone of our belief. It is what a decent man does. If I'm called a heathen for saying that, then I can only say some people need to read the Book more closely."

Master Pieters shook his head. "You're playing with fire. One of these days, you'll run into trouble. You will find that the Regent has banished you, disowned your estate and robbed your family. I know you as a friend and I would hate for that to happen."

Nellie had collected all the plates—few leftovers here —and could finally get out of the room.

She had heard the rumours that the Regent's advisor didn't have much good to say about the church, but this was the first time she'd witnessed it.

His outburst troubled her, because she, too, had never understood why it was all right for the monastery to sell wine while the shepherds condemned those who drank it.

She had always thought the shepherd meant to condemn those who drank it to excess, but then why did the monastery sell wine to those very people, those in the palace? Monks were poor, she knew that, too; but surely they could produce other things than wine?

When everyone had been fed, the plates taken away and tea brought upstairs, Nellie had time to go to church.

The prospect filled her with dread. She had not thought about her father, the book and dragons for most of the day, but she wanted to ask her trusted friend, the

Shepherd Adrianus of the church in the commercial district, about it so she would not feel guilty about having done nothing with her father's information.

But the fact that her father still controlled her six years after his death made her angry, too.

She debated whether she would take the book. To be honest, she would love to be rid of it. The book, the pipe, the monocle all reminded her of things she didn't want to remember. The church could have them, including the key, which probably belonged to the church anyway.

So she packed the lot into a carry satchel, and then went to the kitchen, where she collected the bowl of leftovers, that she'd saved from going to the pigs, in a hessian bag.

It was time for her to go.

CHAPTER 6

BY THE TIME Nellie pulled the door of the servant corridor shut behind her and stepped into the palace yard, the weather had taken a turn for the worse.

A biting wind blew the first snowflakes of the year over the city. They whirled against the darkening sky, dark specks that blew through the street in little eddies. It wasn't cold enough yet for them to settle, and they melted as soon as they hit the ground, but they were a reminder of the season to come.

Nellie clutched both sides of her coat against the wind with her left hand. The hessian bag she held in her right hand was too big for her coat to fit over the top, but she could hardly carry its contents in plain sight. The guards would ask where she was going with a couple of half-eaten loaves of bread and a bowl of cooked potatoes, some with the congealed gravy still attached. It would be obvious even without the coat of arms of the royal family on the bowl that the food came from the palace kitchens, and they might accuse her of stealing, even though anyone who knew Nellie would know that she wasn't a person who stole things.

Not bowls at least, and not food, either, except for left-overs from the ridiculous dinners that the Regent hosted, destined for the pigs while common people in the city went hungry.

In the gathering darkness, Nellie walked across the marketplace, where most merchants had gone home for the day, into the commercial district, where only the occasional shop showed signs of activity. Some shops had been boarded up, the owners leaving when they could no longer pay the rent or after one of the Regent's sweeps against magic.

Nellie stopped at her beloved church, an unassuming building tucked away between two stately merchant houses. The church tower was taller than the houses, but invisible from here because the street was too narrow.

She looked over her shoulder. Dusk was fast falling, and the street was almost deserted. Feeble light radiated from the windows, but the city guard who came to light the street lamps had not yet come. Lately, it had been far too common that no one lit the lights at all.

Nellie climbed the steps to the church door, opened it, and let herself into the darkness within.

She didn't like how the door was closed, although she understood why it was necessary. The church should be welcoming to everyone, open all day to people seeking solace and guidance from the holy Triune, people wanting to say a quick prayer after a day of work, or before asking a loved one's parents for her hand in marriage, or for the health of a sick child. Such people wanted to spend a moment in reflection in the cool and dark space, just themselves with the Triune and the heavy smell of incense.

Once the church had been like that. These days, the scent of incense was laced with an uncomfortable smell that reminded her of the poor house, where her father would sometimes visit on church business when she was little, though he didn't like it that she came.

It smelled of unwashed clothes and sweat. It even smelled of piss, a smell that hit you in the face and wouldn't let go, a smell reminiscent of suffering, of dirty, muddy refugee camps, of stumbling through the rubble of the destroyed city to find something to eat.

Those were uncomfortable memories.

The smell was in sharp contrast to the mild whiff of incense that the Shepherd still burned at the altar.

That candlelit pool of peace seemed a world away.

Here, in the darkness, where in normal times people would stand because they were too poor to pay for a pew or because they were late to the service, she could hear and feel, rather than see, the presence of people. She could smell the poor people who had come for a service but had stayed because it was cold and they could no longer afford to heat their homes. It was all right if one came to the church to make the children warmer and less hungry, right?

Often those people couldn't pay the rent at all, and they all came to the church because they had nowhere else to go. More people kept turning up at the church each day, because they heard it was a safe place to sleep, away from the weather and things like foul magic; because magic might be banned but that didn't mean no one was using it. People did evil things when they were desperate.

When Nellie's eyes became a little more used to the darkness, she unpacked her hessian bag and set the items she had brought onto the table where the shepherd used to leave the box of candles for patrons to use next to the box for donations, if you took a candle and had a coin to spare.

But there had been no candles for a long time, and the

box of money had long ago disappeared into the back room of the shepherd's house. Even before that, Nellie suspected that it no longer contained money.

"I've brought bread and potatoes," she said into the darkness.

The smell of cold boiled potatoes and cold gravy rose from the bowl once she took the lid off. It was not a nice smell, and it reminded her of the foul rooms where she had to tiptoe in after dinners ended and collect the dirty plates and dishes, the half-eaten chicken legs and spilled sauce, the unfinished potatoes and cold carrots. The place always stank of wine and sweat, though all the guests were gone save those too drunk or too fat to be dragged to their beds. Sometimes they sat in their own piss and slept in their own vomit, and Nellie had to pull the plates from under them, because Dora would kill her if the plates weren't clean by the next day.

And Nellie always put the scraps in a bowl and the plates on a tray and she carried the bowl downstairs. The bowl would breathe the smell of cold food as she carried it all the way down down into the basement and out the back door, through the yard where the pigs would oink-oink as soon as they heard the door. She had to walk across the yard with its muddy puddles without slipping, and sometimes a potato or two would fall out, and she would pick it up, muddy and all, and put it back into the bowl.

That was the food she was giving to these poor people.

It made her stomach churn.

A few people had come out from the darkness behind her. Now that her eyes were used to the low light, she could see the beds they had made for themselves against the back wall. My, there were so many more people than a few days ago.

"Thank you so much for thinking of us," the old woman Mina said.

As usual, Mina was impeccably attired in a dark dress, done up to the neck with a modest lace collar which looked only a little bit the worse for wear. She held herself straight, and assumed her position by organising the poor children in line for their share.

Mina was a few years older than Nellie, with no family to support her. Her husband had died several years ago, leaving her nothing but debt. Nellie saw herself in Mina's face. A comfortable life was such a fragile state that sometimes only a single thing needed to change and suddenly you were living in poverty on the streets.

Not that Mina hadn't tried to find work. She'd mended clothes and looked after children but, these days, the well-off who paid for such things had tightened their belts as well. And, if there was a choice of seamstresses or nannies, why not get a pretty girl who charged less than an older one with more experience? Why get an old woman who would only ask more money?

Mina took the bowl of potatoes, emptied it into a rusty old pan, and gave the bowl back to Nellie, who put it into her bag, which she set under the table, hiding the incriminating palace emblem from view.

She met the eyes of a man leaning against the back wall. His eyes were sunken and his skin sallow. He had an untidy beard that was knotty and dirty. He looked at her like a predator ready to spring. She didn't know him. He must be one of the jobless dockworkers. Many of them hung around the city, because they came from the surrounding villages. Nellie had heard some of these people had so much trouble from bands of rogues that travelling back to their homes was not safe, if even their villages still existed.

They had no money. Some would beg for jobs in the

marketplace. They were desperate and hungry, and they were becoming a danger in the city. How long would it be before they overpowered the women and children to get food?

She said to Mina in a low voice, "Now remember, this is for the children first."

"Of course, I'll make sure of that. No one will lay a finger on this food until the little ones have eaten."

Not that Nellie didn't want to help the men, but there were so many of them, and she could not carry that much food from the palace. Not without being noticed. Not without getting into trouble. And to be honest, the men frightened her.

"It looks like you got a lot of new people," Nellie said, while a sense of unease crept over her.

"Oh yes," Mina said. "New people join us all the time. The landlords keep putting up the rents and some families can't afford it anymore. They're ill or looking after little ones or old people. Many reasons."

While they were talking, a few women, all dressed in many layers of clothes, handed out the food to a group of dirty children. It disturbed Nellie to see how many children lived in this church, and some of them were so young.

"Don't be impatient, and wait for your turn," a woman was telling the children while ushering them into a line. "Show me your hands—no, no, you two, you have to wash your hands before you'll get anything. And all of you, say a prayer to thank the Almighty for this food, and thank Him for sending Nellie, because without her, you'd be hungry."

The two children who had been told to wash dunked their hands into a bucket of water, and then ran off to join the others on their way to the statue at the front of the church for prayer.

"And don't run," the woman called after them.

Her voice was familiar.

The woman put her hands at her side. "Those kids . . . they need to understand that we're in a church." She turned around.

Nellie gasped. "Jantien, what are you doing here?"

"Nellie!" The woman gave her a shocked look.

It had been a while since Nellie had seen her. When Nellie's parents were still alive, Jantien had lived two houses down the street. She was younger than Nellie, but the two families got on well because they were all church people. Last Nellie heard was that Jantien got married.

She felt a stab of horror, as all the people who had taken refuge in the church up till now had been there for reasons she understood. "How did you fetch up here? Where is your husband?"

Jantien looked aside. Hardship had deepened the lines on her face. "He had to leave."

"Leave, why?" It was a strange thing to say. Good husbands didn't leave their families in poverty. "Was he unwell? Was his family unwell?"

Jantien's husband was a tailor, she remembered. He even owned a shop in a good part of town because he did quality work.

"He's well enough, as far as I know," Jantien said.

"But?"

"He had to leave. I better say no more about it."

Nellie didn't give up so easily. "But . . . he had a shop, didn't he?"

"Yes, he did."

"Did he get involved with bad people?"

"No, nothing like that. Look, you wouldn't understand, living in the palace."

"I understand what it's like to have no money and I know from experience what it's like being on the run—"

Jantien opened her mouth.

"—but I understand that it's hard to talk about. How long have you been here?"

"Only a few days, I hope to find someone who has room for us."

But clearly she couldn't entertain too much hope, because if there were better places for homeless families to stay, then all these people would not sleep in the church.

"How many children do you have?"

The group of children now knelt at the altar under the leadership of the Shepherd Adrianus, who must have come in through the back entrance.

"Six. The oldest is twelve."

Nellie felt sick. Imagine having to live here with these dirty people with six young children. "I'm really sorry. I'll look around for ways to help."

But the palace had already taken all the people it could absorb into the servant staff and, as far as Nellie knew, the palace didn't have an endless supply of money, either. Neither did it have places for children to live.

"It's all because of the Regent and his evil men," a rough male voice said. He spoke so loudly that his words echoed in the church.

Mothers hushed their children, and women scurried to the safety of the darkness.

Mina pulled at Nellie's arm. "Don't pay attention to him. He's bad news."

Yes, Nellie knew of the raving rants Bert would have while standing in the middle of the marketplace with all the people going about their daily business around him, doing their best to ignore him.

Some said he was possessed, but he had correctly predicted some of Saardam's misfortunes.

A number of weeks prior to the Fire Wizard killing King Nicholaos and Queen Cygna, he had predicted the coming of a firestorm. During that long winter of the Fire

Wizard's harsh rule, he had predicted that the king's son Prince Roald was still alive and that he would come back, and when that had indeed happened, he had even predicted that a great evil would bring down King Roald and Queen Johanna.

He had to be in his sixties, a weathered, wrinkled, grizzled old man. In his youth he had been a soldier and had lost his right leg, cut off at the thigh. There were many stories about how this happened, all of them involving opponents with giant swords, or wild animals. Nellie suspected the truth to be more mundane, but the fact was he had only one leg and used crutches that went clack-clack-clack on the stone floor of the church as he dragged himself along.

His skin was raw and flaky from living in the cold, his eyes were watery, and he had only two brown chipped teeth.

He shuffled up to Jantien and pointed at her with a crooked finger and a long, dirty fingernail.

"It is because your dear husband had magic," he said. "That's why they took him away. The Regent's men seek the ones they don't like, and then start the rumours that they have magic and lock them up and those people are never seen again. No, don't shake your head because you know what's true. And especially you, Missy from the palace." He looked at Nellie, shuffled to her and pointed the dirty hand at her. "She knows this. She knows!"

Mina pulled Nellie further to the side. She whispered, "Don't listen to him, he's crazy."

Bert laughed. "You're afraid of me, you dumb woman?" He flapped his hand at Mina. "Get out of her way and let her go. She's not as dumb as you are. She knows I speak the truth, because she has seen what I'm talking about. I am telling you this Regent is evil. He and his henchmen are destroying us. They are destroying all we built. They drove the eastern traders out of the harbour; they drove the river peddlers away. So they did, and now we have no trade, huh? You go to the markets and what do you see? Some crappy cheeses and worm-eaten apples. There are no more beautiful sausages from Florisheim, no more fabrics from Lurezia, no more spices from faraway lands. The harbour is empty. There are no more iron ships; they've all gone to Anglia. There are no more riverboats, because the traders don't come anymore. The Regent and his henchmen have chased them all away. We should get rid of this fat, selfish man. We need the royal family to come back."

"Stop talking nonsense," Mina said. "They're all dead, so don't go talking about raising the ghosts, because you know where that leads."

Bert laughed. "You're afraid woman. You're afraid of me."

"I am not. I'm protecting the children."

He repeated in a faux female voice, "We're protecting the children!" He laughed again, long and loud. "The children don't need protecting. Or: the only thing the children need to be protected from is your own little minds. Let the children run. They will be fine. They will see that this pig of a Regent is only here to stuff his own face, and to assume the royal mantle that belongs to the last surviving member of the royal family."

By now, several of the women shouted at Bert to shut up.

"No, you are just afraid. We could have the power to change our fortunes because we did it before. When Queen Johanna ruled us, she did everything right. She brought in the rich traders, invited the kings from Burovia, Lurezia, Anglia. She brought in the money. She had plans to teach all children how to deal with magic, good or evil. She was going to teach the young kids with magic how to control it. And she never got to do any of that, and it killed her. You know why? Because of these idiot men in their idiot robes and their idiot three-headed god, because somehow they got it into their little heads that their god prohibits magic, and I've been through the vile Book of Verses more than ten times, and do you think I can find it? So do not talk about children. The children can see what you cannot—"

A woman yelled, "You are in our church! You can accept its teachings or leave!"

"You fools! It is only from within that you can change. I cannot change you. You must change yourself. When you step out of your little minds, I can help you find the only member of the royal family who is still alive. We could bring him back and have a royal family again if all of you were not so afraid. You're cowards, that's what you are!"

Mina yelled back at him. "I don't want to hear any of your stories about Prince Bruno either. Don't go putting nonsense into people's heads."

"But he is alive, I know it."

Then a clear voice said, "Wise and compassionate people don't shout at each other in the house of the Triune."

Shepherd Adrianus.

Everyone turned around to him

With his intelligent grey eyes and dark beard, the shepherd painted an authoritative figure. He was in his late twenties, a popular up-and-coming figure in the church.

He stepped between the squabbling parties, putting a hand on Bert's shoulder. "The Triune will appreciate if you were to keep those opinions quiet, and not to accuse other people."

Mina said, "Once he gets going, he picks out one person and then tries to frighten them."

"The Triune does not want His authority to be used to

frighten people. He wants us to accept one another as we are. Bert, good man, why don't you come over to the house for a talk?"

Bert sniffed and harrumphed. "All your weaselly words will not make any difference. The prince is alive. Everyone knows it. The guards know it too, but they are too afraid of a handful of fat men in dresses and their henchmen, never mind that they have a lot of money. They can hire armies and pay for their bodies, but they could never pay for their hearts. Prince Bruno is alive, and the city would come up in arms if they knew about it. We don't want priests, we don't want this stinking Regent."

"Calm down, good man. No one here will harm you. Will you promise to come for tea later?"

Bert sniffed again. "Only because it's you, mind. I have nothing with priests, but you're a nice man."

"Thank you, Bert."

Bert limped back to his corner past the table where he stuffed a cooked potato into his mouth. Mina breathed in deeply, put her hands at her sides . . . and then let out her breath.

Bert was Bert and there was no arguing with him.

In the scramble, one child had dropped a filthy rag doll. The shepherd picked it up and held it in the air. "Who owns this lady?"

"That's not a lady, it's Koos," said a little girl.

"Here then, look after Koos."

The girl was reunited with her doll.

With a few sentences, the shepherd had defused a potentially nasty situation. It was no wonder that the church had promoted him from deacon to shepherd and given him his own congregation.

"Oh, hello, Nellie. I see you've brought food from the palace."

"Not much today. There will be a lot more later this

week." For occasions such as important banquets, the kitchens always cooked far too much food.

"I will send a few choir boys to help you carry whatever you can get."

"Thank you."

Nellie had come for prayer, so while the shepherd talked to the children, she knelt before the statue of the Triune.

Three entities made up the Divine: the Father, who represented wisdom in the present life, the Ghost, for those who lived their lives in dubious pasts, and the Holy God, who ruled in the afterlife.

The statue had the body of an ox, or sometimes a dog, and three heads, one for each of the parts that made up the holy Triune. This statue was a work of art, chiselled from knotted and veined wood, imbued with golden lacquer and adorned with gemstones and gold paint.

The light from the flapping flames of the oil lamps made it look ethereal, warm and friendly.

She became aware that the shepherd had knelt next to her. It was typical of how he moved: quietly, but startling no one, and never drawing attention to himself.

"How are you keeping up?" he asked. "Happy birthday."

Out of all people, he would know when her birthday was, because the church kept all those records.

Nellie had almost forgotten about the reason she had come. Her birthday, her father's book and the box she carried in her satchel. "We're very busy."

"What did you find out about that letter from your father's solicitor?"

"I was going to ask you about that."

"Then come. Let us have some tea. I'm cold. I just made tea and I would hate for it to go to waste."

CHAPTER 7

NELLIE FOLLOWED the shepherd through the side doors of the church. They came out in the alley that ran between the church and the next house. It was a dark place, with uneven cobblestones, and she had to be careful where to put her feet, especially where it was wet. The alley ended in a small courtyard, with an entrance to the house where Shepherd Adrianus lived. It was a simple building of a single floor, with a parlour, a kitchen and—she assumed—one bedroom, since shepherds took their vows to the church and couldn't marry.

They climbed the steps into the dark hallway where it smelled of musty carpet, and went into the living room to the right, where the candlelight bathed everything in a golden glow.

It was warm in here, with a fire blazing in the hearth.

"Take your coat off, sit down," Shepherd Adrianus said.

He went to the cabinet against the wall and busied himself pouring tea. A moment later, he placed a cup in front of her, steam rising from the surface.

"It's become a lot busier in the church," Nellie began.

"Indeed."

"Did anything happen that sent people running to the church?"

"Food is getting scarce and expensive. Many families have been hanging on, waiting for harvest to bring better times, but the countryside is unsafe and farmers don't come to the markets from as far as they used to. Heaven knows rogues and bandits may have destroyed some small farming villages. There is not much food. The landlords are pushing up the rents and men are losing their jobs. It's coming to a crunch at this time of the year. Likely, it will get worse in the next months."

He was right about that, too.

"You're running out of room in the church," Nellie said.

"Yes, and there is not that much extra food you can bring."

Nellie wasn't even feeding a significant number of outcasts—some were in the poor house, some begged, some stole and others lived off the charity of others—but she understood their plight. As winter progressed, there would be more of these people and less food for them.

She said, "Bert was really getting into it today."

He sighed. "I should tell that man to respect the church and to stop spreading untruths, but then he would sleep in the street, and I don't want that either. But he *is* getting rather troublesome."

"If he couldn't stay in the church, he would steal things, because how else would he survive? He could beg, but few people have much to share." In fact most of the poor peddlers had vanished from the streets because there was nowhere for them to work.

"We'll just have to keep feeding them, because, no matter how far these people have strayed off the right path, they can always be brought back when we show them the goodness of our hearts. If there ever comes a time that we stop caring about our fellow human beings, that is truly the end of humanity."

"You're a good man," Nellie said.

"We do the best we can," the shepherd said.

Then he rose from his seat. "Do you want more tea?"

"I wouldn't say no to that." It had been cold in the church, even with the doors closed, and Nellie hadn't realised how chilled she had felt. And although it had seemed so when she came in, it wasn't actually very warm in this room at all.

The shepherd brought over the teapot.

The light from the hearth lit him side-on, highlighting all the unevenness in his skin. He was still young, but his face had turned much older in recent months.

It bothered him, Nellie knew, to have all these people in his church. She imagined that he didn't like the children running around the altar, and he didn't like the way the smell of poverty hung in the sacred space. He definitely didn't like Bert making statements that amounted to sacrilege.

But the shepherd was a peaceful man. He never argued and never shouted.

The Holy Triune was good, and forgiving, and He did not turn people into beggars.

He poured and gave Nellie her cup. While he set the teapot back onto the tea light, she warmed her hands on the porcelain.

"Bert says some odd things," Nellie began, because she needed to bring the conversation around to her father's book and the dragon box, but it was as if the whole room and the shepherd's demeanour screamed against her mentioning it.

"That, he does. He is full of strange tales; we all know that."

"His stories have often turned out to be true."

"Oh, there may be some truth in it, but a lot of what he says is dangerous speculation. It gives people ideas. They easily believe things and sometimes spread rumours just so they can get the attention of their neighbours and friends."

Nellie took a deep breath. "I heard something else and was wondering if it's true. I hope you don't mind if I ask."

"Asking is always good. It shows that you have the intelligence to think for yourself and not blindly follow the opinions of others. But if it's about Bert's statements, I wouldn't be the best person to answer your questions. I am never up to date with the latest gossip."

"It's about the church."

He raised his eyebrows.

Nellie took another deep breath. "And it's about my visit to my father's solicitor. He gave me a box that contained my father's diary, and while I was looking through it, I found some disturbing comments."

He folded his hands on the table as he often did when listening to her.

"My father said that at the time he worked for the church, the shepherd would buy secret artefacts and instruments of evil to research them. Is that true?"

The shepherd paused before replying. Nellie didn't like that pause. Then he said, "I know the church has a large library that includes books one wouldn't expect to be in a church. The Guentherite monks will send their brightest students to read those texts and see the evil within."

"Have you read those books?"

"I have. I know you're curious, but I have read them so that my congregation doesn't have to."

"What about other things that are not books?"

"There are some of those, too, but to be honest, most of them become worthless if you separate them from the belief that makes them evil. They serve as obscene reminders of what the human mind is capable of and excesses we have to stamp out."

And, of course, this was the problem, because the church refused to acknowledge that magic existed.

"My father worried that some of those items would fall into the hands of those who wanted to do ill with them."

"Oh, I understand, but your father was close to the Shepherd Wilfridus, and would not have grasped the reality that the items are inaccessible for most people. Even I would have to ask permission to go down in the locked section of the crypts and, to be honest, it's a very musty and dark place, and not as interesting as it sounds." He chuckled, but with little conviction. "Your father was a fantastic bookkeeper, but should have kept to keeping books."

Nellie nodded. That sounded like her father. But the shepherd's reply insinuated that her father *hadn't* kept to keeping the books. "Just to make sure, there is no dragon?"

He gave her a sharp look. "A dragon?"

"My father said—"

"Your father didn't know everything." Wow, that reply came too quick.

"He said there was a box that contains a dragon. I've seen those boxes. The queen used to have one given to her by the eastern traders. Her magic was wood, so a tree grew in it when she opened it. My father said the church acquired a box with a dragon in it and people had been killed and parts of the crypts burned down while trying to open it."

"I have never seen such a thing." Much too quick.

"Did parts of the crypt burn down?"

"They did, but that was because of a neglected candle."

"Did two church deacons almost get killed?"

"They did, but that was because they were reading in

the next room. The only exit was past the fire. There were a lot of rumours concerning this event, because the deacons had been reading books they shouldn't have, but between you and me, they were not the type of books that your father was thinking about."

"Does the church have a little box, the size of my hand, with eight sides and a pretty lid?"

"I honestly don't know. It might be in the crypt, but if it were important, I'd be aware of it. Why the concern about this box?"

"Because . . ." Nellie spread her hands. She didn't know anymore. Because her father had thought it was important. Because he would never lie, and if he had seen a dragon box and knew the church had bought a dragon box, then there was a dragon box.

But six years was a long time, and so much could have happened.

Maybe someone had taken the box and . . .

No, that thought didn't fill her with hope either. She had much rather that the box was in the crypt. "Maybe it's still there but people forgot about it."

He smiled, weakly. "That could well be, and, honestly, I wouldn't worry. There are a *lot* of things down there. And there are many who will tell any kind of lie to cover up their own misdeeds even if they concern mere acts of the flesh. Unfortunately, this *does* happen more often than I would like to admit. I'm much more inclined to believe that the two deacons in question were involved in an indecent act, knocked over an oil lamp and then blamed a dragon for the resulting fire."

When he said it like this, yes, Nellie could definitely see how that could happen.

"I try my best to keep the church honest and its servants acting honourably, and to me, that is a greater priority than ancient relics that may or may not exist, and that, if they exist, have no power beyond the minds of the people who believe in that power. This is why it's important not to repeat those rumours, because repeating gives them power. And many people want power over us. We in Saardam have a lot of things that the barons and kings of surrounding nations want. We have a vibrant port city that allows our merchants to access the low countries and the lands across the sea. We have a city that is free of those who seek to rule through evil magic. We have—only just— a Regent who fosters peace and is not embroiled in endless feuds with surrounding royal houses. We have the blessing of a peaceful Triune who respects all people and does not seek revenge. We are lucky. We've had bad times, but we are extremely lucky. Think of the poor people in Florisheim who have to bow to the Red Baron, the evil Baroness Viktoriya and her haughty daughter. They have no church to visit except the Belaman Church, where the priests wear gold-rimmed robes and demand that people donate a tenth of their meagre wealth in return for a blessing by someone drunk on the wine that the monasteries are forced to give to the church. If they protest against the rich and fat men in their opulent buildings, they may be whipped, or the church will send their magicians to mete out terrible punishment. Those poor people would love a church like ours, but the Triune cannot go where evil exists. The Belaman God is a vengeful god and does not approve of forgiveness. Their god holds the poor common people of those places in a powerful grip, and the more the Triune looks kindly upon them, and the more the people want to come to share our freedom, the harder the Belaman Church squeezes. Those people are locked inside the stone walls of their cities, because they are made to believe their church protects them, and are made to believe that evil men have evil magical relics that have the power to destroy. But who unleashes the fear of the ghosts that supposedly roam the countryside? The priests of the Belaman Church. Who punishes a wayward priest who fathers a child with an innocent maiden with such vengeance that the poor fallen priest murders the maiden, cuts the babe from her womb and hangs the head out to dry as 'proof' that evil magic made him do it?"

He now referred to the ruby-studded dried infant's head that was the relic that had prompted the unrest—started by the girl's peasant family—that had been the origin of the Church of the Triune.

"The Belaman Church priests are afraid of us, because we give the people hope, we give them a decent life, and we ask for nothing to enrich ourselves or the church."

He sipped from his tea before continuing.

"Regent Bernard may not be the most-loved man, but he has a nose for how to run a country, and people will come around to appreciating him and his family. He is not an unkind man. He will be good for the city."

"Does that mean he will finally be crowned king?" Nellie dreaded that day. The regent was not an evil man, but with his nightly banquets and his disregard for less fortunate people in the city, he was a long way from *good*.

"That's not for me to say. Shepherd Wilfridus has several monks dedicated to finding the best course to take with that issue."

When she asked previously, he had told her a complicated story about having to check the protocol to make sure that there was no other claimant to the throne. When King Roald was suddenly killed, and his successor Princess Celine died with him, a merry search had started for who had the most right to the throne.

"Is the delay because the church needs to check rumours that Prince Bruno is still alive?"

He chuckled. "These rumours have been around for a long time, and they're just that: rumours. If he were still alive, he'd be fourteen by now, on his way to becoming a strapping young man. He would not keep quiet. And even if he were still alive, he is not the king's son, so the church might not allow his claim on the throne anyway."

But the people of the city might think differently. Although she wasn't sure, because with his glossy dark hair and strange eyes, he was a *foreigner*.

"We live in a hard time," Nellie said.

"We had it too good for too many years," the shepherd said.

Nellie said no more. It was not up to her to question the shepherd's judgement, for he was a man much wiser than her. She knew, however, that whenever there had been good times, it had been because the Triune had inspired people to make it so. It had never happened because people waited to be saved. She knew that after the Fire Wizard had destroyed the city, the Triune had inspired her Mistress Johanna to return with Prince Roald, who could not have done this by himself. Heavens no, he would have preferred to hide in the garden or a monastery.

She knew the Triune had inspired Mistress Johanna to accept the eastern traders and stave off attacks by the Red Baron because he feared their eastern magic and wanted to get his hands on their iron ships. She knew it had been the Triune who had inspired Mistress Johanna to make the deals with the surrounding rulers that the city became the hub of trade, and not contested by any of the surrounding nations.

The Triune inspired people. But the people did the things. And if there had been bad times in the city, it was because people were not doing things and not caring as much as they should. Maybe it was because they were not listening to the Triune.

But no, she didn't think good times needed to be

punished. People who strayed off the path caused bad times.

She sipped from her tea.

Well, this had been a most unsatisfactory discussion.

She was wondering how she could bring the discussion back to her father, but then came the sound of footsteps from outside, and someone came into the front door of the house without knocking.

The shepherd looked at the door. He did not look alarmed because he probably recognised the visitor.

He got up to put his empty cup away.

The Shepherd Wilfridus came in.

"Oh!" Nellie got up from her seat and gestured to it. "You sit here. I was just about to go."

"Be at ease, child," the Shepherd Wilfred said. "I've come for a chat with my friend. I'm not in the habit of chasing away faithful citizens."

He met her eyes.

Shepherd Wilfridus was a man who seemed too tall and strong for his position. He was at least a head taller than Shepherd Adrianus and was wide in the shoulders as well as his waist. His hair had only recently started to go grey, and most, at least the part above his ears that formed a half circle around the bald top of his head—was still rust brown. He had to have southern blood because his eyes were brown.

The penetrating look in those eyes always made Nellie uncomfortable, as if he knew the inappropriate thoughts and the questions she had.

Speaking of questions—Shepherd Adrianus wouldn't tell Shepherd Wilfridus what she had asked, would he? That would be too horrific for words.

Nellie rose, her legs trembling. "I was about to leave. I have a lot of work to do tomorrow."

Shepherd Wilfridus gave her melancholy smile. "Yes, and you work very hard."

He must have seen her serving at the Regent's banquets, because he often attended those feasts, where Nellie would rush up and down the stairs from the kitchen with dishes and plates and other items. It always disturbed her to see the shepherd at the main table with the Regent. She wished he wouldn't come because those banquets put on by the Regent should not have church approval. Not while people in the city went hungry.

Nellie bowed to Shepherd Wilfridus and then Shepherd Adrianus, who stood by the hearth, his hands clasped before him, the knuckles white.

The silence in the room was thick as Nellie picked up her coat and her satchel with the box and the book from the stand near the door and left the room.

She was still in the dark hallway, doing up her coat, when the men started to talk. At first their voices were soft, but then Shepherd Adrianus burst out, "I don't know! You've asked me this many times already. If I knew, or if anything had changed, I would tell you."

Shepherd Wilfridus said something else that Nellie couldn't hear.

"They are not thieves," Shepherd Adrianus said. "If they were, they wouldn't need to come to the church for help. Heaven knows, they might live in stately houses."

Thud.

"You play with fire!" Shepherd Wilfridus said, his voice like a clap of thunder. "It's like you fail to understand our delicate situation."

"Oh, I understand it well enough, but these people are not thieves. They are poor, that's true. They may smell, that's also true. They may even have snatched an occasional apple from a market stall, but they have no interest or use for those items you are talking about. They wouldn't even recognise their value. Go into the church and ask them yourself, and you will get the same answer I'm giving you: these people are poor, but they are not thieves."

Nellie retreated from the door. The two men would probably come out soon, and she had no business being here, *eavesdropping* on the shepherd. And she hadn't even found the courage to show the shepherd her father's book.

CHAPTER 8

NELLIE LEFT the shepherd's house as quickly as she dared. Down the steps, into the court-yard and across the alley. She collected the hessian bag with the empty bowl in it from under the table in the church vestibule and set off for the palace. A steady drizzle fell from the sky, making the cobblestones slippery.

As she passed the church, the sound of voices drifted out, but she kept walking. She felt guilty that she couldn't do more for Jantien and Mina and those poor children. The shepherd was right: with the coming winter, things would get worse. Many more people would find themselves without a home.

At one point some people sheltered in the main church, too. One of them had reportedly stolen some-thing. But why did that make all the poor people thieves?

But she could still hear the men's voices. They had definitely not sounded like they were friends.

The rumours that there was no love lost between Shepherd Adrianus and Shepherd Wilfridus had always been strong. Once she had heard someone in the kitchen —was it Wim?—talk about an argument the two men had after a service when they thought no one could overhear them.

Apparently there had been a lot of angry sniping between the two, although Wim didn't know why.

And so her thoughts went around while she walked through the streets.

Few people ventured into the miserable weather. Most of the citizens stayed inside and covered their windows with thick blinds to keep in whatever warmth still lingered from autumn.

Nellie pulled up the collar of her coat and was reminded of the content of the box that was still in her carry satchel. Her talk with Shepherd Adrianus hadn't really revealed anything useful.

He'd seemed disturbed when she spoke of her father's book, but had asked no questions. She hadn't liked the small moments of silence.

Then he'd taken the conversation in a different direction. Yes, she understood that it was necessary to guard the church against those who wanted to do it ill, but stories of church officials doing disgusting things and then trying to cover it up were not uncommon.

As the Book of Verses said, the flesh was often weak.

But she hadn't asked about those things. She'd asked about her father's involvement in particular, about the church buying items of dark magic, about dragon boxes.

Because one thing bothered her in particular: if the church believed magic didn't exist, they might have an interest in the old relics for curiosity's sake. But why would they pay a lot of money for an empty wooden box that might not even have belonged to Prince Bruno, anyway? Without the dragon, it was just a box, worth the price of the wood.

So, if the church was prepared to pay a lot of money

for the dragon box, then they had to believe there was some kind of magic in the box.

Hmmm, what did this mean for the other relics? She had heard the church owned the ruby-studded infant skull, which was meant to be a symbol for rebirth and cleansing. That book of evil magic, *The Arts Of The Arcane,* would have no value if you believed the contents were all nonsense.

At least that was her practical thinking.

She might be completely wrong about this, but when it came to money spent, she wasn't often wrong. People spent money because there was value or because they could brag about having expensive items. Since the church was not putting the items on display in gold-rimmed cabinets, there had to be value. Did they keep those things in the church crypts?

Nellie arrived in the marketplace. The big main church loomed dark and forbidding on one side of the square. Once, when mistress Johanna was young, the church had been a simple building made of wood. Mistress Johanna insisted on wearing clogs into the church, and sometimes Nellie could still hear the clomping sounds on the wooden floorboards. People would act scandalised about it, and Nellie remembered pleading with mistress Johanna to wear proper shoes. Looking back on it, Nellie hated how meek and dumb she would have looked. The Church of the Triune was *about* common people, and people should feel welcome inside its walls no matter what they wore.

The old church had burned to the ground when the Fire Wizard occupied the town. He started rebuilding it, initially for the Belaman Church.

If you looked at the walls closely enough, you could see where Johanna and Roald had been victorious over the Fire Wizard and the complicated design of the church had been scaled down in favour of a plain stone building.

The main church was *very* plain. Its walls were straight; the doors were simple. There were no arches and carvings, no elaborate ironwork on the door. The roof was simple, the tower simple—though very tall and containing an impressive set of bells that made the air vibrate when you stood at the bottom of the tower.

Like the church she visited, it was always open. Nellie climbed the steps to the church door. She turned the handle. The metal coldness of it, wet with almost-frozen rain, bit into her skin.

The handle creaked.

The door was very heavy, needing all her weight to open it a crack.

A waft of stale air only slightly warmer than outside drifted out, laced with the scent of incense and burning tallow. That mixture of scents would forever remind her of the long days when she sat in the pews as a child, looking at the backs of the people in front of her because she was too little to see the altar. She had counted the knots in the wood in the backrests of the bench in front of her, because she was so bored and because her father would be angry if she wriggled too much.

Most of the giant church hall—with a row of pillars supporting the roof on either side of the aisle—was shrouded in darkness, but a golden glow of light surrounded the altar.

Nellie's footsteps echoed through the empty space as she walked along the aisle. The pews, rows and rows of them, disappeared into the darkness on both sides.

At one point, people also sheltered in this church. Now they were gone and this big dry space just went to waste, because one of them had allegedly stolen from the church and Shepherd Wilfridus had kicked them out.

This was the church where Roald had been officially crowned king, where everyone had gathered on that glorious day in midsummer to baptise little princess Celine. The pews had been full to overflowing, with people standing at the back and along the sides and outside in the marketplace, waiting for the royal family to come out.

Today, in the dark and alone in this giant building, Nellie could still hear the echoes of the voices of those people, the cheering, the tolling of the bells.

Those people were dead and everything was gone. It was hard to believe.

The altar was a plain wooden lectern set on a platform two steps up from the church floor.

Behind it stood the big statue of the Triune that had once graced the pond in the palace gardens in the time of King Nicholaos. It had been dragged out of the palace garden—causing damage to the paving—and thrown into the harbour during the reign of the Fire Wizard. After the wizard had been ousted, it had been retrieved and cleaned. King Roald didn't want it in the palace, because he didn't like the statue—his dislike of the church was an ill-kept secret—so Queen Johanna had donated it to the church as a symbol of the resilience of Saardam and its people.

Despite the cleaning, the stone of the statue had acquired stains that no amount of scrubbing could remove. The face of the Father bore several dark streaks that made it look like He was crying. The Holy God had lost part of His nose. A dark stain marked the neck and upper body of the Ghost.

Children forced to sit still for long services in these pews said it looked like someone had stabbed the Ghost and blood ran over his chest. They would make up macabre stories about it. The adults said it was a divine marking.

Whatever you thought, the statue had possessed a macabre air since it had first been commissioned by King

Nicholaos. The faces of the three-headed being were contorted with emotion, looking up at the sky for salvation while straining to break free from ropes wound around the lower half of the body.

Many people said the statue gave them shivers, and that had not improved with the time it spent at the bottom of the harbour.

The darkness and utter silence, and the long shadows cast by the sparse lamps, rendered the statue dark and threatening. It loomed over the altar and the front pews with open mouths in stifled screams, as if some evil creature had tossed these three people into a snake pit and cast a spell to turn them into stone as they screamed in fear and pain.

Nellie knelt on the padded benches placed in front of the statue for that purpose. Even when she folded her hands and bent her head, she felt that the statue was watching her.

Please, Triune, give me the strength to continue helping the less fortunate of the city. Please help Jantien find a better place to stay. Please let her find a job, no matter how small. Please help Bert to be moderate so that he doesn't anger people and get kicked into the street.

She spoke very softly because the Triune could hear thoughts and one didn't need to speak in order to pray—it just felt better if you did.

But even her soft whispers echoed in the vast space of the church. Several times she halted. Were those soft footsteps, or mice skittering in the darkness? Was someone spying on her, waiting behind a pillar to rob her?

No, she was surely seeing things. The church was a *safe* place, even in the darkness.

She rose, clutched her satchel with the box and the book, but left the bag with the bowl to fetch later and grabbed a lantern that stood near the side of the altar. She knew it was there and had seen the shepherd use it to walk around the church.

She took off the glass covering and lit the wick with the flame from one of the candles.

Then she carried it down the two steps to the side of the church, where a staircase disappeared into the ground.

A section of the church crypts were open to the public.

Apart from holding the church's library and, if her father was to be believed, a stash of evil items, the crypt held the graves of the members of the royal family, and this section was always open, so that the citizens could come to pay their respects.

Nellie walked down the stairs, going slowly because the flapping light in the lamp cast weird shadows that made it hard to see where the steps ended. As she descended, the air grew warmer.

She came out in a broad passage where both the walls bore large plaques behind which past kings and queens had found their last resting place.

King Nicholaos lay buried here with Queen Cygna, and their son King Roald with Queen Johanna. These plaques looked new.

After the tragedy that had destroyed the royal family, Nellie had filed through this room with many other people, touching the inscription on the stone. Tears had flowed freely. The young royal family was loved by many. No one knew how they had died because no one in the audience room—where they attended a musical performance—had lived to tell the tale.

There were no plaques for either child—Celine, aged six and Bruno, aged four, because only reigning monarchs were buried in the crypt. They did, however, have grave stones in the cemetery at the back of the church. Rumours said that both graves were empty, because Princess Celine's body had been burnt to cinders, and Prince Bruno's had never been found.

Empty wall space at the end of the passage was reserved for future kings and queens.

Regent Bernard could declare himself king, but without the blessing of the church he would never be one, and would not be buried here. What would happen if he died?

Would Casper be his heir or would the church find someone else?

A metalwork grate closed off further access into the crypt. The metal bars of the grate were delicately shaped into leaves and roses with thorns, but the metal had turned black with age.

Nellie stood in front of the metalwork, looking into the darkness, peering through the bars.

The passage continued on the other side, but was lined with statues and ornate wooden cabinets. When the church was rebuilt after the fires only this room had survived.

This was the secret room that her father had mentioned.

In the few times she'd been here, she had never considered what might hide behind these bars.

There was a small door in the metal grate. The hinges showed signs of frequent use. An ornate lock with a hole for a key held the door shut.

Nellie pulled it, but it only rattled a bit.

She wondered . . .

Shepherd Adrianus said that he needed permission to come here. He was much concerned with the indecent behaviour of churchmen, with good cause. He genuinely didn't seem to know much about the things stored here. But did the fact that her father knew exactly what was inside mean he had a key?

Nellie put down her lamp, slid the satchel from her shoulder and took out the box.

She picked up the old ornate key in the bottom of the box. With trembling hands, she inserted it into the lock.

It turned.

The door opened.

CHAPTER 9

NELLIE HESITATED at the door, a sense of trepidation coming over her as she stared into the darkness. She shouldn't be here, and if she were sensible she would turn around now and leave this place immediately.

But if she did, she would forever worry about what she could have learned and done if she had gone ahead.

If the Shepherd Adrianus was right, nothing here was of value—just old books full of nonsense and lots of dust. If this was merely a place where junior members of the church came to read about or perform indecent acts then she could understand her father's worry. But in the palace hallways during banquets, she had seen enough debauchery and fornication to last her a lifetime, and since they involved two people who both agreed to take part, she thought there were more important things to worry about. Indecency did not frighten her.

She stepped inside and pulled the door of the little gate shut so it didn't fall into the lock but looked like it was closed. Then she turned around and walked into the secret crypt.

The corridor was short, with blind walls, moisture-stained bricks and the end. Dark wood cabinets on the right-hand side contained old and dusty clothing on hangers: ornate moth-eaten robes and faded habits of types she had seen none of the shepherds wear for a long time.

In between the wardrobes were two doors but, on investigation, both ended up in the same room: a low ceilinged cellar with rows of pillars supporting the roof. Rows of dusty barrels took up most of the floor space, some with markings or names. Wine, she presumed.

It was too dark for her to see the far end.

In the left-hand corner stood a set of sturdy shelves that held bottles with dusty labels. A few newer-looking wine barrels remained on the ground next to the shelf.

To the right, a wooden partition closed off a section of the cellar, and access to that area was through an arched passageway. She found the library on the other side: a room with rows of bookshelves, a few glass-fronted cabinets with rare works, and a set of couches in the middle.

My, she had never seen so many books. Shelves and shelves, most neatly catalogued by subject. The category labelled *the Verses* contained many different versions of the holy Book.

She pulled out a heavy tome adorned with gold paint. The pages were thick and lush, covered with illustrations. Why wasn't this gorgeous book upstairs for all to see?

But on closer inspection she noticed that those beautiful painted letters, the intricate borders and pages of paintings of luscious scenes, all included at least one couple naked, engaged in the act of reproduction. Some of them were almost tastefully hidden behind the first letter of the page, others much less so.

One achingly beautiful illustration showed a couple on a windowsill overlooking a forest with mountains in the background. The woman leaned back with her legs wide, showing in intricate detail the lush covering of curly hairs between her legs, the fleshy lips that protruded from the fuzz and the soft pink opening glistening with moisture. The man's part was not a finger's width from answering that invitation, strong, engorged with a raised vein along the side.

Playful sunlight hit both lovers side-on, drenching the countryside in vibrant colour and casting a glow over the woman's hair and her perked-up breasts.

It was so beautifully done that Nellie wanted to take the page, but so confronting it chilled her. She closed the book and put it back on the shelf, her heart thudding, aware of her own miserable life in which she had never married, never given herself to a man beyond an odd kiss and never experienced the pleasure of being loved.

One book lay separate from the others on a shelf as if it saw regular use.

The book's spine proclaimed the title: *On the Art of the Human Anatomy*.

When she turned a few pages, it was clear what sort of anatomy the book referred to in an almost instructional way with black and white illustrations.

Nellie leafed through the pages with an increasing sense of horror.

Did men really do that to each other, standing behind each other with their trousers around their knees?

Did they really tie up women on a table by the arms and legs and insert various objects into their private parts? The woman in the illustration held her mouth open—in agony, Nellie assumed, because this couldn't be pleasant.

Did they do that to animals, too?

Did they get a woman, presumably a beggar off the street, and sit her on a chair in front of a group of men who watched as she performed indecent acts on herself?

Did they do this to young boys and girls? The poor boy

was crying, the tears dripping down his face. Was this meant to suggest to men that it was normal that the child cried, and not to worry about it?

Did they ask a young girl to sit on her knees in front of a man and take his private parts in her mouth?

Did these men take advantage of poor and homeless people by treating them like this?

This was disgusting. She put the book back.

The next section of the library contained books about nature and herbs, and then a section about human diseases, with intricate drawings of internal organs. A heart, lungs, the inside of the stomach, a womb cut half-open showing the child inside.

There was a thin book about *The Birthing of Infants* that started off by saying that women didn't like it if the church interfered with their practical knowledge, and that the birthing process was a heathen affair during which practices by midwives could invite demons and lead to possession of the mother and child by evil.

There were pages of illustrations of birthing positions and how those favoured by midwives—usually in a chair—were evil because the child was born "into darkness".

It then included positions that were approved, including—fully clothed!—women on elbows and knees and flat on their backs surrounded by men who looked suspiciously like priests.

The illustrations were crude, and whoever wrote this had obviously never witnessed a woman giving birth.

On one shelf, she even found the fabled *Arts of the Arcane*, the book mentioned by her father.

It was a thick book that contained long dissertations about dark magic, about the church—the Belaman Church in this case—and the poisons and herbs with their effects and time before recovery—or death.

There was a chapter on the different types of magic.

Wood magic, wind magic and water magic were common, but other types of magic were mentioned that Nellie had never heard about. Apparently, some people derived their magic from the food they ate. About these people, the book said, *They are often dangerous spies and in the employ of rulers. Not uncommonly, they turn on their rulers and are almost impossible to contain. It is an ill-kept secret that the great outbreak of illness in the Skandian town of Laivi was caused by a spurned food magician.*

The next chapter dealt with food magicians and how to use or detect them: one could detect the presence of magic using quicksilver, because it was repelled by magic. One could make potions that countered the effects of food magic.

It had a chapter on exorcism, including images of how the victim might faint or vomit violently.

Nellie shuddered. She had almost forgotten about having seen that during her travels with mistress Johanna.

The next chapter was called *Beauty in Death* and it detailed how to dress up dead bodies for funerals, including a detailed description of sewing together a man who had been mauled to death by a bear. Of a woman perished in illness, it said to dress her up nicely and paint her pallid face in case the husband wanted to—

Whaaaaat?

Nellie turned the page.

Necromancy.

All right, that was enough for her.

She put the book back, feeling sick, her mind whirling with disturbing thoughts. The church was right to keep all this out of view of the public. By *evil books* she had assumed books about magic, but that made up only a small part of the library and was mostly about herb lore, although there was a book called *Manifestations and Banning Of Ghosts* that she had no desire to see.

Good grief.

This place was the collection of everyone's worst nightmares.

A thin book with a plain cover contained mostly sketches of children, with an occasional picture filled in ink. Wait—that was Prince Bruno and his older sister Celine. This book had to have come from the collection of the court portrait painter.

Nellie leafed through the pages, thinking of those happy memories and sun-filled days.

The children in the drawings grew older, and then suddenly, an empty page.

The pain of loss stabbed through her heart.

Nellie was about to shut the book when she noticed there was another drawing on the next page, in a much more severe style. It showed a boy sitting in a cane chair. Nellie judged him to be about nine or ten. He wore a shirt that was too big for him, with the sleeves rolled up and thin, stick-like arms poking out.

His face had lost its childish chubbiness, but it was unmistakably Prince Bruno.

Nellie stared at the picture, heart thudding. It could be that the artist had tried to imagine what the prince would look like if he had still been alive. Or it could be that the prince *was* still alive, as Bert said.

But if so where was he?

The box. She was here to check if the church had the dragon box.

She blew out a breath as if it would blow the disturbing images from her mind.

The room contained a single glass-fronted cabinet with three sections containing three shelves each, displaying a variety of items that glittered in the light of the lamp. Nellie crossed the room.

By the Triune, the infant's skull with the red rubies was

in the cabinet. The glow from her lamp made the stones glitter deep inside the eye sockets.

When she came closer, the glow pulsated as if there was a beating heart hidden inside.

Nellie took in a sharp breath, and froze, her heart racing. Was this thing alive?

The light remained steady.

She moved the lamp up and down and from side to side.

Phew. The pulsating effect happened because of the way the light reflected in the cut facets in the stones.

She stepped closer to the cabinet because she needed to see what else was in there. A dragon box would be about the size of her palm. If it was in this room, it would be in this cabinet.

She peered in through the glass, holding up the light—and the red eyes pulsated. Was it really because she moved the light?

The glow of the lantern reflected in the polished side of the skull. Weren't skulls normally white? Why was this one black?

She did not like this thing. Wherever she turned, it was as if those eyes watched her.

The ruby skull had bewitched priests. It had enticed people to kill and attempt necromancy. The person who saw this thing and still said there was no magic was truly resistant to it. This skull embodied magic. It proved that magic was real. It oozed evil magic, through the glow of the eyes, and the throbbing of the surrounding air.

It wanted her to take it out of its cabinet and into the daylight so it could turn daylight black. It wanted to be free from this prison and wreak havoc upon the world.

She had to force herself to turn away.

The cabinet contained all manner of dark and obscure items: teeth from all kinds of animals; the skull from a bird much larger than she had ever seen, the black hooked beak still attached; a silver cup with engravings of skulls and bones, blackened through age; a spindly metal instrument with a knob and a little arrow attached that you could move across a dial; a spoon-shaped flange that looked like it might have a medical purpose, but Nellie hated to think what; and a set of two cups made from a ram's horns.

No dragon box.

But wait . . .

On the left-hand side of the middle shelf in the third cabinet section, a spot was empty and a piece of paper with something written on it in loopy handwriting lay there. When she held the light up at a certain angle, it showed an octagonal shape in the dust, about the size of her palm, where something had been until recently.

The note said:

If you have removed this object from this cabinet, may the Lord of Fire have your soul and devour it.

Nelly did not recognise the handwriting, but putting things together, she figured that it belonged to the Shepherd Wilfridus and that this was the item that someone must have stolen from the church.

On the other hand, how could he suspect the beggars, because how would they get in here when not even Shepherd Adrianus had a key?

Maybe a careless monk had left the door unlocked?

But the thief must have known what they wanted, because if they were simply looking for evil, the skull would be the most obvious object to take. If they were after money, there were many silver and gold objects in this cabinet that were worth more than a wooden box, no matter how pretty.

This thief would have had to resist the magic of the ruby skull to pick up the unassuming box instead.

Where was it now?

She looked around, not really expecting to find it. This dank room, the darkness and the sheer evil of the place pressed on her: she needed to get out, now. There was nothing here for her.

She picked up the lantern, suddenly very afraid.

She left the library, past the racks with the barrels of wine and the dusty bottles.

Creatures rustled in the dark.

Nellie went back to the crypt room, let herself through the gate and pulled it into the lock behind her.

Phew.

She strode through the burial chamber, climbed the stairs, but coming out at the top, a faint glow of light lit the wall in the staircase—there was someone else in the church.

She peeked around the corner. At the statue of the Triune stood a monk named Gerard who had been helping the shepherd for a few months now, a young fellow with ginger hair.

He sank on his knees on the padded bench and folded his hands in prayer.

Nellie scooted out of the doorway to the stairs. She turned down the wick until the flame flickered out, placed the lamp where she had found it, picked up the bag with the bowl, and walked across to the statue, her heart racing.

The monk looked up.

"Oh," he said. "I didn't know anyone was here."

It surprised her how young he sounded.

"I visited the crypt to pay my respects to my mistress."

"I understand."

"I'm sorry if I disturbed you."

"No, you didn't."

"Well then, I had better go."

Nellie turned to the aisle, desperate to get out of this place.

"What is your name?" Gerard said behind her.

"I'm Nellie."

"Nellie, do you believe the Triune always knows what is best for us?"

"I do." What was this? How did he know she had doubts about the church?

He smiled. His teeth were white, but they stood at all kinds of different angles. With the light hitting him side-on, his face looked very soft, his chin still without wayward hairs that would eventually thicken into a beard. "Good. The Triune always knows what is best. It is not up to us to question His orders."

He *knew* something. He knew about her father's book and his misgivings about the church. Or he knew about the rumblings in the kitchens that questioned whether the Regent would ever be crowned king, and that if he wasn't, the church obstructed the process.

Nellie nodded. Her legs felt like pudding. "Yes, the Triune knows what is best for us."

"Then be on your way, child. It's late and tomorrow is another long day."

His blue eyes looked innocent, but Nellie couldn't stop thinking about the woman tied to the table while men put objects in her private parts.

Did he take part in those activities, too?

She'd had enough. It was a bad idea to come here. As fast as she dared, she walked along the aisle back to the church door and into the freezing rain. In her imagination, she could hear Gerard laughing.

Why had she even gone down there?

That book from her father was nothing but trouble. She should burn it tonight.

But what a position this left her in.

If she had found the box there, she would have been happy that the church was looking after it, and that some people in the church might be disgusting, but they were not interested in dark magic.

But the box had been *stolen,* and the shepherd wanted it back.

She *couldn't* burn the book.

CHAPTER 10

THE PALACE LAY DARK and forlorn on the other side of the city's main square. A tall fence with an elaborate gate surrounded the forecourt. It was open during the daytime, but the guards closed it at night, and anyone wanting to go inside had to give a reason.

Two men stood by the guardhouse for that purpose, gilded by the glow of light from a street lamp.

They greeted Nellie as she came up to them and opened the gate for her.

Nellie walked through the deserted forecourt, past the side of the palace.

It was dark in the corridor that ran through the servants' quarters, except in the kitchen. A few of the workers sat around the table with a pot of tea between them, a group of weary faces looking up at Nellie.

Nellie walked into the scullery and set the empty bowl —the one she had used to carry the food to the church— on the bench. It was dark and humid here and smelled of rancid fat. Creatures—mice probably—scurried in the corners.

Back in the kitchen, she poured herself some tea before sitting down with the others at the table.

"How was church?" Dora asked.

"There were more people than before," Nellie said. She didn't need to explain. They all knew she was talking about the poor who came for shelter. "I spoke with the shepherd." She wrapped her hands around the warmth of the cup.

To her surprise Els was still in the kitchen. The two sisters normally went home after dark.

Corrie said, "It must have been cold in the church, because you look like you've seen a ghost."

"Just tired." She desperately didn't want to talk about the crypt.

She sipped from her tea.

Dora and Corrie spoke about all the things that needed to be done tomorrow.

Peeled potatoes sat in pans in the corner of the kitchen bench. Plucked ducks hung from the ceiling. A crate of carrots stood on a stool—off the ground so that the vermin would not find it attractive. There was no more room in the kitchen's mice-free pantry.

The bakers had set bowls of dough to rise near the fire. They would be the first to come in here, rising after midnight to start their jobs.

Everything was ready for the arrival of more guests tomorrow, and compared to the things she had seen in the crypt, all this mundane normal stuff passed by her in a haze.

Els was also quiet.

"Why are you still here?" Nellie asked her.

"I waited, because I need to ask you something."

"Oh?" That didn't sound good, and the girl's eyes glittered in the lamplight as she said this.

"Come." Nellie rose, gulped the rest of her tea while standing, put her cup down and walked to the door.

Els followed her out of the kitchen, down the corridor into the linen room.

It was cold here. Light from a lamp in a sconce outside the door fell into the room, revealing the folding table where, during the day, the laundry girls would fold serviettes into nifty shapes.

"You know about herbs, right?" Els said.

"A bit. I can help with some things, but if you want something special, you will have to go to—"

"Please, I need to get juniper berries."

"You need . . ." Nellie stared at her. Those were used to bring on a woman's bleeding if it was late.

Most nights, Els' mother could be found in the taverns in the harbour, traipsing up and down the stairs in the company of drunk sailors with fat purses.

Nellie had taken the two sisters into the palace to save them from going down the same path.

"It's not for me," Els said, seeing Nellie's expression. "It's not for my sister either."

"But for a 'friend'?" Nellie asked.

"No. Men are disgusting. I'd rather become a nun."

"You might try going to church first."

But Els' mother was from Scandia. Scandian people were known to be heathens. In fact, the only one Nellie had ever known to visit a church was King Roald's mother Queen Cygna.

"Now you're just being smart with me."

"You're asking for a poison. I need to make sure you're serious."

"I am. It's for my mam. She has been vomiting in the mornings. With pap injured and spending all his earnings in the tavern, we can't afford any more brothers or sisters. We scarce have money for ourselves. Last time I gave it to her, it worked real well, even if I had to wash the blood out of the bed. I was going to get some berries from the woman at the markets, but she stopped coming. But I'm not looking after any more new babes, and I'm certainly not helping my mam bring any more children into the world. Do you know how hard and disgusting that is, with all the blood and the screaming and trying to keep the young ones out of the bedroom because they don't have to see that? It takes forever, and then the mess. What do people even do with all of it? It didn't fit in our slop bucket, so I had to dump it in the harbour, at night to keep anyone from seeing me do it, because we can't afford to pay fines for dumping waste either."

It was hard to believe that this girl was only fourteen.

A careless youth was a luxury only afforded by the rich.

Nellie went to the cupboard to the side of the laundry where the soaps and bleaches were kept as well as a supply of homemade remedies for common ailments.

Nellie knew the most about herbs of the kitchen staff, so she had taken on the official role of dispensing the medicines and replenishing them.

She took out a glass container with a fat cork stopper. A small layer of black shrivelled balls coated the bottom. "There are few left. Hold out your pocket and I'll give you all of them. I'll buy some new ones next time I'm at the markets."

She upended the jar into Els' apron.

"Make a strong tea and soak these in the hot water. Drink several times a day."

"Thank you. You are so good to us."

With that, Els scooted out the door, and Nellie watched her go down the corridor, her thick plait dancing over her back. Poor girl. Her family really wasn't terribly fortunate. Work in the harbour was poorly paid, seasonal and dangerous, not in the least because the men who worked there were likely to pick up the sailors' preference for liquor. Drunk men couldn't work, spent what little money they had on booze, and neglected their families. They often took to the whores.

Els' mother came from a small village along the frigid northern coast of Scandia, was sold as captain's pet and dumped in Saardam when she was with child.

To Els' father's credit, he fell for the fair-haired beauty, married her and looked after little Els and all the other children she conceived while selling herself at the docks to feed an ever-increasing brood of ragtag brats from many different fathers.

Els took after her northern captain father. Strong in body, strong in opinions.

With any other family, without the whore mother and the drunkard father, she could do well, but she had been doomed at birth.

Nellie returned to the kitchen and collected a bowl of cream, then walked down the cold and dark corridor to her room. She lit a candle in the moist and stuffy darkness.

The black and white kitten poked its head out from underneath the bed.

Funny how quickly those cats learned.

Nellie picked it up, and it hung in her hand with its paws dangling between her fingers, little more than a bag of loosely connected bones.

She set both the bowl and the kitten on the floor where it proceeded to lap up the cream.

Nellie put the candle on the shelf above her bed and picked up the Book of Verses from the table.

A well-worn bookmark sat at the spot where she had left off reading last night, at the parable of the farmhouse door in the Book of Union.

It described how a teacher tells his young pupils that when the Father came home, he closed the door. The

Ghost, being a soul of no corporeal substance, walked through the wood. While the Father and the Ghost had travelled together, the Father did not appreciate this intrusion. So the Ghost did not argue and agreed to sleep in the barn.

So the teacher asked his pupils what this story meant. Most of them said they thought the Father didn't like ghosts in his house.

But one pupil, a little girl, said, "The story is not about ghosts. It's about friends. We're happy to share with friends, but even friends don't need to know everything. A good friend respects that. So the Father and the Ghost are very good friends who respect each other."

The little girl, whose name was Rose, made frequent appearances in this chapter.

She was what the Shepherd Wilfridus would call a good obedient little girl. She watched and thought before she spoke and never yelled or pleaded.

Nellie loved the stories of Rose and she wondered what Rose would have to say about what she had seen and heard today.

Would she say, "The church is the house of the Triune, and the people should respect it," even if the church kept books that showed such horrible things? Would she see why the Triune, the Holy Union of the God, the Father and the Ghost who occupied the church in soul but not in body, needed to have all this dry and empty space to itself while families slept in the street? Would she understand why families were cast into the street while the Regent held lavish banquets?

Would she understand the need for the men of the church to take delight in reading these horrid books?

Nellie sank to her knees, leaning her elbows on the bed and looking up at the candle flame on the shelf above.

"I pray to your soul, oh wise Rose, to grant me understanding, to divest me of my anger and find acceptance with the decisions of those wiser than me."

But she did not find inner peace.

Nellie tried to sleep, but after tossing and turning, got up, lit her lamp and took the Book back out of its drawer and sat in bed, her legs covered by the blankets, and leafed through the pages.

She started at the beginning, at the creation of the world, and worked through the books of the prophets, the teachings and all the way to the parables.

On the small slate that Mistress Johanna had given her when she was learning to read and write, she copied all the references that referred to decency and magic.

They lay together as man and wife and begot a child. Except the couple in question were not married. It was all about the prophet son. That his parents weren't wed was immaterial to the story.

Love is only such when freely given between men and women both. That seemed to suggest that the Triune was fine with two men or two women coming together. Yet both shepherds told the people otherwise whenever an occasion presented itself.

Thou shalt not touch a girl until she has blossomed into a woman. In a story where a man, who had forced himself on a neighbour's daughter, had been punished by death.

The book in the crypt not only suggested that men touched children, but it was normal that a child cried and the tears should be ignored.

The magic of the Triune can only be experienced through complete faith. That was about the magic of faith, not real magic.

Once a person's soul has passed into the afterlife, it must be left in peace. It has happened more than once that in his grief, a husband has placed items on the deceased body of his wife that stopped the soul from making the peaceful journey. Her ghost remained a terror to the neighbourhood forever. Clearly, the church knew that ghosts existed.

To those who work hard, their craft will become second nature, but only to those who possess the soul of their art comes the true genius. That even suggested that the church knew about artisan magic, which turned a competent tailor into a modiste, which turned a musician into a composer and made the queues grow outside the baker's shop, because the bread and pastries weren't just good, they were magical.

So who had come up with the interpretation that magic didn't exist and that those who practiced it were— by that reasoning—liars and evildoers?

The last chapter of the Verses was the Book of Wilhelm. Her father used to like reading from it, but Nellie never touched it.

It described how, in the old world of peace and justice, an evil originated from the misbehaviour and unbelief of men. Yes, it said men specifically, because women didn't count. Moreover, Wilhelm stated that women were *spawn of the night, born to lead honest men into temptation*.

The book started:

With the passing of time, life was so good that men became lazy. They ate and drank all they wanted and were too often led astray by the pleasures of sin. There came to be a brand of harlots who would hide in the darkness of alleys at night, who would lure decent fathers from their families with promises of pleasure.

It detailed the fall of a town's mayor who spent all his money on whores and whose wife was then granted permission to end the marriage, rendering him homeless, because her family owned the land on which they had built their house.

It said these types of things "started happening all over", and that men needed to be taught a lesson.

The worst of the harlots was a woman named Rasa who "had skin and hair white as the ghosts of her victims, and eyes red as blood."

She travelled around the countryside "collecting men's seed" and murdering them afterwards to turn them into ghosts. Having grown bored with normal men, she turned her attention to rulers, magicians and saints.

She visited kings with the blood of thousands on their hands, necromancers, the lord of the sea who held in captivity the souls of those perished in the deep, and the church on the mountain where the saint of the sky touched her with a lightning bolt.

After many months, she had collected so much evil that her womb swelled with it and made her ill. She returned to her cave in the mountains and stoked a fire so hot that the rock melted. She squatted in the pit. The flames burned her skin until it was black. She screamed until her voice was gone, but the inferno was not hot enough for the evil to emerge. So she took her knife and slashed open her swollen belly. Thus, onto the burning coals, a terrible child was born. He was misshapen, had claw-like hands, glowing red eyes and the tongue of a snake. With her dying breath, she fed him the milk of evil from her breast. He drank until the last drop and then ate the body of his own mother. Such was the evil of the Lord of Fire.

Nellie shuddered.

The next few pages described how people realised that something terrible had happened, and that they had to defend themselves. Kings announced rules against men taking up with women of ill repute, but it was too late.

The world had fallen, and only the coming of the Last Prophet would save people from doom.

Of this prophet, Wilhelm said:

The Prophet will speak the truth and no sane man will doubt it.

The Prophet will walk into a town and the bad men will flee.

The Prophet will walk into a palace and the people will make him king.

This last section, more than anything, made Nellie dislike Wilhelm. She didn't believe the world was bad. She didn't believe most men were bad, and she didn't believe anyone should ever believe another person without doubt.

Then again, she had never met a prophet.

CHAPTER 11

THE GUARD'S NAME was Henrik.

Nellie had known him since they were both children. He used to live a couple of houses down from where she lived with her parents back when she was a little skinny girl with a plait on either side of her head.

He was one of those boys who grew tall without being lanky, which, with his thick blond hair and broad shoulders, made for a strapping appearance. Of course he'd joined the palace guards as soon as he was sixteen. Boys like him seemed to have been born for it. He had looked so dapper when he first came through the street wearing his guard uniform. Nellie and her shy friends would dream about how he would ask them to come for a walk, but being a couple of years older, he probably never noticed she existed.

Well, wasn't that a silly time?

Henrik now knew her as a kitchen maid and said hello to her sometimes because he was a nice and proper polite man. His face had acquired a good number of wrinkles and his hair had gone grey, but his back was still straight, his shoulders still broad, his uniform just as pretty and his buttons just as shiny.

She still didn't speak to him because he never came to the kitchen so he never knew of her silly girlish dreams and how she and her friends used to giggle after he'd gone past. Oh, she'd rather die than tell him she had ever done such a thing.

But here he was in the kitchen. He'd come up behind her while she was running back and forth from the cupboard to the trolley in the hallway because they needed to set the tables. When she turned around she almost bumped into him while carrying a stack of precious gold-rimmed plates and she nearly dropped them.

What a disaster that would have been.

Fortunately, she wasn't prone to uttering bad language, because if he had done this with Dora, *she* would definitely have said a few bad words, and of course one didn't swear at palace guards.

He steadied her with a strong hand. "Now hold on to the palace tableware."

Nellie took a deep breath and another one to make sure that yes she still held all the plates and disaster was averted.

"You frightened me, sneaking up from behind."

"My apologies. I announced myself, but it's very noisy in here."

He was not wrong about that.

As usual on the day of a big event, the kitchen had descended into mayhem.

Dora was yelling at one of the boys. A man delivering firewood was walking in and out to deposit the wood next to the hearth. Each time the door clanged shut behind him, the pigs in the yard started their oink-oink-oink because someone needed to feed them.

Two of the young girls were cutting up carrots with big

knives going chop-chop-chop on the board while they were chatting and laughing.

"I asked if you have a moment to spare," Henrik said.

"Me?"

"I don't see anyone else." His face creased into a smile and, to her eye, lost forty years of age. He was again the dapper young man, a bit skinny, but broad in the shoulders and straight of back, who returned from his first day working as a palace guard, and was showing off his spiffy uniform to everyone in the street.

And as she had when she was a young girl, and he deigned to look in her direction, Nellie was sure she was mistaken and he was looking at someone else. But deep in her heart, the little girl inside her sang, *He wants to talk to me!*

"All right then." Her voice sounded high to her own ears. This was stupid and embarrassing. She was far too old to be behaving like a giggling adolescent girl. "You're making me curious." And now she was sassy.

He laughed. "It's nothing serious. I know everyone is terribly busy down here."

"That's right. Don't disturb us too much, or there won't be any food."

He brought his hand to his brow. "Yes, ma'am."

By the Triune, was he joking with her?

His smile faded. "Madame Sabine asked for a herb woman."

Nellie shook her head. "I'm not a herb woman. You'll want to ask Graziela." In fact, she didn't understand why he hadn't done so already. Graziela came to the palace often.

"Graziela is unavailable," he said. "So I asked around for someone else. People mentioned you."

"I know a bit about herbs, but not as much as Graziela."

"Then come. It may be enough to keep Madame Sabine from bothering us for half a day."

Nellie could relate to that.

Madame Sabine barely came out of her room, but made sure that everyone knew when she did.

Nellie took off her apron while following him into the hallway. Her young helpers Els and Maartje were coming the other way and raised their eyebrows.

"Keep putting out the plates," Nellie said. "I won't be long."

At least she hoped with all her might that she wouldn't. There was so much still to do.

She followed Henrik up the stairs, past the stream of servants walking in and out of the hall, past the guards who stood at the main doors, past that group of young nobles with Casper and Frederick and Baroness Hestia in their midst, who sat on the couches in the foyer.

They were just talking, though, watched with sharp eyes by the guards.

Lord Verdonck was considered a voice of authority, and he stood at the door, welcoming arriving nobles.

Another couple of guests were entering the foyer. Two men carried a travel chest up the palace steps and stacked it against the wall. Lord Verdonck informed the chest's owner that servants would arrive shortly to take the luggage to the guest's quarters. Did the lord care for a drink?

He was ushered to one of the smaller dining rooms.

Henrik led Nellie to the broad marble staircase where a couple of women were polishing the banister.

Upstairs, others had lowered the large chandelier so they could replace the burned-out candles.

Nellie felt the questioning eyes of all these servants on her. They knew she worked in the kitchens. They wondered what she was doing here, especially in the company of a guard.

Nellie did not come to the family's private quarters often any more. When Mistress Johanna was queen, Nellie used to sleep in one of these rooms, these days occupied by the Regent's courtiers, stiff and formal people who had accompanied the family from Burovia.

Nellie remembered the happy, homely air of this floor, where King Roald had a room dedicated to his study of natural creatures and Queen Johanna had an office where she looked after the laws and finances of the country. She remembered the well-respected visitors who used to come up the stairs, the mayor, merchants from the city itself and all the surrounding nations, including the far east.

She could almost see Prince Bruno at his desk, not doing his homework as he should, but drawing beautiful works of art. She could hear the music coming from princess Celine's room, where, young as she was, she devoted many hours to violin practice. In hindsight, the haunted melodies she played—music no one had heard before—had been a foreboding of what was to come, but back in those days, life had been happy.

When Regent Bernard arrived, after two months during which the royal family's quarters lay abandoned, he cleared out all the family's beautiful things that had sat as they left them when going to performance where Celine was to play a piece and where, by all accounts, her magic had burst out through the music and killed everyone in the room.

The Regent sold the furniture, gave away the memorabilia, and burned the books that—as he said—were full of evil magic. He brought in his own things, all in stiff Burovian style with red velvet and elaborate armrests and dark wall coverings with tapestries of hunting scenes.

Madame Sabine's room had once been the queen's office and library.

Henrik knocked on the door, and when a female voice answered, opened it.

"I'll wait here," he said. "Call me if you need something."

"Thanks."

Nellie entered the room.

Mistress Johanna's books and shelves, the big desk and the comfortable chairs were all gone. In their place stood a giant fourposter bed with a thick mattress and frilly bedspread. Next to it, against the wall, was a dressing table with a large mirror and a huge variety of pots and jars. The chair in front of it was so elaborate it looked painful to sit on, although Nellie knew that Madame Sabine often did.

The inhabitant of this room sat on the couch in front of the hearth where a lusty fire burned. There was a tray of tea and teacups on the table, and the room smelled of sweet cakes. It was a smell that Nellie associated with the consort's room. Madame Sabine loved her sweet cakes and had the soft, fleshy body to match.

Nellie bowed.

"Do sit down," Madame Sabine said, gesturing a beringed hand at the couch opposite her. She spoke with a Lurezian accent, because that's where she grew up, and she had the dark curly hair that showed her heritage.

Nellie's cheeks glowed. It was hot in here compared to the kitchen.

Madame Sabine wore a dressing gown with open sleeves, which displayed her fleshy, pale-skinned arms, something the local women would consider scandalous.

Nellie didn't want to sit down. She had not been invited to sit in this room since the queen's death and didn't know what to make of this reclusive, pampered woman. She didn't want to look at—but couldn't look away from—Madame Sabine's dimpled thighs, visible in the space where the sides of her gown fell apart.

And she *had* to sit, because Madame Sabine was the Regent's wife, and when she ordered something, it had to be done. So Nellie sat at the very edge of the couch.

The floor was waxed and polished to within an inch of its life. The light from the window reflected in the gleaming surface.

The windows were meticulously clean, and the collection of porcelain, gold, silver and glass statues against the wall bore not one speck of dust. A poor girl came every day to clean all these, many of them grotesque figurines from the Belaman Church, which Madame Sabine attended.

"You asked for someone with herb knowledge," Nellie said, keen to get this over with as soon as possible. The sickly sweet smell made her feel queasy. "Tell me what you need. A soothing tea? Calming oil? Something to soothe your mind before going to the banquet? I don't know as much about herbs as Mistress Graziela, but I will do my best."

"Ah, the banquet," Madame Sabine said. "I have such terrible indigestion that I fear I won't be able to attend." She put her hand on her lower stomach which, had she been a younger woman, might have been swollen with child, rather than with too many sweet cakes.

"I can give you something for that, too," Nellie said, straining to get up.

"No."

Silence.

Nellie met her eyes. "You don't want me to help you?" Then why had she asked for Nellie's attendance?

"I do, but it's not about the ruddy herbs."

"I'm sorry?"

Nellie searched the room for evidence of glasses of

wine or empty carafes. Surely, Madame Sabine had to be drunk to be using such sailor's language?

Had she perhaps disagreed with Graziela?

"You heard me. It's not about the herbs, but asking for herbs is the only way my darling husband will get me someone to help me."

This was getting ever stranger.

Madame Sabine rose, with a groan, heaving all her frills and wobbly bits off the couch, and let the dressing gown slip from her shoulders. Underneath, she wore only an underdress that was white and so thin that Nellie could see her smalls and singlet through it.

Nellie stifled a gasp. She was not unused to her mistress undressing in front of her; Mistress Johanna had done that many times. But that was a long time ago, and Mistress Johanna had not been so . . . voluptuous.

"I guess I can't excuse myself from my own son's banquet, much as I detest these occasions where men get drunk and the women spread nasty gossip about each other. So. I need someone to help me get my corset on." As Madame Sabine went to the clothes wardrobe, she turned her back on Nellie, and Nellie almost let out another gasp.

Across Madame Sabine's back, visible through the sheer fabric, were a number of horrific scars, like bright red slashes across the soft skin of her lower back.

They were about the width of a thumb and ran parallel to each other across the small of Madame Sabine's back.

They looked terrible, horrific, and excruciating. Whatever in the Triune's name had caused those? Had she been struck with a whip?

Madame Sabine returned with the corset and gave it to Nellie, meeting her eyes. Daring her to say something or ask?

But Nellie had not kept out of harm's way by using her

mouth. She had earned her succession of jobs through keeping it shut so that was what she did now.

She helped Madame Sabine put on the corset. It was big enough to fit two women her own size. The laces were very long and tangled up easily, and Nellie's hands were sweaty, because it was warm in this room and she was dressed for the cold kitchen, but also because looking at those terrible scars—and pulling the laces tight over them —made her nervous. She kept wanting to ask if it was painful, but that would mean acknowledging that the scars were there. Maybe Madame Sabine wanted that—and Nellie didn't want to hear about the terrible injuries that had caused these, because it could not have been anything good.

Meanwhile, Madame Sabine chatted about how much she disliked the dinner guests.

"You must have gone into that room where Baroness Viktoryia was holding her tea party where they all gossiped about me."

Nellie wasn't sure if it was a question or a statement. If Madame Sabine didn't want the other women to gossip about her, wouldn't the best option be to turn up to these events?

"I can only guess what they said. That I'm ugly, or only from a low family. I wonder which of them is going to try to poison me this time."

Apparently, at a previous occasion, Madame Sabine had accused one of the Regent's cousins of putting poison in her food, but plenty of other people disputed this. For one, Nellie knew Wim tested everything that entered and left the kitchen for this reason.

"I wish I could just stay here and let the men have their orgy, but yes, I know, it's my son's birthday, even if I barely recognise the cuddly boy I loved. Have you seen him recently? Have you heard the way his father teaches him to talk? Have you seen his behaviour?"

Nellie had seen this and she was glad she stood behind Madame Sabine, and could pretend to be busy with the laces of the corset. It was not appropriate for servants to comment on the behaviour of nobles in front of other nobles.

Madame Sabine continued, "And now my darling husband wants him married. I feel sorry for the poor wench who will have to put up with such a brat as my son. I hardly recognise him anymore, the way he's strutting around in that dreadful peacock suit, rubbing his dick against any girl who comes close enough—what is your name?"

Nellie gasped, both from the crudeness of Madame Sabine's words and the sudden change of subject. "Nellie."

"Cornelia?"

Shudder. "No. Just Nellie."

"All right. *Just* Nellie, do you think I should wear the red dress or the green one?" Just like that. One moment she accused her son of disgusting things—her own son, by the Triune—and then she asked a frivolous question about a dress.

"Uhhh. I like the red one."

"Me, too. Red is a nice colour, don't you think? If someone stabs me with a knife, the blood won't show up as much as on the green one, and they won't even need to change my dress before they put me in state surrounded by pretty flowers."

Excuse me? What was wrong with this woman? Nellie missed a few loops on the corset and had to undo the laces to fix her mistake. Her hands trembled.

Madame Sabine chuckled. "Silly me, you wanted to say there are no flowers at this time of the year, so that's that. I better not get stabbed in the heart, don't you agree?"

"Yes . . . uhhh . . . I agree." That was one of those questions where you didn't know whether to say yes or no, and what was her obsession with the subject of death anyway?

Finally, the corset was done.

Madame then took a rose red dress out of the wardrobe and Nellie had to help her put it on. The dress showed rather a lot more skin than was customary for the local ladies of the court, but the scars were hidden under the corset.

"This is good," Madame Sabine said, while looking at herself in the mirror, shaking her head so her curls danced around her head. Despite a proliferation of flesh, she was not unattractive. "No matter how much my darling husband's guests hate me, I will look respectable. Don't you think?"

At one time, Nellie would have done anything for a dress like that. But those corsets weren't comfortable at all.

"You look good, Madame."

She laughed aloud and clapped her hands together. "Haha, you don't have to be so timid. Tell me what you really think. Do I look like a dressed up cow?"

"Not at all, madame."

"Well—I think I do. The noble women of this town all say so behind my back."

"I don't agree with that at all."

"You don't have to agree. But this dress *is* ridiculous, and this room is ridiculous. Look at all these frills!" She grabbed the bedspread and pulled it onto the floor.

Nellie stood petrified. She had no idea what to do or say except to keep silent.

"My *husband* wants all of this. My *husband* orders these things, because 'I should look like a proper woman.' But it's ridiculous."

Wouldn't the solution be to order her own clothes?

Maybe the Regent wouldn't let her?

"Do you still need me, Madame?"

Madame Sabine turned to Nellie as if she had forgotten she was there. She laughed. "No, you can go. I frighten you, don't I? A woman who speaks up does that to people, even other women. When you were a girl, didn't you get told not to yell, and be all hush-hush, and by the gods not to offer anything that looks like an *opinion* on anything that isn't a piece of clothing?"

Nellie wanted nothing more than to get out. She wanted to run to the door, sprint out of the room and down the sweeping staircase—

"Wait."

She froze. Turned around, her heart thudding.

"My husband can't control me. He can ban me from having anything to do with the guest list for my own son's birthday. He can tell my sons I'm not good in the head. He can spread rumours about me that aren't true. But he can't control me. He tells me to keep my opinions to myself, not to speak to the staff and cover up all of our sordid disagreements. You'll probably expect me to tell you to keep quiet about the things I've told you, but no. I *want* you to tell other people. If someone asks you about me, I want you to tell them exactly what I said."

Nellie nodded, her mouth too dry to speak.

"Yes, Madame."

And then she was free. She opened the door and walked out as calmly as she could.

"Let me accompany you down," Henrik said.

Nellie had forgotten that he would wait, and gasped. "Oh, you frightened me." Nellie clutched her chest.

"Are you all right?"

"Uhh. Yes."

"She can be a bit of an odd one sometimes."

Only sometimes?

They walked back down the private quarters to the upstairs landing, where the servants were hoisting up the chandelier, and into the foyer where Lord Verdonck was welcoming another guest.

The group of young nobles was no longer hanging around, but Casper stood on the gallery watching, his hands in his pockets and legs wide. Els crossed the foyer, swaying her hips. He followed her with his gaze fixed on her backside. *Rubbing his dick against any girl who comes close enough.*

Shocking.

Disgusting.

The truth. She'd have to keep an eye out for Els with her pretty smile and her blond hair. If he tried to touch her, she'd slap him in the face and knee him in the groin and nothing good could come from that.

"Look, I'm sorry to have gotten you involved," Henrik said as they went down the second staircase to the kitchen.

"It's all right."

"No, it is not." He stopped her by putting his hand on her upper arm. "She has upset you. I'm sorry. She is a strange person. But she was furious and demanded someone help her now that Graziela has gone."

"What do you mean, has gone?"

"She has left town. No one knows where she is."

"Is this because she has artisan magic?"

His eyebrows flicked up. "Do you know about that?"

Nellie hesitated. "I have a friend who . . ." No, she couldn't say much about Jantien, because Henrik might even know the men who had driven Jantien's husband out of town by order of the Regent. "A friend's husband had to leave because of it. He had a tailor shop."

He nodded, his face grim. "The Regent has ordered that any person who uses 'unnatural qualities' leave the city. Madame is angry with her husband, even if only because of Graziela."

"I'm sorry." She didn't know what else to say. If anything, *he* had to carry out the Regent's orders, and that would be so much worse if he didn't agree with them.

"No. I am sorry. I am weary of the games and politics of the rulers. I don't believe anything good will come from this. At least I'm aware of the rules and can stay out of the way. I don't like it when people get involved who need not be." And after a short silence, he said, "I hope you had a nice birthday at least."

CHAPTER 12

NELLIE SPED DOWN the rest of the staircase and didn't stop running until she was in the corridor.

Her cheeks glowed, her heart thudded.

She had wondered how Dora and the others had known it was her birthday. Wim had even said a guard told him.

That guard was Henrik, but how did Henrik know?

How? How?

Unless back when she was a young girl and had admired him from a distance, he had taken more notice of her than she realised and remembered things about her.

Unless she had been wrong that he never saw her back then.

He was a married man, by the Triune. She remembered the day he married a girl called Martha. They looked so pretty together. She was a nice girl. They had two daughters. What was he even doing talking to her like this?

Nellie's heart was still racing by the time she came to the kitchen.

The smell of bread pervaded the kitchen.

The kitchen workers had cut one loaf up and were sharing it for their morning break in one corner of the big kitchen table while the rest of the table was taken up with food that still needed to be prepared.

Someone had brought eggs for making pastries and sauces. A basket contained chicken eggs and duck eggs and goose eggs.

The fire was already going, and the pig hung to roast. Two kitchen boys turned the handle.

A man delivered a crate with jars of plums and a basket of apples.

There was so much food, you'd never know that people in the city went hungry.

"Come sit down for a break," Dora said.

"No time," Nellie said.

She grabbed a piece of fresh bread from the table and continued on to the linen room to put her apron back on.

She was *afraid* of the questions, she realised. Afraid of what she should say about Madame Sabine. There was clearly something wrong with the consort. Why did she talk like that about her husband and son? Why did she have those horrible scars? Why did Nellie have to see that and then be told to tell everyone?

Madame Sabine was trying to make a point, but what was it?

Els and Maartje came into the kitchen, both giggling.

"Really? Is that what he said?" Maartje said.

"He did. And he asked me for a dance and I said I was too busy, and he said he would—" Els stopped talking when Nellie stepped in their way.

Nellie pointed to the door to the scullery. "Dishes."

Els huffed. "Yes, yes."

The two sisters scurried into the scullery, and then Maartje said, "What's wrong with her?"

Nellie strode to the door. "I heard that. I told you I

want no trouble with any of those young guests upstairs. No matter what they say, they don't care about you, they are not worth getting in trouble for, and you are far, far better than they are."

"We were only joking," Els said, putting on a sad face. Oh, she was a good actress.

"But I was not. There is a lot of trouble brewing with all these important people here. I want no trouble from you."

"But we are only talking."

"That doesn't matter. Whenever these men have an argument, they try to blame it on someone else. You have to keep your head down and do the work so that they don't notice you to put their blame on."

"But what if what they do or say is wrong or disgusting?" Maartje asked. She was far darker of skin and hair than Els, and not as smart or dangerous.

"You keep your head down."

"But what if you don't want to because it's unfair?"

"You keep your head down. Don't forget who is paying for your food and who owns the roof over our heads."

"But what if they do something to a friend or your family?" Trust Els to be contrary, always wanting to have the final word. And yes, she would protect her sister if anyone tried to harm her.

"Has any of that happened to you?"

"No, but—"

"Then don't worry about it until it does. And when it does, see me. Keep quiet, because making a fuss only creates more trouble for everyone, including the people you are trying to protect. Remember that."

They nodded, albeit sullenly. Nellie would love to see the thoughts in Els' head, because her thinking would have moved far past these sorts of things.

"How is your mother?" she asked.

"Oh, she is fine, thank you so much."

Hmm. Nellie didn't miss that Maartje raised one eyebrow. She could see the girl think, *Our mother?*

Also, *fine* was not the way one would describe the cramps women got when juniper berry tea took effect. They were ill for days whether the remedy worked or not. And most often, it didn't.

So either the berries were for herself—which was hard to believe, because she didn't seem to have suffered any cramps—or for a friend. But why not speak the truth? Nellie would have given them no matter who was the recipient.

She resolved to keep a closer eye on the girls.

The girls continued to clean dishes in silence.

Word came from upstairs that people were starting to fill the hall, and so Nellie helped the kitchen hands carry the first dishes upstairs. They arrived at the top of the stairs to raucous applause from all the guests waiting in a long line to be allocated seats. Most of these people were locals. Nellie recognised some city councillors, some merchants, the palace's account keeper, the cousin twice removed of the Estlander Duke and some other minor nobles.

It was the only time when nobles got out of the way of servants: when the latter were carrying the food.

Inside the hall, the tables glittered with clean glasses and silver tableware. My, Nellie didn't think she had ever seen this many tables in this hall. There were chairs for the orchestra next to the dais where the table for the Regent and distinguished guests stood, but the area that would normally be free for dancing was filled up with tables.

Because they couldn't yet sit until the Regent had arrived, most of the guests congregated around the drinks table. Two young monks were serving wine. Nellie recognised Gerard as one of them. He was scooping ladles of wine into glasses that were snatched up by eager nobles as fast as he could fill them. Was he old enough to drink wine?

The assembly of guests was a riot of colour.

Men in velvet coats with frilly collars and cuffs, women in narrow-waisted dresses of many different colours. Wigs and pearls and gold-buckled shoes, lots of pale skin and an occasional bare shoulder.

In the midst of all this splendour, Nellie spotted a long dark brown robe, worn by Shepherd Wilfridus, talking to one of the local well-off merchants. Nellie understood why he was invited: as protector of the church, Regent Bernard could hardly not invite him, but she didn't understand why the shepherd accepted the invitation.

She could still hear the coldness in his voice. *They are thieves.*

Jantien and her six children went hungry while these men came here to eat and drink themselves stupid.

While Nellie wrestled through the throng in the foyer, a man yelled, "There is a thief in the palace!"

People moved aside to let the speaker through, a nobleman wearing a red jacket. Nellie didn't know him.

Two guards pushed through the crowd. "What was stolen?" one of them asked.

"They made a mess of my room. They tipped over my travel chest. All my clothes are on the floor. Do you know how much those jackets cost? All lying in the dust."

Dust? That was outrageous. The palace staff made sure there was not a speck of dust in any of those rooms.

"Are you missing any items?" the guard insisted.

"I haven't noticed, but they made such a mess of my travel chests, how could I tell whether something was missing? They searched through my things—"

"They stole nothing?"

"It makes no difference whether they did. They upset

everything in my room. The Regent is supposed to employ honest guards—"

A voice came from behind. "Dear Phillip, are you in any way suggesting that my guards are dishonest?"

Regent Bernard stood on the stairs dressed in a clean and elaborate military uniform that had never seen a day of battle. He wore a red cloak around his shoulders, very much like the royal Carmine cloak.

Nellie's heart skipped a beat.

He wasn't going to use this occasion to have himself crowned king, was he?

Madame Sabine stood next to him, holding his arm. She held her head cocked and smiled vacantly at the crowd. Her red dress almost blended with the cloak—the colours were so much alike. The red velvet of Frederick's red coat was darker. Casper looked out of place in his peacock blue suit. He held his back straight. His cheeks still glowed with bright red blotches, and while he stood on the stairs with his family, he glanced aside and smiled.

The nobleman bowed. "Exulted Regent, I am not suggesting that your guards are dishonest, although the same may not be said about any of the guards brought by the other guests. Somebody has been searching my room."

"Watch what you're saying!" another man yelled in the crowd. Nellie couldn't see who it was.

The Regent laughed. "I can see there will be plenty of entertainment tonight. Now forget about your petty grievances and let's celebrate."

The crowd parted to let the family through. When they passed, Madame Sabine caught Nellie's eye. The penetrating look in her eyes chilled her.

The nobleman called after the party, "But my room! My clothes!" The interest of the crowd had shifted, though, and people pushed past him to follow the Regent into the hall.

Back in the kitchen, she collected several large plates on a trolley which she wheeled out through the kitchen yard around the side of the palace into the forecourt where there was a ramp for this purpose. It was still very busy in the foyer, with most of the young nobles hanging around here. Nellie could see Casper and Frederick with their parents at the dais, looking very bored, but the other obnoxious youngsters, including Baroness Hestia, were all in the foyer.

On the other side of the foyer, the nobleman Phillip was still complaining to two guards in a loud voice, "I told you they emptied all my possessions on the floor. I demand that my shirts be cleaned!"

Nellie pushed the cart across the side of the foyer, avoiding both these groups, and was about to go through the door, when a hand reached out from behind a pillar and stopped the cart.

Henrik.

Nellie's heart jumped.

"I want to warn you to be careful," he said, his voice low. "Keep an eye out, be vigilant. Something is brewing."

"Is this about people stealing from private rooms?"

"That, and other things. Many people in this hall don't like each other. Someone has been upsetting people's rooms, and likely it's one of the guests. Watch out, tell me if you see anything untoward, and make sure that none of you get involved."

Nellie nodded. "Thank you." And then she hesitated. "Thank you for telling Wim that it was my birthday."

"You figured out it was me?"

"No one else would have known." She met his smiling eyes. "How did you know?"

He laughed. "How did I know? How could I not know? You were the prettiest girl in the street."

"I was not."

"You were, but your father was standing over you like a mean guard dog. None of us boys dared come anywhere near you."

"You are just flattering me."

"No, I am not."

And she saw in his eyes that he was not joking.

Well, that was a little . . . upsetting. "I sat on the porch on that day you came home from the palace wearing your new uniform. I thought you looked very good, and that you were now a serious man and would not talk to young girls anymore."

Henrik laughed, and Nellie laughed, albeit uneasily.

Els came walking past and raised her eyebrows at Nellie, as if she wanted to say, *What was that about not getting involved with men?*

Nellie remembered that she was supposed to be serving, so she left to go to the kitchen, still feeling uneasy.

She remembered playing with Henrik—amongst a big group of other children—when she was little.

On second thoughts, her father *did* keep her away from other kids, *because you're old enough to help your mother in the kitchen.*

What if it hadn't been about helping her mother at all?

She remembered vividly the day she heard Henrik was getting married. She had already been living with Mistress Johanna, but the news had made a little sad spot inside her. Not that she had hoped he might marry her, but because it didn't look like she would marry, ever, because maids who lived with the family they served rarely married, and Nellie needed to live with the family because her own family had no money.

When Nellie came into the kitchen, Els and Maartje laughed at her.

Els could never keep quiet about things like this. "What did you say to us about not getting involved?"

"I was talking about our safety."

"You're so serious. He was flirting with you."

"He was warning us."

But as Els grumbled and continued into the hallway, Nellie felt ashamed that Els was right.

Yes, he was flirting, and she should be ashamed. He was married, by the Triune. She should do her work and keep vigilant.

She made the trip into the hall with the trolley a few more times. Each time she came downstairs, Dora was shouting at the kitchen hands. Roast ducks had to be carried to the hall. The table waiters were out of bread. Why was there no cut bread ready to be taken upstairs? Why were the carrots not done yet? Who had forgotten to check on the plum sauce? It had become too dry and burned in the bottom of the pan. And so on, and so forth.

Nellie walked into the hall just as the Regent was ending a speech for the birthday of his son. Everyone in the hall erupted into raucous applause, except Madame Sabine.

She sat next to her husband, wearing the red dress and looking like an overstuffed sausage, and stared over the heads of the guests.

Nellie remembered her strange behaviour in her room that afternoon. What was up with that woman? She didn't fit into the mould of what Nellie expected noblewomen to do. She said she was from a low family. Why did Regent Bernard marry her? What was behind her recklessly unhappy behaviour? Why did she have those scars?

After the Regent's speech, Casper was finally released from his chair. Because there was no room to dance in the hall, the orchestra set up at the back entrance, and guests danced in the garden room, where it would be cold and empty.

Nellie watched out for Els and Maartje while still embarrassed about having been caught off guard.

Fortunately, Henrik had been given duty elsewhere. She didn't see him anywhere anymore, and she assumed that he had gone to investigate the stolen items, because there was quite a lot of activity in the back of the guest quarters, but it was too dark, it was too far away and she was too busy to find what it was about.

Afternoon turned into evening. The line of plates to be taken upstairs was continuous. When one end of the long table was done, it was time to clear plates at the beginning, and then the next course needed to be brought out.

She and her young helpers looked after just one row of tables. There were six more rows, each with at least fifty noble self-absorbed, demanding guests in various states of increasing drunkenness.

Because there was so little room, the servants had taken over the task of filling glasses. Gerard was still on duty with the ladle, having stacked one empty barrel of Guentherite wine on top of another.

There were the usual mishaps. Glasses fell over, food was spilled, guests were too drunk to make it out of their seats and collapsed. Others became boisterous and rude. They fought, but were mostly too drunk to do each other damage.

Over the years, Nellie had become good at deflecting angry questions, ignoring rude remarks and dodging questing hands. She rarely felt shocked about the behaviour of these people when they were all together in a room and drinking a lot.

She was pleased to see that both sisters Maartje *and* Els behaved sensibly. Els took over from a servant girl bringing around wine, and she and the Guentherite monk Gerard formed an efficient team.

But glances into other parts of the hall showed her that

not all the servants were so lucky. A commotion broke out at the end of a table on the other side of the hall. A couple of the guests had risen from their seats and were yelling at each other and attempting to trade blows, with little harm done because they were too drunk. A few palace guards came in to take the involved parties to different parts of the hall and found themselves the target of other angry outbursts.

Meanwhile, the group of young nobles with Casper had reformed near the entrance to the garden room. Some had split off into couples, but few were dancing.

One could scarcely hear the music over the yelling.

At the main table on the dais, the mayor of Saardam was in a heated discussion with the merchant next to him. Madame Sabine sat next to the mayor, leaning her chin on her hand and staring into the hall. On the other side of the merchant sat Shepherd Wilfridus. He had just taken a plate laden with a duck leg, plum sauce and roast vegetables. His gaze darted over the guests in the hall and met Nellie's over the half-eaten duck leg in his hand. Grease glistened on his chin.

Down in the kitchen, Dora yelled at her kitchen hands. Bring this, bring that, don't let it burn, take it upstairs. The fire roared, pots boiled on the stove, and people ran around checking this or that pan.

Nellie only ventured into the part of the kitchen where the finished dishes stood.

It was mayhem down here, almost worse than upstairs.

Nellie went back up with a plate of vegetables.

The disturbance in the corridor that led to the guest quarters was still not resolved. It looked like someone had tossed a guest's entire luggage into the hallway. Chests stood open and people stood bent over the contents. A couple of guards stood in the hallway, but didn't appear to be getting involved with the goings on.

Some banquet guests were coming out of the hall into the foyer. A nobleman with a sweaty face remarked to Nellie, "Phew, it's so hot in there."

It was, and it stank of sweat and stale wine, and the noise grew ever louder. The floor felt sticky with spilled food and wine.

Els was just replacing an empty glass with a full one when one of the guests waved his arms. He hit her elbow, and she dropped her tray which fell into a plate with roast duck legs. Duck legs and wine flew everywhere. It splashed all over the dishes and the table and the laps of the surrounding nobles. That wouldn't have been so bad, if one of them hadn't been an elaborately dressed woman, who copped a big splash of wine in her hair and down the front of her yellow dress.

She stared at it, mouth open, and started screaming.

A number of surrounding men laughed. The poor woman's husband got up and yelled at them to shut up and have respect for his wife and then started yelling at Els.

Els' face had turned red, and it wouldn't be long before that sharp tongue made its appearance.

"Now wait a moment." Nellie strode around the table and pushed herself in between the angry man and Els. "Calm down. It was not her fault."

"She threw the tray. I saw it!" Too much wine reddened his face.

"It was an accident and we're sorry." Nellie touched the shoulder of the poor woman who was now crying, all wet with red wine down her front. "Come, I can help you clean up." She glanced at Els. "Quick, go downstairs."

Els ran.

Nellie took the poor woman out of the hall. At the start of the corridor a couple of rooms had been reserved for guests to recuperate or to enjoy quiet time.

One of the rooms was occupied by several men in a

business meeting and from another came a sound of vigorous vomiting, so Nellie chose the next room, where she settled the poor woman, now shivering in her cold wet dress, on the couch next to the fire.

"I'll just run to the linen room and get you some dry towels."

She sped through the hall to the rooms with the cleaning equipment and clean linen.

It was dark in the room, and, because the door had been shut, extremely cold. A light outside the window cast a pale yellow glow over the table where the servants folded the laundry. The shelves with towels stood on the right.

But hey, what was that?

As she crossed the room, from the other corner came a small sound, like the sharp intake of a breath, and a shifting of fabric, the movement too loud to have been made by a mouse or even a cat—because they would often find cats or even nests of kittens in here.

Nellie stopped walking. "Anyone here?"

No one replied, but when she continued and reached for the towels, she could hear a soft sniggering. She turned around, and in the pale light, could just make out the folds of dress fabric spread out over the end of another table. On the dress, an elaborate bun of straw-blond hair. And the pale oval of a young man's face.

The fabric rustled and a woman's accented voice whispered, "Never mind, it's only a servant."

Baroness Hestia.

The young man grunted and the rustling of fabric resumed.

Heavens.

Nellie's heart thudded.

She grabbed a handful of fabric off the shelf, not caring how many towels she got, clutched them to her chest and ran out of the room.

Was that really Casper?

Good heavens. What did he think he was doing?

Nellie's knees still felt weak by the time she returned to the noblewoman. She gave her the towels and helped her clean up as best as she could and then helped the woman back into the hall. She was a local lady and wanted to go home. A few people had started to leave, all of them locals. A woman complained loudly about the behaviour of the young guests.

The commotion at the end of the guest quarters was still going, and Nellie picked up rumours from passing men that someone was looking for something supposed to have been stolen.

A line of guards stood at the door to the main hall, all of them with serious, tense expressions on their faces. She couldn't see Henrik. Nights like this weren't much fun for her, but wouldn't be a lot of fun for him either. Maybe she should ask him tomorrow what all this searching of rooms was about.

The noise in the hall was just deafening.

Shepherd Wilfridus stood at the table, yelling at a man next to him. His face was red, and he had to steady himself on the back of his chair with one hand.

Madame Sabine still stared into the crowd.

Should Nellie go up to the dais and tell her that her son was screwing around with one of the guests? As if she knew that Nellie was thinking about her, Madame Sabine stopped staring and met Nellie's eyes. Then she pushed herself up from her chair. Her husband turned to her and said something. In a flash, Madame Sabine picked up the untouched full wine glass at her plate and tossed the contents into her husband's face. Then she strode out of the hall, to loud laughter.

Several people rushed to the Regent's side with cloths to clean the wine, but he brushed them all aside.

He rose and yelled after his wife, "You can run, but you can never escape the truth, my darling."

Because he had such a loud voice, a lot of the guests fell quiet.

Madame Sabine paid him no attention, but kept walking.

Nellie had been collecting empty plates, but she had to stop because everyone else fell quiet, and one could not continue to make noise with plates while nobles were quiet.

"Thank you for your concern," Regent Bernard said, into the sudden silence. "My dear wife can be a little feisty, but rest assured, I am used to it. Why do you think I've chosen to wear red clothing today?"

A ripple of laughter spread through the hall.

Nellie thought of the scars on Madame Sabine's back.

CHAPTER 13

WORD REACHED the kitchen that Madame Sabine wanted tea.

Dora let fly a string of swear words that would make a sailor blush.

"Tea, huh? She wants fucking tea? Why the fuck does she think I have time to make fucking tea? And she wants fucking cakes, too?"

"I'll bring it," Maartje said.

"No, I will," Nellie said. She would not send either of the sisters to that woman's room, no matter how much she hated going herself.

Nellie collected a pretty teapot and made the "fucking" tea in the midst of the chaos. She put the pot and a dainty cup on a tray and walked up the stairs, dodging servants coming down with empty trays, dodging drunks stumbling through the foyer, and breathing the fresh—if biting cold —air that came in through the open front doors. She pretended not to notice the young couple who stood hidden in the shadow of a pillar, their mouths glued to each other. A Guentherite monk—not Gerard—walked across the hall, money jingling in his pocket. He sauntered out the front door and relieved himself down the side of the steps.

But by the time Nellie reached upstairs in the Regent's private quarters, the noise had quietened to a background murmur, occasionally punctuated with a crash of tableware or loud laughter.

She couldn't wait for this whole circus to be over. The palace stood stiff with tension, people disliking each other, people accusing each other, people yelling at each other, people behaving badly. Something awful was bound to happen before sunrise.

She knocked on Madame's door.

"Excuse me, here is your tea."

For a while, nothing happened. Nellie got angry that she pandered to this woman whose aim seemed to be to make the servants understand how little their time was worth.

But then the door opened.

Madame Sabine herself looked out. "Oh, it's you. Come in." She opened the door further.

Nellie wasn't sure what she had expected.

Part of her expected to find Madame in tears about the events downstairs, whatever the Regent had said to her that had made her run out, with her face blotched and eye liner running down her cheeks.

Another part expected Madame to have taken off the red dress and be in need of assistance with the corset.

She had definitely not expected Madame to be dressed in a man's chemise and trousers and a long coat, with her hair tied back so it looked as if it were short.

"Don't look at me like that," she said. "Put the tea down and help me pack this chest."

Nellie crossed the room, sidestepping discarded

clothes and piles of other items. Boots, a man's hat, a raincoat.

She set the tray on the table and helped pack the clothes and other items from the bed into a travel chest that stood on the floor.

"Are you going for long?" And where was she going, anyway?

Madame Sabine looked at her. "Tell me this—Cornelia, wasn't it? If you had a husband like mine, would you feel inclined to stick around when he and his friends got drunk?"

"I . . . don't know."

"Of course you know, everyone knows. Don't you think I haven't heard the talk on the streets? My husband cares about me not a bit."

Nellie didn't believe she had ever heard of Madame Sabine mingling with the citizens, let alone hearing the talk on the streets.

Sometimes she rode her white horse through the streets, usually after dark. That horse would pull her coach on the rare occasions she went out during the daytime.

"When my husband invites his fawning nobles and ridiculous priests to get drunk at the expense of this pathetic country that can't afford it, I don't want to be around, and he doesn't want me around either. I wait out the debauchery out of town. I don't want to have anything to do with my husband's business or the nobles who fall on their knees to beg him for favours. Do they have no pride? Don't they see that my husband himself is under the influence of these priests?"

"But people will gossip about you."

"Let me tell you a secret: I don't care. I don't care about this town and the stupid nobles. I never asked to come to this ruddy palace."

Nellie stared into the fire, afraid to say something out of place.

"You wonder why I came then, don't you? I was happy in Burovia where I was not too far away from my family in Lurezia and could visit them. We have a nice comfortable house on a hill where we can see the deer darting at the forest edge. I have *friends* and business contacts there. But one day my dear husband comes along to say we're moving to this place Saardam. I told him: who goes to Saardam? It's a backward place. I asked him why and he said he'd been made Regent and it was a great opportunity for us. Well, what a great opportunity it has been. My husband still doesn't get he's a puppet leader. He says the nobility loves him. They do, but only when he feeds them. I bet as soon as he stops giving parties, they'll turn around and kick him out. Those nobles get no say in the matter anyway."

No, ultimately, the decision about succession lay with the church, and they were taking their sweet time with it.

"I have seen the letter from this shepherd where he said they wanted someone to step in while they figured out who was the most rightful heir to the throne. It wasn't my husband, that has always been made clear, but the position was too hot for any of the real contenders to allow their rivals to take it. So: this stupid oaf who happens to be my husband takes it. Because he likes the pomp and the parties. He likes pretending. I don't know why he still thinks the church will make him king. They have told him subtly and less subtly that they are not going to. But they're also not making headway in picking a new king. Prince Clement from Burovia is married to a friend of mine. He's one of the first in line, but he's heard nothing about the succession. There are some Scandian royals claiming the throne because of Queen Cygna, but they're not going to get in. Rumours are that the church can't find the documents that Cygna signed that she and her family forfeited the right to lay claim on Saarland's throne and assets—not that there are any of those. That's the excuse those priests use, anyway. That they can't find the documents. That they need *ten years* to search for them. Yet my husband can't see that this is ridiculous. Why does he even want this town, in which every second person you meet in the street stinks of manure and every woman who calls herself civilised can only ogle at me? There is no culture here. Everyone is buttoned up to the chin, and so many women wear these ridiculous bonnets."

"Is my bonnet ridiculous?"

Madame Sabine whirled around. "Yes!"

Nellie gasped from the sudden outburst. She raised her hand and touched the offending piece of clothing. "Really?"

"I understand why you wear it in the kitchen, because we would not want hair in our food, but when you go to the markets? You all look like you came from a nunnery. This town does not appreciate style. This town *is* a nunnery. You're all so obsessed with this stupid church you can't see you're living like you're dead already. Where is the colour, where is the music, where is the fun—no, don't answer that. You wouldn't understand."

"I *do* understand." Nellie knew she *shouldn't* get angry—mind, she had told her young helpers this many times: don't get involved, don't answer back, they're rich people and they are always right, even if they're wrong. But she couldn't help herself. "You've been here only a few years; you don't know anything about us."

Madame Sabine gave her a shocked look. "What was that?"

Nellie's heart jumped. What had she done now?

Madame Sabine took a step closer. "What did you say?"

"I'm sorry. I . . ."

Nellie wanted to run out of the room, down the stairs and back to the safe kitchen. Madame was still the Regent's consort and what she said was law in the palace.

Madame Sabine said slowly, "Your words were: you don't know anything about us."

Nellie nodded and cringed. She had to force herself to look up from the floor. "I'm very sorry. I shouldn't have said that."

"But you did. That is the first time any of you have said anything that's not 'Yes, Madame, I will do it immediately, Madame.' It is astonishing, how a town such as this accepts a stranger like my husband, because the church makes it so."

"I'm sorry."

"Stop apologising! I like it. There is life in you yet."

"There is plenty of life," Nellie said. "We had many different people in Saardam. There even used to be a Belaman Church in town. We had the only office of the Eastern Traders in the lowlands, and our people traded with every country up the river."

"Where are all those people now? I'm not seeing them. When I go out into town, I'm seeing dreariness every-where. I'm seeing closed shops, I'm seeing beggars."

Nellie knew she was right. "After the royal family was killed, the shepherd made a rule that outlawed magic. Many people got scared and left." The Eastern Traders and the Anglian trade office nextdoor had closed. Li Fai and Christopher Fossey had been good friends. The pastor of the small Belaman Church, a pretty and ancient building in the middle of the commercial quarter, had left. The river trading family of Master Deim from Gelre, who were rich and generous, had also left. The list included several gifted modistes from Lurezia who made outrageous dresses that all the noble women gossiped about, and a wine seller from Burovia whose wines were so expensive that no one could figure out who bought them. There even used to be a Phenician spice trader in town who sold spices that turned food vivid yellow or bright red. They were all gone.

"Yes, there you are. The church said it. They made all these people leave. They killed the life in your town. When did the last ocean ship come into port?"

"There have been some."

"Only the ones owned by people in Saardam, and even they have found it hard to compete against the much better-financed ships leaving from towns further down the coast."

That was true, Nellie knew.

"It's all because of this ridiculous church and the churchman, who comes to talk to my husband and insists on talking to him alone, who puts ideas into his head and mouth and who has all of you dancing like little puppets on a string."

Nellie gasped. "You should stop talking about shepherd Wilfridus like that! He's a good man."

"Is he? I suggest you banish all that church claptrap from your mind for just a few minutes and look at what he does." She met Nellie's eyes with an intense expression.

Nellie was too angry to think. How dare this foreign harlot speak like this about her country?

Madame Sabine snorted. "Anyway, I've had enough of my husband's partying. Since neither he nor my sons appear to realise the damage they're doing to their own reputations, I'll make myself scarce while he attempts to get any of the local clique that calls themselves nobles to put a knife in his back. When that happens, don't come running to me because I'll tell you, 'I told you so,' because

I did tell you so. I don't want to be here when it happens. I've told the boys to get the horses ready."

"Won't your husband be angry that you're leaving?" Nellie didn't know what to think. A wife's position was to support her husband, wasn't it? Queen Johanna would never leave King Roald by himself for an occasion like this, and he was just as likely to say or do stupid things, even if he never touched any wine.

What a strange and selfish woman was this.

Madame Sabine flapped her hand. "Nah. Believe it or not, my husband enjoys these parties. It keeps him busy. He won't even notice I'm gone, and he knows I hate them and the people who come to them and those people hate me, so it suits us both for me not to be present."

There was a knock on the door and a man's voice said, "Madame?"

"Here we are. The horses are ready."

Madame Sabine went to open the door.

A male voice said something that Nellie didn't hear.

Then Madame Sabine said, "No, I didn't hear that. Is it serious?"

That didn't sound like it was part of the preparations.

"He fell ill not so long ago."

"Is there anyone with him?" Madame asked. Her voice sounded concerned now.

"Not at the moment. We have called for a physician, but they are hard to find after dark when everyone is drunk."

"No word from Graziela?"

"I'm afraid not, Madame."

"Don't let any of my husband's men near him. Especially anyone from the church."

"It's not my place to deny people entry," the man said. "I can't deny entry to people ordered to come by your husband."

Madame let out an audible sigh. "Fine. Wait here." She came into the room, pulled the tie out of her hair so that her curls danced over her shoulders, she took off the coat and put her dressing gown on over her shirt and trousers, and gestured to Nellie. "Come with me. You know about herbs and remedies."

CHAPTER 14

NELLIE FOLLOWED Madame Sabine out the door with dread in her heart. She needed to return to the kitchen. Dora would wonder where she was and Els and Maartje would have to work that much harder the longer Nellie stayed away. Moreover, she didn't *want* to go where Madame Sabine was taking her. Sure, she knew about a few herbs and remedies, but was nowhere near as well-versed in them as someone like Graziela.

The man outside was a young fellow from Lord Verdonck's party. He wore leather trousers and a jacket with fur lining and tall boots that suggested he was a coachman.

He led them down into the foyer.

The kissing couple was gone. A few guards lined up on either side of the door. Henrik was one. His eyes met Nellie's, full of concern.

From the bottom of the stairs, the coachman turned right, towards the guest quarters. They walked past the quiet recovery rooms which were empty except one where a woman sat on a bench fanning herself.

At the start of the guest quarter corridor was a short passage that led to a small room where brooms and buckets and other cleaning equipment was stored.

Inside the passage, half-hidden from the light of the lamps, stood two people. The long golden plait belonged to Els, and she was talking to a young man in a dark brown robe: the monk, Gerard.

Neither of them looked up. What was Els doing with him in a place where few people would notice them?

With a *monk,* who was supposed to be unaffected by the attractions of female flesh.

And Els wanted juniper berries *for my mam* because, clearly, whores had nowhere better to turn to end unwanted pregnancies than the herb cabinet of the palace servants' quarters.

Nellie, that girl has well and truly led you up the garden path.

The young coachman knocked on the door of Lord Verdonck's room, meeting another man inside.

"How is he?" the coachman asked.

"No better, I'm afraid."

Nellie guessed the second man to be in his late twenties. He was tall, but broad in the shoulders as if he'd been trained in swordcraft. Like Madame Sabine, he wore travel clothing: a long cloak, a plain shirt and leather trousers for riding.

She didn't know this man, but presumed that it was Lord Verdonck's son, Adalbert, or another noble from the lord's party.

Madame Sabine ran into the room. "Ronald!"

She dropped to her knees next to the four-poster bed.

The man who lay back in the pillows, with sweat glistening on his face, was Lord Verdonck. Blood dripped from a cut on his forehead and had seeped into the collar of his white shirt.

The air was stifling hot from the fire and laced with the sour stench of vomit.

"What happened?" Madame Sabine asked. She sat on the bed, using a cloth to wipe the Lord's face.

He whispered, "My dear, I am so sorry. I seem to have fallen ill."

Well, that was . . . revealing. And it explained a lot of the strange happenings, like why this man, a dissenter against the church, was still employed as the Regent's advisor.

"My lord says he felt unwell before dinner," the young coachman said to Nellie. "We were getting ready to leave, but he collapsed in the hallway and cut his head. We carried him inside, but he's in a right state."

"I've brought you a herb woman," Madame Sabine said in a soft voice, stroking Lord Verdonck's face.

Everyone in the room looked at Nellie, including the lord, whose eyes were bloodshot and watery and whose skin was pale as death.

Nellie's courage sank. Whatever herbs she could offer, this man was too ill to benefit from them.

They'd need someone with herb magic, someone far more skilled than she.

She didn't want to be in this room. Whatever plot these people had hatched, it was against the Regent and against the church, and she wanted no part in it.

If the Regent found out she was here, there would be hell to pay.

But she had no choice.

The stench of illness hung around the bed like a cloud. The lord's shirt was drenched with sweat. There were specks of vomit on his shirt as well as bloodstains.

A cup of water stood untouched on the bedside table while the contents of the bowl that stood next to him amounted to nothing more than some yellowish slime.

Clearly, he'd been vomiting for quite some time.

Where to begin? Clean up the mess, she supposed.

"Does your head hurt?" she asked.

"My stomach." He placed both his hands over his lower belly. His voice sounded raw. "The cramps are something terrible."

By the Triune, what to do about that? She knew about simple remedies, but had no idea how to treat serious illnesses.

Nellie bent down to look at the wound on his forehead. It was dirty with dust and dried blood; she could at least clean that up. The table next to the bed only held a night lamp and an old, square bottle of gin with a goat on the label. She could use it to stop the rot in the cut, but it was empty.

She asked for water, and when it turned up, wiped his face. Then she tore a clean length of fabric from a rag in her pocket and wound it around his head.

Through all of this, the lord hung apathetic in the pillows. He appeared to want to vomit when Nellie moved his head forward—his hair was soaked through with sweat —but nothing came out except a dribble of dark slime that ran down his chin.

This man wasn't just unwell; he had been poisoned.

"What caused this?" she asked.

"Not the food at the banquet. My father hardly ate anything and already looked unwell."

If it wasn't the food, it could be the drinks.

The Guentherite order had supplied the wine. The Guentherite order were not part of the Church of the Triune, but definitely had a good relationship with them. There were several monks in the palace.

Wim in the kitchen tested the wine. They had all "tested" the wine. Yet she was sure that the kitchen would be blamed nevertheless.

Lord Verdonck moved his lips, but no sound came out. He appeared to want to say something and grabbed onto her arm with surprising strength. His hands were cold.

"Get out, my dear." His voice was only a whisper. "Go without me. Take it to safety."

"You must be mistaken. I'm Nellie."

Madame Sabine was talking to the young coachman. Their voices were low and full of concern.

Adalbert Verdonck—who looked quite a lot like his father—sat on the chair by the hearth, glaring at Madame Sabine or his father. Whenever Madame Sabine looked in his direction, he stared into the fire. There was no love lost between those two, for whatever reason.

Nellie was done with the bandage. She folded back the cover, intending to cool the patient down, noticed that he was still in his clothes and that he had soiled the bed. My, what a stench. She recoiled and took a step back.

Phew.

The others stared at the mess.

Lord Verdonck's eyes held a sad expression.

Nellie had an eerie thought. Sometimes, hunters or farmers brought birds to the kitchen that were still alive. They would come in a basket that Wim would carry into the yard, an axe dangling on his belt. The birds would be quiet and would look at Nellie with their beady eyes. They knew they were going to die.

The same expression hovered in the lord's eyes.

He knew he would die and could do nothing to stop it. Nellie couldn't stop it, either.

"Have you got something to ease his stomach pains?" the young nobleman asked. "At least we can get him into the coach."

"He's not fit to travel home like this," Nellie said.

"We have to go," the lord's son said. His eyes were intense. "This place is not safe for us."

No; if someone had poisoned him, she understood that. But . . .

"At least let me clean him up." By the Triune, she had never seen anything like this. "Get him out of bed and take his bottoms off. I'll find clean clothes." The lord's travel chest stood on the other side of the bed.

The two men and Madame Sabine pulled the sheets off the bed, and Nellie opened the heavy lid of the chest.

Inside the chest lay all manner of clothing: a heavy coat, spare shirts, a jacket. She took them all out in search of clean trousers.

Ah, there they were—but what was that?

In a corner of the chest lay an octagonal box, made of fine polished wood. Her heart skipped a beat. Was that. . . ?

In her mind, she saw an octagonal shape in the dust.

The magic box she had seen on Mistress Johanna's desk had been much more elaborate, made of inlaid wood with mother-of-pearl. The shape surely had to be a coincidence.

Still, she draped a shirt over the top of the box and returned to the bed, where the men had pulled the lord to his feet and Madame Sabine had undone his belt.

They pulled off his boots and socks and then his trousers. He moaned through it all, with slime dribbling down his chin.

His underwear was soaked in watery shit and blood-stained urine.

"Phew," the coachman said.

While the men helped him lift his legs, Nellie pulled down the soiled trousers, which was hard work because they were wet and stuck to his skin.

The smell made her feel sick.

But she got to his knees and asked the men to lift his

leg so she could pull the trouser legs off. First the right one, and then the left—

And there she stopped.

Across the back of his left calf, he had a scar: a broad red mark about the width of her thumb.

Nellie pulled his trouser leg further down and found two similar scars, parallel to each other, as if a giant cat had scratched him across his calf. Just like the scars on Madame Sabine's back.

And then she knew what they were: dragon scars.

This could mean only one thing: that box in the chest was indeed the dragon box that everyone was looking for.

By the Triune.

That was why the guards had been searching the guest's rooms.

The church had not been experimenting with the box, *he* had, and Madame Sabine, and now the church was looking for the box, knowing one of the guests had it, upsetting the nobles' rooms as they searched the entire palace.

The trousers were off.

Nellie wiped his legs and gave the young men a clean pair of underpants, although she wasn't sure how long they would stay clean. Then the trousers.

"Wait. I'll get a shirt to put in his underwear to keep him clean longer."

Nellie turned back to the chest. Sweat rolled down between her breasts, and not just because it was hot and airless in this room.

She crouched by the chest with her back to the two men. She picked up the shirt she had draped over the box and grabbed the box within it.

"I'll just fold this into a wad," she said, with her back to the others.

She let the box slip from the shirt into the pocket of her apron that was big and also filled with two spoons, the rest of the rag she'd torn the bandage from,, some buttons and pins and other small items. Then she grabbed a second shirt, rolled that up and stuffed that into the pocket as well, letting the ends hang out over the front to hide the shape of the box in her pocket.

Between the four of them, they dressed Lord Verdonck in clean clothes.

Madame Sabine kept asking if Nellie thought he would be all right.

So the two of them had thought to elope with this object of great magical value that belonged to the church?

They had thought to take it out of the city, to Lord Verdonck's estate, which lay in the fertile lands to the south.

Nellie feared much that the lord would not be all right. If he had been poisoned, there would be hell to pay, and he would have a long road to recovery, if he recovered at all.

But they got him into his clothes and eased him back onto the bed after draping the covers over the soiled sheets. Nellie pitied the girl who would have to deal with those tomorrow morning.

The lord's son left the room to find someone else to help his father to the coach.

"Can I go back to the kitchen now, Madame?" Nellie asked.

Madame Sabine turned aside as if she had forgotten Nellie was in the room. "Yes, that's fine."

Nellie fled the room, past the guards who stood outside the door, through the foyer where some guests were going home, and past the entrance into the hall where the music played and the drunken shouting continued.

It was not until she had reached the kitchen that she realised the enormity of what she had just done.

She had *stolen* something—something that belonged to the church and had been stolen from the crypt, that the church had bought for safekeeping.

While Nellie continued to work, the corners of the box poked into the skin under her apron. She probably imagined it, but the box felt *warm*.

She wanted to be rid of this horrible thing.

She joined the line of servants carrying dishes of puddings into the big hall. The guests left much of the food uneaten, and she couldn't imagine that anyone could still be hungry. As usual, the odd guest had fallen asleep at the table.

A growing number of guests were already leaving.

They were locals, and most did not look happy. As Nellie passed the groups on their way to the doors, she caught words like *scandalous* and *outrageous*. They might have been talking about the behaviour of the young nobles, or about the fact that people's rooms were searched.

The guard level in the hall had increased. Several palace guards stood at the door, demanding to check the coat pockets of everyone who left.

Many of the nobles objected to being asked.

"What do you think?" she heard one indignant man say, in a slurred voice, "that we steal the palace silverware? It's not that nice. It hasn't been polished for months. The tableware at my home is much nicer. I wouldn't lower myself to steal second-rate things. You know this man, this foreigner who sits on the throne, is a leech. It's inappropriate to hold festivities like a king while he's only a pretend king. If he wants to be our king, he had better behave like one."

His wife was pulling him by the shoulder. "Come on,

let's go," she said in a low voice. "You don't want to get into trouble, do you?"

"I'm not the one who will get into trouble!"

The wife hissed, "I don't understand you. All night you've been talking as if Regent Bernard is your best friend. What has gotten into you?"

The husband took off his coat so that the guards could check the pockets, but the look on his face spelled thunder.

The guards found nothing of interest and returned the coat to him. He huffed while putting it on and the pair left through the front doors, still arguing.

Now that she knew what the guards were looking for, Nellie felt conscious of the bulge in her apron pocket.

After all the guests were gone, the drunks dragged to their rooms or removed from the palace by the staff, the plates cleared, the tables wiped and the floors mopped, Nellie could finally go to her room.

She made sure the door was shut before she took off her apron, sat on the bed and dug the box from her pocket. The polished wood gleamed in the light of the lamp. Compared to the box that mistress Johanna used to have, it was a simple thing, although well made. She didn't remember seeing this box before. Then again, Prince Bruno was only four, and no doubt his mother or his father would have kept it somewhere safe on his behalf.

The wood felt warm under her fingers.

It seemed to say, *Open me if you dare.*

Nellie let her fingers slide along the crack between the lid and the bottom of the box. An ornate clip held the lid in place. Her fingertips traced the sharp outlines of the metal.

With a soft *mrrreeooooow*, the kitten jumped onto the bed. It climbed onto her lap, pushing its head against the box.

"No, don't do that, I might drop it," Nellie said.

She rose from the bed, picked up Lord Verdonck's shirt, wrapped the box in it, tied the parcel up with the sleeves and tucked it into the back of her clothes cupboard. The kitten watched her from the bed, meowing occasionally.

CHAPTER 15

ALTHOUGH TIRED, Nellie found it hard to sleep that night.

She couldn't help thinking about the box in her cupboard, the box that two deacons of the church had opened, setting fire to the crypt. The box that contained the dragon that had given Lord Verdonck and Madame Sabine terrible scars. The box that was now in her room in the unlocked wardrobe where people could accidentally stumble across it.

It was as if the air became stifling with imaginary heat.

Nellie had seen Li Fai's dragon once, a terrible creature with a long, sinuous body and a large mouth with vicious teeth. It was about the size of a horse, could fly and blew fire from its nostrils.

Back then, it had defeated a great evil sorcerer, so she had seen it as a *good* creature, but magical creatures existed under the command of their masters, and whether they performed good or ill depended on the master.

If this dragon had belonged to Prince Bruno, who said *he* would have done good with it?

And who commanded a dragon without a master?

Then she worried about Lord Verdonck, wondering if he and his son and coachman had left the palace and if Madame Sabine had gone with them, and whether they missed the dragon box.

More than the box itself, Nellie feared the bad things that other people could do with it.

She gave up on trying to sleep and lit the lamp on her little table.

The kitten bounced off the bed and sat at the door to the cupboard, miaowing, as if it wanted to investigate this strange thing.

Now she had the box, did her father have any instructions about what to do next?

She sat on the bed and opened her father's book on her knees.

She found the page where the dragon box was first mentioned and read backwards from that.

In the pages she had previously only skimmed, she found references to the good artisans of the city, which included the bakers and the tailors and the people who worked in the harbour, and cooks and the carpenters.

The city needed these people, her father said. It was in art that people had the ability to work their magic and make wonderful things. He did not believe all magic should be banned.

Strange, she had never thought of him as a supporter of magic. Quite the opposite, in fact, even if only because the church banned magic and refused to acknowledge its existence.

In a roundabout way, he even mentioned the sorceress Juliana as a woman who lived in the artisan quarter and whom many feared, but who they turned to when they had an illness.

He said about her:

Certain artisans with dubious qualities have a great

interest in the items acquired by the church. It is not always clear how they know these items are in the crypts, but one woman is very insistent in her complaints. She claims to be the rightful owner of many of these objects, and although that is nonsense, she has a disturbingly accurate knowledge of what is there. It seems she uses a spy within the church, although we have not been able to ascertain who this is. The woman in question is known as a witch, and no self-respecting churchman would speak to her.

And on the next page, she found,

The witch claims the box has healing properties, and this is certainly untrue. Not only that, but Brother Alfred, who first attempted to open the box, would still be alive, since he was subjected to the full force of magic. But alas, he died of illness the same year. When handling the box, it can seem to be warm, in all likelihood caused by the anger of the creature hidden within. Maybe the man who holds it close to his person can derive benefit from this warmth, so as to make him less susceptible to common illnesses, but to be honest, that is extremely doubtful.

Yes, Nellie had noticed the warmth. Healing properties? It had done nothing for Lord Verdonck's health. What about this man called Brother Alfred? Nellie remembered him vaguely, a monk who had regularly come from the monastery to visit the church. He had been well into middle age when she was much younger.

What was the box supposed to have done?

She put the book down and went to the cupboard. She took out the bundle of fabric with the box inside. The kitten followed her every step, almost making her trip.

Slowly, she peeled the shirt away.

The gleaming wood of the box reflected the light from the candle.

This box was not the same as Mistress Johanna's. It

was made of a darker wood, and while Mistress Johanna's had carvings of flowers, this one was plain.

Nellie shivered.

She remembered the fire demons that had destroyed the city. She remembered them hovering over the roofs of houses.

She definitely wasn't going to open this box, but she was curious to know what was in it. How could a dragon hide in a little box like this? Surely, it couldn't be a very big dragon. If it wasn't a big dragon, it couldn't be a dangerous dragon.

She ran her fingers over the smooth wood. It didn't feel warm to her. Her fingertips traced the outline of the clip that held the lid in place and started pushing the clip up.

She caught herself. It was trying to trick her. It *wanted* her to open the box. She must put this thing away.

She would wrap it up and take it to Shepherd Adrianus' house to ask what she should do.

She rolled the box back in the shirt.

The little kitten found the movement of the fabric very interesting. It jumped onto the parcel and tried to claw at a dangling sleeve.

Nellie batted the paws away.

"No, this is not for you to play with." The kitten had become so much stronger already.

Nellie picked up the kitten and lowered it to the floor, rose from the bed and returned the box to the shelf.

The little kitten didn't give up so easily. It jumped back onto the bed and from the bed onto Nellie's dress. Because its claws were so sharp, it climbed up the dress and jumped into the cupboard, using its claws to haul itself in.

But with the weight of the kitten, the pile of clean aprons, towels and sheets tumbled into a heap on the floor, including the shirt that held the box. The kitten's attempts to free itself unrolled the shirt from the box, and being octagonal, the box rolled on its side across the floor.

The kitten chased after it.

Nellie dived after the kitten and noticed that the clip on the box had come undone.

No! *No, no, no.*

Her fingers touched the box, but it slipped from her hands.

The lid fell off.

No, no, no.

Nellie brought both her hands to her mouth and stared at the box in horror. "Oh, look what you have done—"

Inside the box was—nothing, except soft red silk covering the inside of the bottom and the lid.

Well, that was strange.

Phew. She'd worried for nothing.

And then another thought: this was a ruse. People looking for this box thought everything was about the box, but the dragon was no longer in the box. Someone had taken the dragon out and hidden it.

She chuckled, though her heart thudded.

She picked the box up and ran her fingers over the silk lining and felt in the corners of the fabric to check if anything hid in the folds.

Nothing.

The dragon was gone.

That was a relief.

She would never know the full history of it or how it came to be in Lord Verdonck's position. And, what was more, she had no idea why the church would want this thing.

It didn't matter. Because she would not give it back to Lord Verdonck, and she didn't have to think about what she would do with this dreadful thing anymore, because it was empty. It was empty! This box was a ruse. She could use it to store her hairpins, or other things.

She was about to put the lid back on the box when something caught her eye.

What was that?

Inside the fabric, a little point glowed, like a flame without a candle.

She lifted the box closer to her eye, and the effect disappeared. But when she held the box further away again, the point reappeared, brighter and bigger.

What was that?

She poked her finger into the interior of the box through the glowing point. She felt nothing. She saw nothing on her skin.

But the point of light became brighter.

This was magic. She should shut this thing and hide it somewhere before someone came and saw this. But she couldn't bring herself to do it. It was as if a giant hand stopped her and forced her to stare, frozen, at the bright spot.

And then: poof! The bright spot grew into a ball of whirling flames. A shape moved within, a curled up crea-ture like a chick inside an egg. It opened a beady eye that focused on her. That creature looked all too . . . real.

Nellie gave a squeak and dropped the box. It fell onto the mat by the side of her bed, with the lid and the bottom of the box sticking up like the halves of an empty clamshell.

The kitten mewled and ran over to sniff the box.

"No, don't!" Nellie pushed the kitten out of the way. The spell on her was broken, and she slammed the lid onto the box.

But just before the lid closed, the fire creature slid through the tiny gap. It whirled through the room, sucking in more fire as it passed the candle flame.

No, no, no!

Nellie picked up the box and chased after it, snapping the two parts of the box together like a pair of grasping hands.

And missing.

Going right through the glow but capturing none of it.

The kitten bounced onto the bed, onto the table, trying to bat the fire creature when it passed. *Playing with it.*

Everywhere the fire passed, it left black marks. Nellie even had to stomp out a fire on the rug.

This thing would set the whole palace on fire.

The fire creature skittered to the ceiling. It now had distinguishable legs, and wings, too, all radiant with fire glow.

Nellie climbed onto the bed. With both sides of the box in either hand, she reached out and slammed the box shut to catch the creature—and missed again.

The fireball scooted to the corner of the room near the door.

"Oh no, you don't." Nellie jumped off the bed and snapped the box together again.

The creature whizzed to the other side of the room, above the shelf over the bedhead. Nellie tried to catch it with the box, dislodging the hairbrush that lay on the shelf. It fell onto the bed and clattered on the floor.

The creature flew to the other side of the room. Any moment now someone would come in to investigate the racket she was making in the middle of the night.

The fire dragon escaped her twice more. She dragged the bed to the middle so she could reach all corners of the tiny room.

The creature darted from corner to corner, making the bedspread smoke until Nellie put the fire out.

"Stop it, stop it, you'll set the palace on fire!"

The creature darted away.

"Stop it!" She didn't want to shout too loudly. People would come into her room.

And still the fire dragon grew.

It already didn't fit in the box anymore. If she waited too long, it wouldn't even fit in the room. She needed something other than the box to catch it. A sheet or a towel from her cupboard would do, or an apron. She had a spare one she pulled from the shelf.

The dragon sat on the little table next to her books. It had already become less glowy and more solid. The skin looked like that of a snake. It shimmered gold and red. The eyes were orange and had long pupils, like a cat's. It had two round nostrils that flared at the end of its snout. It had pointy ears that moved as if it was listening, like a rabbit.

Nellie could feel the warmth coming from the demonic construction.

For a moment, neither of them moved.

She would have one chance at catching this creature with the apron which she had unfolded and held up in front of her.

Then the dragon sniffed like it was a horse. It blinked its eyes, and cocked its head, regarding Nellie, who stood frozen.

The kitten sat on the bed, also watching, but twitching its tail as if getting ready to spring.

Nellie whispered, "Come on, help me."

The kitten mewled.

The dragon turned its head.

Nellie lunged forward. She tossed the apron over the dragon's head and wrapped the garment around it. The creature's body felt solid and warm through the fabric.

She transferred the bundle to her bed and wrapped the apron's straps around the parcel.

There.

Nellie got to her knees and reached under the bed where she kept her chest with the last of her personal possessions. She opened the lid, tipped out the contents— her mother's winter coat, a set of cups that had belonged to her grandmother and a couple of table cloths she had no use for but couldn't bear to sell.

She collected the bundled-up apron from the bed—and found that it was empty.

What?

Heart thudding, Nellie looked around. Where had the dragon gone?

The box lay open on the bed where she had left it. A little glow floated into it like a downy feather drifting on the breeze.

Nellie grabbed the box and slammed it shut over the glowing spot.

Phew.

She found a ribbon in her cupboard and wound it several times around the box. That dreadful thing would not escape again.

Tomorrow evening, she would give it to Shepherd Adrianus so he could return it to the safety of the crypt.

She wanted nothing more to do with this thing, and she wanted no one else to have it.

CHAPTER 16

NELLIE WOKE UP with a shock when a couple of people walked past her room talking. They probably weren't that loud, but only sounded that way, because she had been so fast asleep—and by the Triune, she had slept in. Not even the kitten on her bedspread had stirred.

There was so much to do. Dora would be angry with her.

Nellie scrambled out of bed, lit the oil lamp and searched for her clothes.

It was still quite warm in this room.

That brought back the surreal memories from last night.

Nellie checked that the dragon box was safely tucked away in her linen cupboard, which it was.

She dressed to get ready for work: her underdress, her overdress, her apron, her long socks. She hesitated when putting on her bonnet. It looked ridiculous, Madame Sabine had said.

What would she look like without?

On the shelf above her bed stood a little mirror that

had belonged to her mother. It was stained with dark blotches where some paint on the back of the glass had come off.

Nellie undid the pins to her bun.

Her hair fell past her shoulders.

It had never been pretty. It was thin and had an ashen colour that was neither the radiant silver of Els' hair or the golden blond of Queen Cygna. Now that it was mostly grey, it was stiff and stubborn, even if that made it easier to pin up.

Bah, suggesting that she shouldn't wear her bonnet was easy for someone like Madame to say. She had a head full of lush curly locks, none of this dirty-looking, wiry, lifeless rubbish.

Madame Sabine also didn't like hair in her food, so Nellie put on the bonnet, and tucked all the stray hairs underneath.

She made sure the cupboard was properly shut so that nothing would look out-of-place if someone checked in her room. The kitten was again trying to climb in, so she picked it up and took it into the corridor, making sure that the door to her room was also closed.

It miaowed and scratched at the wood.

"No, you're not getting in when I'm not here."

Nellie left the kitten sitting there.

In the kitchen, activities for breakfast were in full swing. Dora had started cooking soup for the midday meal.

"Hey, Nellie, you're late." She laughed, holding up the ladle.

Els and Maartje were filling plates with pastries.

The scene in the kitchen was surreal, the happy atmosphere that usually hung around after a busy night, the sense that the worst was over and that life could go back to normal now. Even if there were still a lot of guests in the palace, the big event was done.

They knew nothing about the claims of poisoning yet. Definitely no one knew of the dragon. But how long would the happiness last?

Nellie poured some tea and cut a slice of the freshly baked, delicious-smelling bread. She couldn't bear to break their contented mood. The bad news would come down to the kitchen soon enough.

"Is Wim in yet?" she asked. He would know.

"I've seen him briefly this morning. He was doing something in the storerooms. Why?"

"Just wondering, because he wasn't here."

She didn't ask any further. She never spoke much to Wim and had no reason to be interested in where he was.

After a quick bite to eat, Nellie and her helpers brought all the clean plates back upstairs.

There were fewer diners now—only those who were staying at the palace. Most of them were only now coming out of their rooms, ambling down the hallway that led to the guest quarters.

The servants had opened the doors in the big hall to let out the foul stench. The breeze that came in from outside was cold and made the tablecloths on the far side of the hall flap.

Clean tablecloths, for breakfast for the remaining guests. Some young helpers were already putting out plates on the tables, those plates that had been washed and dried by Maartje and Els after the partygoers had gone home or to their rooms last night.

There were of course far fewer people to be served than at the banquet, so the tables all stood in the middle of the hall.

One by one, the guests arrived.

Most of the pretty nobles looked a little worse for

wear. Not quite as nicely dressed, their hair messy. Some were not wearing their wigs.

The Regent sat alone at the table. Neither his wife nor his sons had joined him. A young girl had the task, every morning, to bring porridge with honey upstairs for Madame Sabine. Nellie had seen her leave the kitchen with her tray.

The girl had not come back with the full bowl, so Nellie assumed that Madame Sabine had not left the palace.

There was no word about the condition of Lord Verdonck.

Breakfast was a much quieter affair than dinner had been. Most of the guests were rather subdued. They sat in groups with the people who had travelled with them to the city, and the tables had a lot of empty seats. Nellie also noticed some women who had not been at the banquet last night.

Madame Sabine had not been the only one with a distaste for noisy drunken banquets.

For Nellie and the servants, serving was an easy task, bringing up bread and tea, butter and jams and honey, cheeses, and milk and porridge for a plentiful breakfast.

Nellie was in the hall pouring tea when Adalbert Verdonck came in.

He strode across the hall and along the aisle between the two lots of tables. He wore riding clothes. His hard-heeled boots made sharp clacks on the marble floor.

Compared to these sorry partygoers, he looked so proud and straight-backed. He had not been at the banquet last night, Nellie realised.

Everyone in the hall fell quiet. Some people turned around and looked at him.

Adalbert stopped in front of the Regent's table, giving a stiff bow.

"What is the matter, young man?" the Regent said. "You look like you've seen a ghost."

"I demand answers. Why has my father been treated like this?"

"Whatever are you talking about?"

"My father has been poisoned!"

A murmur broke out among the guests. Amidst the shouting and men getting up and arguing, Nellie spotted a noblewoman pushing her plate aside. That was food she and Dora had cooked. There was nothing wrong with it.

The Regent held up his hands. A semblance of quiet returned. He started with a grandiose gesture and a dismissive tone. "I don't see how you can conclude that your father's condition is caused by poison—"

"That's clear to me. You only need to go into his room to see that. I will spare these good people the details, especially the ladies, except to say that he is gravely ill. I demand an explanation and an apology. I demand to know who under this roof did this."

"Calm down, man. He probably suffers from indigestion. Wait a while and he'll recover."

"He is *not* fine. He was poisoned some time yesterday while eating food you provided."

The Regent's face grew red. "That makes no sense. Why would I want to poison my closest advisor?"

"I can think of many reasons."

"Wait, young man, before you commit the foolish act of accusing your host in this palace."

"You are not *my* host. My father is your advisor. Without my father, you would not be sitting here and you would not be holding these lavish feasts. I'd like to remind you of King William of Anglia's words: *You will not sit at the table with evil men, and eat their food, because your stomach will turn to water and your water will turn to blood and you'll die before the two days are up.*"

"Don't be ridiculous, man. I employ a man who tests all the food before it comes up into the hall."

"Does he taste the wine?"

The Regent scoffed. "The food and the wine, he tastes all that passes through the kitchen. The wine comes from the Guentherite monastery, and you can hardly—"

"Did he taste this wine?" Adalbert Verdonck asked, more insistently.

"They are *monks*. Are you really saying we should distrust religious men? What has the world come to?"

Nellie made her way out of the hall. She sped across the foyer and down the stairs, panic clamping around her heart.

The wine.

They had drunk some wine around the kitchen table the evening before the banquet, but a large crowd consumed so much of it, tasting it all would be impossible.

Most of the wine came straight off the river boat from the Guentherite order, was unloaded by monks, brought to the palace by monks and served by monks. With help from Els, who had shown more than a passing interest in the monk Gerard.

Els, who was up to some mischief with her juniper berries, lying about why she needed them.

By the Triune . . .

But no, she found it extremely hard to believe that a fourteen-year-old girl would be involved with poisoning people.

But there was definitely something going on with Els.

Yes, but let's be realistic, if the wine was poisoned, then everyone in that room would be ill.

But still . . .

The activity in the kitchen was normal, disturbingly normal. Dora, whose work to cook breakfast was done by now, sat at the table drinking tea.

She met Nellie's eyes.

"Anything the matter?"

"There is some commotion upstairs," Nellie said. "They say someone has been poisoned." Sweat rolled down over her back.

Dora's brows knitted together. "Are they sure?"

"They said it was poison. That's all I know."

Dora's frown deepened.

"Is Wim here?"

"No, he's gone out. Is this why you were asking about him this morning?"

Was Wim already answering questions from the guards? Nellie felt cold. "Can I speak to you?"

Dora jerked her head to the back door.

Nellie proceeded Dora into the yard. The weather had taken a turn for the worse, and snowflakes drifted from the sky. It wasn't quite cold enough for them to freeze, but they left a slippery slurry on the mud in the courtyard.

As soon as Dora and Nellie appeared at the top of the steps, the pigs thought they were getting something, and they started to make noises.

Dora let the door fall shut behind her, and the two stood facing each other.

"Is there anything I should know?" Dora said in a low voice. "You were in Lord's Verdonck's room last night, weren't you?"

"Yes, I was called to attend him, because Mistress Graziela has left town. The lord had fallen ill, and they asked me to help, but there was not much I could do."

"What was wrong with him? Are they sure it was poison?"

"It looked that way to me. His bottoms were stained with blood."

Dora gave her an *urgh* face.

"Wim doesn't test the wine, does he?"

Dora shook her head. "It comes from the Guentherite monastery."

"It could have been an accidental poisoning. I haven't heard about anyone else falling ill."

But Nellie knew that was unlikely, in the light of the other events. Lord Verdonck was not a friend of the church. The church delivered the wine. Nellie couldn't imagine the shepherds getting involved with—or even ordering—anything like a poisoning, but those monks might. And there was that cabinet in the crypt room with the dusty bottles. Poisons aplenty for whoever needed them.

Lord Verdonck had stolen or otherwise obtained the dragon box. He was unlikely to have direct access to the crypt, but might know someone who did. Likely, her father's wasn't the only stray key to the little metal door in the grate.

The church suspected that someone in the palace had the box, maybe even knew that Lord Verdonck had it. They might know the dragon had taken a swipe at Lord Verdonck and Madame Sabine. Because both thought they could control magic or had a small ability.

"Whatever is going on, we have to keep our heads down and weather the storm," Dora said. "We have no knowledge of any poisoning, and I hope our word will be enough."

But the implication that it might not be enough hovered in her voice. "To be honest with you, Nellie, that man is trouble."

"Lord Verdonck?" She only knew him as an affable father figure.

"No, his son Adalbert. He distrusts us so much, he brings his own food and eats nothing provided by the palace."

It was true that Nellie had not seen him at the banquet.

The sound of commotion came from the kitchen. A man was shouting, and a woman shouted back.

"It seems someone is down here already," Dora said.

Like a good mother hen protecting her chicks, Dora protected anyone who worked in the kitchen. She turned to the door and went inside. Nellie followed her.

Several guards had come in. They stood around Corrie, one of the kitchen hands.

The woman's face was all red, and she was shouting, "I have no idea what happened. I saw no one who doesn't belong here." And then she saw Dora, and she pleaded, "Please tell him to go away. We have done nothing and have nothing to do with with poison. We cook the food. We also eat the food ourselves."

"A man has been poisoned," one of the guards said, his voice serious. "Your taster is hiding. If you're so innocent, where is he?"

"I don't know. He also works in the yard sometimes, and he fixes things around the palace. He is an honest man. He tastes everything that passes the kitchen. We had some wine, which we all drank, but most of it never came down here." Corrie was almost crying. "Why do you suspect him? No one else got sick, and Wim used to be one of you, didn't he?"

And yes, Wim used to work for the guards before he became injured and couldn't work anymore.

Dora went to stand between her and the guards. "If there is any problem, raise it with me. Stop intimidating my workers. We're busy."

"The Regent upstairs demands answers."

"No, he demands his meals be cooked. You're not to bother any of my people. I have served the Regent for many years and I have done so faithfully, I have cooked many of his meals, and the people here have served at his table many times. The people who work here are trustworthy, and I cannot imagine that they would have the stupidity to jeopardise their jobs by poisoning the Regent's guests. I can imagine even less why any of them would want to hurt the family that feeds them. Now, get out of my kitchen before I set you to pluck and gut the chickens for tomorrow."

The guards, strong adult men with swords, retreated to the door. Yes, they wanted food. Yes, Dora was faithful. Such was her reputation that anyone else would have failed both in stopping the guards dragging off everyone from the kitchens for interrogations.

They were about to leave when another guard came in with a triumphant whoop.

"Look what I have here!"

He pushed a man in front of him.

Wim. Nellie met his eyes. They were filled with despair.

A cold hand clamped around her heart. Did Wim know something?

The guard laughed. "I found him hiding in the laundry."

Wim was shivering. He was a thin man, with one crooked leg and thinning grey hair and pale skin that was almost translucent in places. "Please, I've done nothing wrong. I tasted all the food we cooked here."

"But you didn't taste the wine. Why not?"

"I tasted all that was brought to the kitchen."

"But not the vats that were delivered upstairs."

"Nobody asked me to. The monks brought that wine. Why should anyone suspect it was poisoned?"

"Well, if you are so sure, maybe you'd like to try it now," another guard said. He set a flask on the table.

Wim's eyes widened.

"This was the wine we found in Lord Verdonck's room. We will see if it is as safe as you thought."

"No, please."

"Bring me a cup," the guards said.

Corrie could do nothing but to obey. The man took the cork out of the flask and poured the wine. In the utter, horrified silence, the glug-glug-glug of the wine sounded loud.

Nellie wanted to stop him. Dora looked like she wanted to stop him, too, but in this case she couldn't. Wim *would* have tasted all the wine had it come from anywhere except the monastery.

The guard put the full cup in front of Wim.

"Drink."

Wim shook his head.

"Drink!" The guard pulled his sword out of its scabbard with *zhing* of metal on metal.

Another guard pushed the cup into Wim's hands.

"No, no, please. Anything but that. I have a family!"

"Drink." The guard held the sword poised at Wim's throat.

Wim picked up the cup. Nellie wanted to rip it from his hands. What was the point of treating him like this?

Wim took a sip and set the cup down. His face was pale and glistening with sweat. "It tastes fine to me."

"All of it," the guard said.

"Please." Wim looked like he could faint any moment.

"All of it," the guard repeated.

Wim picked up the cup again. He drank, slowly. The guard motioned for him to hurry.

He finished the wine. By now, tears streamed down his face.

The guard poured another cup and shoved it back towards Wim.

Someone shouted from the door that more tea was

needed upstairs. Corrie set about making it because what happened upstairs took priority.

Wim drank the other cup, too.

The guards watched him for a while. Nellie had to start peeling apples for making applesauce.

Wim sat at the table, looking at his knees. He said a few times that he felt ill, but nothing else happened. Then he said he wanted to throw up.

He tried to get up from the table, but stumbled over his own feet. He landed on hands and knees, and the guards dragged him out the back door where he vomited all over the steps. They made him clean it up with a bucket of freezing water. One of the guards left the kitchen to *tell the Regent*.

Nellie needed to go upstairs, but when she came back down, Wim was still sitting at the table, looking at his knees, expecting to die.

But dying of poisoning was a drawn-out affair.

In fact, each time Nellie came back down, the guards looked increasingly bored. Wim had gone to sleep with his head resting on his folded arms on the table. He slept peacefully. He had no crippling stomach cramps, his insides did not turn to water, and his water did not turn to blood.

He was *drunk,* not poisoned. There was nothing wrong with the wine. But now the guards had told everyone they'd found the culprit.

They had picked Wim as an easy victim to blame. Much easier than figuring out what else was going on in the palace and upsetting the monks and potentially the church.

By the Triune, now she was angry.

Nellie returned to the hall, where many people had gotten nervous and gathered around the dais, and the Regent was trying to calm them down.

"My room has been searched, too," a man shouted.

"My wife just drank the wine in our room," another said. "I will hold you personally responsible if something happens to her."

Nellie collected plates, hoping that she could get most of the tableware to safety before a fight broke out.

"Nellie?" said a man behind her.

She turned around. It was Henrik.

No, she didn't want to talk to him. She seriously didn't. She was too angry.

"I heard the guards gave the kitchen a hard time," he said when he had caught up with her. "Whoa, why the angry face?"

"Wim didn't do *anything* wrong. All the food we cook in the kitchen, he tastes. If it doesn't come in through the kitchen, he can't taste it. It's unfair to frighten him and unfair to make him drink all that wine. He was so scared that he was crying. What if the wine had been poisoned? Would that have been his fault? How could he have tasted it if he never saw it?"

"Whoa, whoa!" He held up his hands. "I'm not accusing Wim of anything."

"Your colleagues in the kitchen did. And then they made him drink two whole glasses of wine. Wim rarely drinks, so he threw up and now they say the wine was poisoned and it was his fault. Problem solved."

"Please, Nellie—"

"Have you not seen what's going on right under your noses? Lord Verdonck is no friend of the church. He's also Madame Sabine's lover. The two were planning to leave last night, a situation I can't imagine the Regent agrees with, so someone poisons him to stop it and gives Wim the blame."

And there was a dragon box in that story somewhere, but she wasn't going to tell him about that. These people were all the same. Somehow, she had hoped he would be different, but he was not. He was just all shiny buttons and spiffy uniforms and total obedience to his boss, whoever that was. Why had she ever thought he was any more honourable than the other people working upstairs?

"Nellie, we are not blaming Wim. But he is one of the people we need to investigate."

"Then investigate him without blaming him. And now, I've got *work* to do. If you want to make yourself useful, drag Wim off to his bed."

She turned around and strode down the stairs.

CHAPTER 17

BUT AT THE BOTTOM of the stairs, another unpleasant surprise waited for her. She almost ran into someone who was coming the other way.

A woman wearing a man's coat with the hood pulled over her hair.

"Oh, there you are."

Madame Sabine.

Nellie's heart jumped. What was she doing here? Was she looking for the dragon box? Did she know it was missing yet? By the Triune, did this mean that Madame Sabine had actually been to her room?

"I went to look for you. Lord Verdonck made it through the night, but he is very ill and will take a long time to recover. We don't feel he's safe here, so we're going to try to get him home. I need you to find him some remedies for stomach cramps so he can make the journey."

"Sure, I can bring him some tea of—"

No, she couldn't. She had given the last juniper berries to Els.

"I . . . I'll have to go to the markets, anyway." Dora was

sure to need something. "I'll bring the tea as soon as I can."

"Thank you. I'm insanely worried. He means so much to me, and I trust you with this important task."

Oh, if she only knew.

Maybe she suspected that Nellie had the box. One did never trust these nobles.

Madame Sabine looked small and lonely walking up the stairs to her room. In the big hall, Nellie knew, her husband was still talking to many of the guests.

Dora did, indeed, need someone to go to the markets. She'd run out of salt and needed saffron for the glazing of the pork legs she would cook tonight, as well as a few other things.

Nellie offered to go.

Dora nodded. "I'd send one of the kids, but if you want to go, be quick, because I need you."

So Nellie returned to her room, checked that the dragon box was still safe in the cupboard—which it was, and it didn't look like anyone had been here—and donned her coat.

Grey clouds chased each other over the roof of the city, and the wind that blew off the Saar delta bit into her skin. At the marketplace, stallholders stood huddled under the flapping covers, casting foul looks at the sky. The question was not whether it would stay dry but whether it would rain or snow.

Many of the stalls selling exotic spices were gone, but one local man still came occasionally. Nellie was lucky that he had come to the markets today. He used a tiny set of scales to weigh out the precious threads of saffron and filled her cloth bag with salt.

While he was doing this, he spoke about the weather. He lived in town where his wife ran the family's shop.

Nellie collected all her purchases into her carry satchel.

Then she remembered something. "Juniper seeds." She had almost forgotten. What would she have told Madame Sabine?

"I'm very sorry, but we are completely out. If you come back next week, I may have some. A pretty young woman just bought all the ones I still had."

"Oh, what a pity. I'll have to go somewhere else." Wait. A pretty young woman. What was the bet this was Els? "How long ago was this?"

"This morning. Scarcely a moment before you came."

"Do you know the woman?"

"I don't."

"Which way did she go?"

"She was very chatty and said she was going shopping."

The shops were in the adjacent quarter, but Nellie still needed juniper berries, and a deep sense of dread had come over her about what Els was up to, so she left the markets.

Several shops in the commercial quarter sold herbs and all manner of dried groceries. The first shop she entered had also run out of juniper berries.

The second shop was very busy, and Nellie didn't want to wait long for her turn, because Dora was waiting for the salt, so she visited a third shop, which also had no berries left.

What had the man at the markets again said about a young woman buying up all his stock?

So she had to go back to the shop where it was busy, and just as she was going in, someone came out.

"Oh, Nellie!"

It was Els, dressed in a warm coat, with her hair done up in a bun. Nellie had never seen her like that. She looked like a normal citizen, not someone whose family was to go into the poor house. That coat was of decent quality, and she wore a scarf, too.

"Out shopping?" Nellie asked.

This was awkward. The sisters' work at the palace didn't usually start until later in the afternoon. It was perfectly fine for Els to go shopping, but something in the way Els had almost sounded shocked when seeing Nellie told her that Els had not expected to see her.

"My mam asked me to buy a few groceries." She was carrying a basket with the lid shut. "Well, I better be going."

"I'll see you this afternoon."

"Yes, bye."

She skipped into the street, and Nellie almost entered the shop, but she turned around instead and waited on the porch, looking around the pillar that supported the corner of the alcove that held the shop's door.

What was the chance that Els had bought the last ones from this shop as well?

Juniper berries could not only be used by women whose bleeding was late. They could be used to make poison.

By the Triune.

The street outside was quite long and straight, and the foul weather kept a lot of the people indoors. Nellie could see Els walking out of the town centre, with her flaxen blond bun bobbing on her head. For some reason she thought of Madame Sabine's aversion to bonnets.

Where was Els going?

As far as Nellie knew, her family lived above a shop near the harbour, which was the other way. She wasn't going to the palace either, or she would have turned right.

Nellie followed her, keeping at a safe distance.

Els continued down the street for a while before turning left into a narrow alley. This part of town had never been affected by the terrible fires. All the buildings were old, many made of wood, although some of those were now being rebuilt. Nellie was not terribly familiar with this area, but when she had lived with Mistress Johanna in the merchant quarter, before Johanna married prince Roald, this had been a quiet part of town where the workers lived. The houses were small and cheaply built.

But these days a newer generation of people were moving in, people who were better off and who replaced the older wooden structures with bigger houses built from bricks.

The street ended in a piece of empty land. With a bunch of sapling willow trees—now all without leaves—it looked like a park, until you noticed the broken and blackened walls poking out from between the dead grass. Yes, Nellie remembered that this area used to house a garden with pens that contained exotic animals. One of them was a large spotted cat that the owner, a dark-skinned man called Mustafa, would walk on a leash. It was bigger than an average dog and it walked soundlessly. Mustafa called it a leopard, and he would allow people to pet it.

There was also an enormous green and red bird with a curved beak, called a parrot, that screeched something terrible. It could speak, but the ship's captain who had owned the bird had taught it a lot of bad language, which young men found extremely funny.

Mustafa was forced to keep the animal at the back of the garden, but its swearing could still be heard in the street.

Nellie wondered where Mustafa and his menagerie had gone. That no one had built on this land meant that he probably still owned it.

Back then, this patch of land was on the edge where the marshy meadows joined the jumble of houses of the city. The land beyond had been too wet to build on. But the city council had recently dug another canal to drain the land.

New buildings had been added on the far side, most for businesses: a carpentry and furniture maker, a coachmaker, and the building that stood next to the coachmaker's yard was so new that it hadn't even been finished. The door and windows had been installed, but the wood hadn't yet been painted. This was where Els went.

Nellie ducked behind the dilapidated remains of what used to be the entrance to the animal park, a little booth—now all rotting and falling apart—where Mustafa would sell tickets and refreshments.

Els walked up to the warehouse's double doors and knocked. A moment later, the door opened from the inside.

A female voice said something, and Els disappeared inside, carrying her basket.

Well, that was interesting, and annoying. What now?

Nellie sped over the bridge across the canal, and up to the warehouse door, but the tiny windows on either side were too far off the ground for her to see through.

A narrow alley ran past the right side of the building, in between it and a wall around the coachmaker's yard. The sound of men's voices drifted over the wall from the carpenters talking and laughing in the workshop.

This alley was where the owners of the businesses took out their rubbish. A bin of sawdust and wood shavings stood ready to be collected by someone who kept chickens or ducks. With the other building as new as it looked, that side of the alley was still tidy and empty except for two empty bins. Despite the tidiness, the air smelled of rotting fruit.

A window in the side was too high for Nellie to see through, but she dragged one of the empty bins underneath, turned it over and climbed up.

From her position, she could see over the wall into the coachbuilder's yard. Business must be going well because underneath a shed with open sides stood two coaches in progress. Coach wheels of various sizes leaned against the far wall. Large vats of water contained timber planks weighed with stones to bend them.

A couple of men were busy polishing the side and door panels of an almost completed coach.

By the Triune, if those carpenters saw her standing on top of this wobbly bin, they would laugh and wonder what she was doing.

She peered into the warehouse window.

The first thing she noticed, when her eyes got used to the semidarkness inside, was an installation made from metal vats with pipes. The installation stood against the wall. From her position, she could only see the top of the thing.

There must be a fire somewhere because the wall felt warm under her hands. Steam blew from a little hole in the top of one of the metal pipes.

On the warehouse floor at the other side of the installation stood a row of bottles on a bench.

Nellie recognised the shape. A glass blower in town made these bottles. They were for gin.

That was another use for juniper berries: making gin.

The city of Saardam had laws about making and selling gin.

Nellie was sure that this factory in an unmarked building that hadn't even been completed yet didn't fall under those laws.

People were sent to jail for making and selling illegal gin. The city levied taxes on liquor because it liked to control how much of it was sold. Also, given half a chance, some people would use it as payment, neglecting their families and, in all, too much gin led to more thievery and more beggars on the streets.

And Els was inside that building where this illegal

activity took place, with some ingredients. Nellie could see her, too. She was talking to another young woman, hidden behind Els. What she said must have been funny, because Els bent over laughing, covering her mouth with her hand.

But this gave Nellie a view of the other person.

It was not a girl. Except she was.

A girl with a familiar face, fairly coarse for a woman but, without the monk's habit, unmistakably female. It was Gerard the monk.

Well, by the Triune.

Not only that, Nellie remembered seeing a bottle of gin in Lord Verdonck's room. Empty.

She felt sick.

Els clapped the monk on the shoulder, they hugged each other, and then she turned around to the door.

Nellie scrambled off the rubbish bin and ran through the alley.

Els had left the building and was just walking across the empty plot of land that had held the animal park. Nellie strode after her and caught up with her in the street by grabbing her by the shoulder.

"What are you doing?"

Els gasped. "Nellie! What are you doing here?"

"I could ask the same about you. Buying juniper berries all over town, dealing with girls dressed up as monks. You know making liquor without a permit is illegal. You could end up in jail."

Els' cheeks coloured. "Who says that's what I'm doing?"

"Then what are you doing in the warehouse back there?"

Her eyes widened. "You were spying on me?"

"With good reason. You lied to me. You took advantage of me. You didn't need the berries for your mother at all. You should be ashamed of yourself. I trusted you."

Els glared at her, her arms crossed over her chest.

"You're only fourteen. I'm trying to help you. You don't want to get involved with anything illegal."

"I don't need help. I'm doing fine by myself."

"No, you're not. You'll be headed for jail by the time you're sixteen. What is this kind of girl-monk you've got yourself involved with? Why were you schmoozing with her at the palace?"

"Do you see everything?"

"Yes, I do. I haven't made it to my age by being stupid. Anyway, if you think you've been hiding your activities well enough, think again. I won't have been the only one noticing your strange behaviour."

Els glared at her and let her shoulders droop. "Will you promise not to say anything to anyone?"

"I don't know about that. I'll decide once I hear the story."

Els breathed out a sigh.

"Gisele is like me: the daughter of a whore. Yes, I know you don't like that word, but that's what I am: whore spawn. My father didn't care. My mother doesn't care." Her eyes burned. "Gisele's mother lives in Lurezia and doesn't care about her. She's lived with the street rats all her life. Stealing food and doing other things you disapprove of."

"I don't disapprove—"

"Oh yes you do, you know nothing, but you're full of judgement. You call it 'help' but it's just telling people how bad they are."

"Fine, if you don't need the work at the palace, you can hand in your aprons, if that's what you want. Then you can be a whore like your mother. You'll do well, until the first babe comes along. I thought you didn't want to live like her so that's why I helped you. But I'm sorry. I must have been mistaken."

She glared at Els and Els glared back. Somewhere deep inside her, Nellie believed Els didn't want to follow in her mother's footsteps at all, and that perhaps this illegal venture was part of it.

"I never said I wanted that and you can't tell me to leave anyway. Only Dora can."

Also true. Nellie bit down on her anger. "Keep telling me about the girl monk."

"She has a name: Gisele."

"I'll decide if I want to use the name once I hear the story."

Els gave her another *fine* look. "The only way for her to survive in Lurezia was to steal stuff. One day, she stole a bag with a monk's habit inside. She was cold, and the habit was made of thick fabric, so she put it on. And when she did that, people in the street treated her differently. The guards left her alone. The pimps stopped bothering her. So she cut off her hair to make herself look more like a boy and worked for the church, because they gave her food."

"While pretending to be a monk?" That was disgraceful and misusing people's trust in the church. "What if the order finds out?"

Els shrugged. "They don't care. As long as she works. For a girl alone, pretending to be a monk is safe. She's strong, so she worked on riverboats. Then, when she came here, she started making gin, because a lot of people want to buy it in the harbour. I met her there. She's funny and she's smart. She lets no disgusting man come near her. She sells a lot of gin in town. Gisele makes the gin and I find people to buy it. I know many people in the docks through mam, and all the taverns always want cheaper gin. We split the money. That's all. There's no evil plots involved, just us trying to survive."

"Did you sell anything to the palace?"

"To the palace directly? What do you think I am? I'm

not stupid. They'll want to know where it comes from. I don't want to get caught. I have no argument with the palace. It's just dangerous to be involved with them. We sell to sailors. They don't talk because if they do, they don't get gin."

But obviously someone was well connected enough to lend them the use of this building. As with everything connected to Els, there was probably more to it.

But it was not Nellie's business for now. "That's all very nice, but I am left with no juniper berries and nowhere to buy them. The Regent's advisor Lord Verdonck has fallen ill, Graziela has left, and it's up to me to get the remedies. Because of your buying up all the berries in town, I can't get them anywhere."

Els grinned. "Then I'll tell you a secret—and don't tell Gisele that I've told you this. If you want anything that's a remedy or a poison, mistress Julianna always has some."

"The witch?"

"If you want to call her that, but don't say it to her face or she'll go crazy on you and charge you three times the price for the berries. She'll have them. She may have better remedies for the noble's sore heads, too."

CHAPTER 18

NELLIE DIDN'T WANT to see Julianna. Neither did she want to go into the artisan quarter, where many houses were strange, reflecting their occupants, the artists, the musicians, the modistes.

But she had promised Madame Sabine to bring her something for stomach cramps, although Madame would be better off finding someone who knew about remedies.

The artisan quarter of the city lay on the western side of town, in between Saardam's centre and the marshy ground between the city and the strip of sand dunes that protected the land from the sea.

In the past, this used to be grazing land, and during the summer months caravans of travelling artistes used to camp here. When the people of the city dug canals to get rid of water, the land became useful for building, even if floods still happened.

When she was a little girl and still allowed to roam the streets, the kids would dare each other to go to the artisan quarter, knock on the doors of witches and other strange people, and run off. They would hide around the corner, watching as the inhabitant of the house came to the door, opened it, and found no one there. Some people came into the street, ranting at the kids, others tried to catch one of the rascals and make an example of them, and others shouted that they would complain to the kids' parents.

The one thing the kids wanted was for some magician to come out and blast them with magic, and the boys even had a plan for what they would do if this happened. One boy brought a silver spoon, because, "My pa says silver stops magic, like, dead." But when they knocked on Julianna's door, Julianna—who had always seemed as ancient as she was now—had not given them the satisfaction of blasting them with magic. The only result of the exercise was that the boy received a hiding for misappropriating the family's precious tableware.

Nellie did not come here often anymore, because the only reason she left the palace was to go to church, and sometimes the markets, and both were in a different direction.

She found that the artisan quarter of today differed greatly from the fearful place of her memories. The buildings didn't look so tall and overbearing now. Neither did they lean forward as if they were about to collapse on her.

In fact, many of the houses were freestanding, and some even retained their yards. In others, the yards had been completely built in. These plots, with jumbles of several buildings on them, often housed at least a handful of families.

The houses didn't look so scary anymore. Peeling paint no longer made a house look like a skull with its dark eyes following whoever came past; now it was just peeling paint on a wall. A gate that creaked in the wind was just that. A dog barking behind a wall was just an animal, not a demon in the shape of a dog. Cats scooting behind rubbish containers were in colours other than black, and the seagulls on the roof were just resting, not plotting an attack on people.

And the spider webs . . . there were not that many, let alone ones containing giant man-eating spiders.

She smiled with those silly memories. Kids were so good at scaring each other with stories that were all made up. Witches, wizards, demons, enormous spiders, goodness.

The place was just a little quirky and old.

What surprised her was how many of the houses appeared to be uninhabited.

She wasn't sure which was the house of the sorceress Julianna, because everything looked so different, but Nellie walked along the main street until she found a sign hanging outside the front door that said "Healing and Charms."

Faded red velvet curtains covered two windows on either side of the door. On the inside windowsill on one side stood a glass jar half full of white powder, the outside and stopper covered in dust. Next to it lay a sheep's skull with the horns still attached. The other was empty, but a round mark in the dust showed that a vase or jar had stood there until recently.

Nellie pulled the hood of her coat further over her head, stepped up to the front door and picked up the knocker, in the shape of a goblin, poking out its tongue at her. The thing was big and heavy, and she wondered if it was made of silver, because silver had magical properties.

The knocker made a heavy sound—*bang*—on the wood. It echoed in a hollow space on the other side of the door.

Not too much later, footsteps sounded from inside the house.

A heavy bolt was drawn back, and the door opened a crack.

"Who are you?" said an old woman's voice.

"A friend sent me here to get juniper berries," Nellie said. She felt rather ridiculous.

"A friend?"

"Just someone I asked because everyone in town seems to have run out. I have money, and if you have other remedies against inflictions, I may buy more."

This was finally enough to convince the woman to open the door.

Nellie hadn't seen the sorceress Julianna for many years. She used to have a stall selling herbs and knick-knacks at the markets, but she had stopped coming long before the current troubles. It wasn't hard to see why.

She looked unhealthy, frail and very old. She was quite tall, a mere skeleton of a woman. Her clothes, all black, hung off her shoulders like poorly arranged drapes. She wore her hair in a severe bun. Her face was wrinkled, and her eyes watery and bloodshot. The hand that hung onto the doorknob was long fingered, like a giant spider, with the skin blotchy and flaking.

Now Nellie remembered another reason all the kids feared her. She had several red blotches on her face, and the boys used to say she had killed someone and the blood splattered over her face and would come not off when she washed. Because that was apparently what happened if you were a witch.

Nellie took a step back.

The woman laughed. "Yes, the years have not made me any prettier, but I'm still the same witch. But now you. Prim lady, knows what's right and wrong, at least acts like she knows, and lets no one forget about it. The church says this, the church says that. Let's do what the shepherd says and never think about why they say this. Because the church is always right. You haven't changed a bit either. How are things up there in the palace?"

Nellie gritted her teeth. She might be a prim lady, but

she was not about to let an old witch insult her. "I wanted to buy something from you. Now you've insulted me, why don't I turn around and take my money back home."

"You might do that, but then you still won't have your juniper berries."

Fair enough.

"Come on inside, because it's cold out here."

Nellie had to steel herself to step into the house that had been the subject of her childhood fears.

Life had been so simple back then. Magic was always bad, as the church was always good and the king was always good. Wouldn't it be easy if things worked that way?

The carpet on the floor dampened the sound of her footfalls and released a musty smell.

Once Julianna had closed the door behind them, it grew very dark inside the hall.

Nellie went first down the hallway.

Julianna walked slowly, taking small steps and sliding her hand along the wall as if steadying herself. Her breath wheezed.

"Just this room here," she said between gasps of air, indicating a door immediately to the right.

It was the one where the dusty jar and sheep skull sat on the windowsill behind those long and thick curtains that blocked almost all light from outside.

In the middle stood a table with a single candle whose flame flapped as the door opened. Three chairs stood around the table. The rest of the room contained shelves and cupboards containing many strange objects. A display cabinet was filled to the brim with skulls of various types of animals. Some, like seagull, horse and cow, she could name, but others looked so unfamiliar that they had to come from exotic lands. What bird, for example, had a head the size of a sheep's? Could it still fly? Why did it have such a broad, flat beak?

Another glass-fronted cabinet displayed devices made from metal: weighing scales, a sextant, a spyglass and many other things that Nellie didn't recognise—things with sharp points and spoon-shaped implements. A ceiling-high cabinet contained many wooden drawers, which each had a little round knob and a label announcing the drawer's content: *wolfsbane*, *arrowroot*, *passionflower*. The top three shelves brimmed with bottles and jars of different sizes, most of them very dusty.

So many cabinets crowded the walls that there was scarcely enough space to walk around the table.

"Sit down," Julianna said.

Nellie sat on the edge of one of the chairs.

The strange smell in the room made her uncomfortable. It was not just the scent of dried herbs and spices. It was faint tang of meat gone bad that she couldn't place. A fluid had stained yellow patches in the ceiling—maybe from a dead rat? Or it could be the carpet, which looked none too clean.

The palace's rugs were taken outside twice a year and hung up over the walls and beaten with a stick to dislodge the dust. She could not imagine Julianna doing that.

Because the silence was so oppressing, she asked, "Is this where sick people come to see you? I was expecting a shop or something."

"Sometimes they do." Julianna lowered herself with painful slowness onto the opposite chair. "I don't have a shop. The only people who bother to come to see me are ones who know what they're talking about. Do you know your herbs?"

The candle that stood between them lit her face from underneath, turning it into a ghostly mask.

"A bit."

Julianna snorted. *"A bit* gets you into danger. It makes you think you know everything, but you know nothing. Many of these herbs and extracts here are deadly."

She stopped as if to let that sink in.

Nellie was beginning to think the whole city could have poisoned Lord Verdonck.

Julianna continued, "Many of these bottles on the shelves behind me contain concentrate of herb extractions, poisons more powerful than you will find anywhere. Give someone the wrong dose, and they will die."

"I understand."

"No, you don't. You *think* you understand. Two different things."

"I understand. Someone in the palace has severe stomach cramps. I'm looking for juniper berries to give him juniper berry tea."

"Hmmm, yes, that's always a good start. It's a pity you didn't bring the person, because there are many inflictions that can cause stomach cramps."

"This man is very unwell. He may have been poisoned."

"No surprise, that, seeing all the things these noble people do to each other. The more money, the more bad behaviour, if you ask me."

She pushed the candle aside and put both her wrinkled and gnarled hands on the table.

"Now give me your hands and let me see your lines of power."

"You must be mistaken. I didn't come here for my fortune. I only want juniper berries."

"I am never mistaken. I can sense great confusion in you. People who are confused are often about to make bad choices. Powerful remedies and herbs give people the power to make a bad choice worse. Give me your hands, so I can divine whether it is safe to give you what you ask for."

Safe? Of course she was safe. She wouldn't do any dangerous things, or heaven forbid, poison people.

"I am just a servant. The man in question is a friend of the Regent's who pays me. Why would I wish him harm?"

"Well, in that case, you shouldn't be fearful of me looking at your state of mind. Your hands." She patted the tablecloth.

Fine! She was *not* afraid.

Nellie held out both her hands, palm up, because that was the way these fortunetellers wanted it, right?

Let this witch "tell her fortunes". If she spoke truth, then there was nothing to fear, because she wouldn't do anything, except give the tea to Madame Sabine and get on with her own work, and try to figure out what to do with a dragon.

Well, yeah, the dragon.

If Julianna lied, then . . . well, she lied, and whatever she said had no value anyway.

Julianna took Nellie's hands in hers.

Nellie had always thought her own hands looked old, with wrinkles and darker spots and one or two places where she'd cut herself and the skin had healed with a scar, but compared to Julianna's, they were positively young.

Julianna turned Nellie's hands over, so that the palms faced down. With a crooked finger, she traced a vein that ran over the top of Nellie's hand. The skin on her index finger was cold.

Then she turned Nellie's right hand over and similarly traced the folds on the palm of her hand.

It was utterly silent in the room.

No noise came from the street or the houses nextdoor.

Something rustled in the ceiling, probably a rat.

"Hmmmm," Julianna said, and a moment later again, "Hmmm."

Nellie wished she'd hurry, because she could stay away

from the palace a bit longer than necessary, but if she stayed away too long, there would be questions, and Dora would be angry.

"I sense a great disturbance in your mind."

"Well, yes, I've very busy and I wish I didn't have to deal with sick nobles, because it's not something I normally do, but—"

"I sense you're on the verge of a great change, a great decision that will influence a lot of people."

"I work in the kitchen. How is that going to make any difference to anyone?" By the Triune, this woman was really as mad as people said she was. "Can I get the berries or not? I've got money to pay for them." *Just let me get out of here.* It was a mistake to come here. Maybe Els even sent her here on purpose. Who knew?

"I'll only give out poisons to people whose lives are stable and who are trustworthy."

"And I am not? Fine. I'll leave."

Nellie pushed herself up.

"Wait."

The voice was so dark and haunting it sounded like it came from the woman's deepest soul, from an entity that was not part of her earthly body. Nellie *had* to sit back down.

A cold feeling crept through her.

No, she should never have come here.

She'd been right as a little girl: this woman was more than a creepy-looking hag.

In her travels with Mistress Johanna, Nellie had seen more evil magic than she had ever wished to see, more than she had ever believed to exist. She had seen ghosts, demonpossessed, fire demons. She had seen necromancy.

She should have known better.

"You served the queen," Julianna said.

Nellie nodded.

"You knew both the queen's children were strong conduits for magic, not through the woman herself, but through their fathers."

That was true.

"You know magical entities have struggled to gain control over Saardam for many years, starting before the time of King Nicholaos. Why do you think kings, barons and dukes of the east lined up their children to marry into the royal family? Why do you think the royal family has met with so much violence? They consorted with a church that seeks to ban magic. Magic is the mainstay of all those who sail the waters and those who take boats up the rivers and those whose produce they sell. Magic is in the creation of things. Magic is the core of the ongoing battle for Saardam. The church may try to deny magic all they want, but several magical lines cross each other in the port —wind magic, water magic, wood magic—and the power in those lines is stirring. When I touch your hand, I can feel the magic singing through you."

"That's ridiculous. I am the least magical person alive."

"Yet you are brimming with magic."

Because of the dragon box. And because of her tussle with the dragon last night. "I have no idea what you're talking about."

"If you speak the truth, you will find out soon. This person you come here to buy these berries for, is he a powerful magician?"

"I wouldn't be able to tell. I am not that type of person."

"Is he poisoned because he is a magician?"

"I don't know! I told you many times: I'm not that kind of person. I'm here to get something for stomach pains, but I shouldn't have come. I didn't ask to be examined. I don't want my fortune told. I need the berries."

"That's what they all say. Fix this, Julianna, and I'll be

gone. But it's not that simple, is it? Because everything is connected, from the people we depend on to the people who ask us for help. Why did this lord ask you to help, and not anyone else? He could have sent for me if he had it in his mind. He could have sent for a priest to pray."

Julianna's gaze was so intense that Nellie had trouble meeting her eyes. Why, oh why, had Els suggested that she come here?

Because the gin business with the girl-monk was run by magicians, and Els, as a fourteen-year-old, was too inexperienced to see that?

Because Nellie, too trusting, had made the mistake, time and time again, of trusting this girl who had shown herself, time and time again, to be unworthy of this trust?

"I understand," Julianna said after a while, and didn't elaborate on what she understood.

"I will give you the berries." She pushed herself up from her seat.

"Thank you," Nellie said, and she did her utter best to make it sound like *You could have stopped wasting my time and given them straight away*. She didn't know if she was successful. Making snippy remarks like that was not her style. It was rude.

But Julianna had been wasting her time, and if she would give the berries anyway, what was the point of all the other nonsense?

Julianna went to a cupboard against the wall behind her and, slowly, with age-trembling hands, opened a drawer and took out a glass jar filled with shrivelled black little balls. She shook a handful into a porcelain bowl and emptied this onto a sheet of paper. She then made a show of folding up the paper into a parcel which she gave to Nellie.

"If the man who is gravely ill is indeed Lord Verdonck, advisor to the Regent, these berries will have no effect on whether he lives or dies, because he will have been poisoned with magic. At any rate, his life is forfeit sooner rather than later. He attempted to interfere with a magic that chooses its own conduit, and that wasn't his to take. If you are really such an innocent little servant woman, none of this will make any sense to you and you can just go back to your kitchen and live your little life as before. However, if you know why I'm saying these things, know that great magic and powerful conduits of magic are not for the little people to play with. It requires a magician of great skill."

Hang on—was she saying *If you have that box, please give it to me?*

Well, by the Triune.

Yes, she bet someone like Julianna would love to have the box and the dragon.

"I assure you, if I ever came across a thing of powerful magic, I would return it to the rightful owner straight away."

Another intense stare.

"Then it seems we are in agreement."

"Indeed." Nellie picked up the parcel with the seeds, stuck it in her satchel with the rest of the shopping, and rose.

She'd show this woman what this *poor little servant* could do. She might not have a shred of magical ability in her body, but she sure knew that glimmer of greed in Julianna's eyes.

CHAPTER 19

NELLIE CAME BACK to the palace kitchens during the chaos of mid-morning.

"Oh, there you are!" Dora called out the moment she stepped into the door. Her face was red from stirring the pan at the stove.

"I've brought you the saffron," Nellie said.

"Must have been very special saffron for the time you were away."

"It was. The usual place was out of stock. Can I—"

"I need you to help the girls upstairs. Corrie tripped on the stairs and hurt her ankle. I told her to stick her foot in cold water. She can barely walk, let alone carry dishes. Where *were* you? What's going on, Nellie? I heard Madame Sabine came down here to speak to you. What was that about?"

Nellie told her of Lord Verdonck's illness and how Graziela was no longer in town.

"Yes, she was clear about her witchcraft. I liked Graziela, but she was playing with fire. I never understood why Madame Sabine had such a good relationship with her."

"I do," Nellie said, and in a few sentences, described Madame Sabine's injuries.

Dora's eyes widened. "All right. That makes sense. Better not say anything more about it. That woman is trouble."

Nellie couldn't disagree.

She had wanted to make juniper berry tea and take it to Lord Verdonck, but the kitchen was so busy, it would have to wait. She boiled water and let a spoonful of the dried and shrivelled berries soak in the pot. She'd take it up to Lord Verdonck's room later. The kitchen was low on staff, since Wim was also out of action, so they needed all hands on deck. The Regent's needs always came first.

As to Wim's health, Dora informed her he had taken to bed with a sore head but he was still very much alive and she expected him to continue to be alive, if not much of a help right now.

Dora continued, "Mind you, the guards have been in here twice asking about him. It's like they *want* him to keel over. I've told them to get out and stop wasting our time if they want any food to be served at all. Why are they so concerned about Wim all of a sudden?"

Nellie understood the reason. If the poison wasn't in the food and wasn't in the wine, then where had it come from? And more importantly: was the poisoner still in the palace?

That was sure to make the guards nervous. They'd turn over every room in the palace until they found the culprit.

The longer they looked, the more likely it was that the question of the dragon box would surface. If Lord Verdonck recovered, he would notice it was missing. Maybe even Madame Sabine would ask about it. They both knew of its existence, and, judging by the scars, had both experienced its power.

Nellie absolutely had to get rid of it as soon as possible.

This afternoon, she decided, she would go to the church and give it to Shepherd Adrianus so he could return it to the crypt where it belonged.

But first, the midday meal had to be served.

More people were present than this morning. Many of the guests who had not been at breakfast had finally emerged from their rooms. Most of them looked distinctly less noble than they had last night.

Nellie caught shards of conversation about this morning's accusation made by Adalbert Verdonck, but to her surprise, most people were curious rather than angry.

Down in the kitchen, she said to Dora, "I don't know about you, but if I'd been at a banquet where people were poisoned, I'd be asking a lot of questions about what I ate."

"Just count your luck they don't. We'd be copping the full blast of everyone's anger."

And the kitchen had done nothing. Besides, all the food that was taken upstairs was also eaten in the kitchen.

Nellie caught other people talking about Lord Verdonck having asked for trouble and that the situation was his own fault.

A noble lady said, "That son of his is a strange bird. He won't even come in here and sit at the table with us, like we're too good for him."

"They're *very* well off, though," another noble lady said. "I heard that the De Ruyter family proposed a marriage between him and their daughter Josefina, and that they refused because the family didn't have enough assets."

A third noblewoman butted in. "*I* heard they're heretics. *That's* why they won't sit with us and marry our sons and daughters. And frankly, I wouldn't want *my* daughter to marry a heretic, no matter how much money and land they have."

There were sage nods around the table.

"It's such a pity that Regent Bernard doesn't have any daughters," the first noblewoman said.

The conversation went on, but Nellie moved further down the table and she couldn't hear them anymore.

The level of support that Regent Bernard got from the local nobles never ceased to surprise her. The Regent had very successfully bought his way into their heads by offering them this food.

When everyone was eating, the Regent got to his feet and asked for quiet.

Great, a speech.

He started a great ramble about his good friends and loyal citizens and that he would always be there for them.

Nellie was stuck listening to it, because she had started clearing the tables, and there was no way she could do that while the Regent was speaking. A few other kitchen servants were also caught up in the crowd. She spotted Els and Maartje standing together and talking in low voices. Nellie wondered what Maartje knew of her sister's activities.

As she watched the two, it occurred to her she was drawn to girls of Maartje's type. Els was too in-your-face about everything. Maartje appreciated the position Nellie had made for her. She would work hard and would stay in the employ of the palace until she grew too old or until she married.

Els, however, would either do something great and would be remembered for all time, or she'd be dead before she was twenty.

Nellie had been like Maartje all her life. What would it be like to be like Els: to be bold and say what she thought? To see the reactions on the faces of the people who demanded respect but deserved none of it?

For a moment, Nellie entertained thoughts of stepping up to the Regent to tell him he'd eaten enough cakes, to tell Shepherd Wilfridus that if he didn't shout so much in church, she might consider going there, or to tell all the nobles in the city that the *must* have noticed that Regent Bernard was only interested in them for as long as they told him he was the best man to have ever lived in the palace, and that they should know better than to sell their loyalty for the chance to come to these ridiculous banquets because it made them look dumb.

Sometimes she wished she could say these things.

Nah, she was too old for that stuff.

The Regent kept on speaking, about how the safety of all the guests was his utmost concern. That they were all his dearest friends and that he valued their relationship too much to risk it. Was this going to be one of those occasions where he went on forever? He had a reputation for doing that.

"While I have your attention, I may raise another subject."

The tone of his voice changed, and people noticed, fell quiet and listened.

"As you are probably aware, my oldest son has reached his adult years."

Some people laughed.

"Oy, where is your exalted son?" someone called out.

A man said something about *a woman's tits* and a bunch of people laughed. Only the men, of course.

If Nellie had to guess, Casper was still in bed with a sore head.

Once, Nellie had wished for that kind of luxury, but now she realised that even if she were rich and never had to get up early, she still would. Because all the people she had respected who were rich got up early. Mistress Johanna and her father both got up early. People who were lazy got nothing done and always arrived after others had already made the important decisions. They might have money, but weren't often very good at *keeping* that money. Because that was one thing Nellie had learned: having money, and estates, and a business, was a lot of work. It was *different* work than the work she did, but it was work, and it was not easy, and you had to be smart.

"Having reached his majority means that my son will inherit my estate if I were to die tonight. Except I have little for him to inherit. My estate is small and my son from my first wife has first claim on it. The Guentherite order who helped me defend my estate against rogues has a second claim on it. Casper and Frederick have lived in Saardam for the better part of their lives, yet there is no part of this town they can call theirs. I intend to do something about that."

By the Triune, this was going in all the wrong directions. It seemed like most other people in the hall also realised this, at least the ones who were not half-asleep from yesterday. A thick blanket of silence fell over the audience. People who had been about to leave sat back down, or stopped on their way to the door.

"It is now almost ten years since the church asked me, in a moment of great distress, to help with the regentship of Saarland. I was surprised and even took it as a joke. I own a moderate estate in Burovia. I am a distant cousin of King Roald and am not favoured by any ruling family. It was just that quality that the caretaker for the crown wanted: not being an enemy of the surrounding countries while not being overly friendly with any of them either. I like to say I have done my job well. I like to say that I've done it very well, considering the circumstances I've found myself in. I've asked for the situation to be made more permanent, and I've been told to wait. What I should wait for appears to be immaterial. Whenever I ask at what time a decision will be made, the answer is always to wait. Well,

I've made a decision, because if I don't make a decision, no one will."

He glanced over the gathered nobles, all of whom watched him intently. From the women with the fancy dresses, to the junior princes, to the brother of the duke of Aroden and his family and dainty courtiers, to the wives and servants and all the other people in the hall.

Also the people who stood at the open doors. These were nobles who lived in the city, those people who had gone home after the banquet and now came back for the continued festivities. Nellie spotted the mayor and his daughter, but also Shepherd Wilfridus and a deacon.

The Regent let a long silence lapse to increase the impact of his words. He looked around the hall, his hands clasped loosely over his ample stomach.

When everyone had fallen quiet, he continued.

"Come spring, we will have another gathering like this. Except it will be a gathering bigger than this one. We will invite all the kings and queens, the barons and baronesses, the dukes and duchesses from all the surrounding countries. There will be a banquet better than the one last night, and it will come after a day of official celebrations when I will be officially crowned king."

At these words, many people in the hall cheered. Some of them jumped up and clapped. Some of them banged on the tables, making the plates and cups dance.

But across the hall, the shepherd yelled, "The Lord of Fire will come to this town before you will sit on the throne!"

He was used to preaching and his voice projected across the crowd much better than the Regent's had.

The mayor called out, "You insult my daughter and you expect me to bow for you?"

Several people in the hall yelled at the mayor. That he

was a traitor, that the Regent had been so good for the city.

Nellie caught the eye of Els and Maartje across the table and the heads of the nobles who were still seated.

"Quick," she yelled, and hoped her voice didn't get lost in the noise. "Get everything off the tables before things turn nasty."

Maartje wrestled through the narrow aisle with the trolley, while Nellie, on the other side of the table, collected a big stack of plates.

Shepherd Wildfridus strode through the hall, his ornate cloak flapping. People ducked out of his way.

He was not the only person making his way across the hall.

Several of Regent Bernard's personal guards formed a barrier between the Regent and the angry people trying to climb the steps to the dais.

Several noblemen had taken to protecting "their" Regent from the angry newcomers. The mayor was shouting at a merchant to let him through.

Regent Bernard was yelling, "Sit down, everyone sit down!"

Despite the loudness of his voice, it barely rose over the tumult.

Nellie and the two girls worked hard to collect the plates. If someone upset the table and a lot of plates broke, she would be accused of breaking them. The tea cups were especially precious, made of the finest porcelain, and there were not that many.

A number of guards came into the hall and walked through the aisle, telling everyone to calm down and be seated. Nellie met Henrik's eyes over the heads of the guests. His expression was worried. He came around the table to speak to her.

"Get everything out of the hall as soon as possible.

Other townsfolk will be in here soon, and I don't think it will be pretty. You better get all the pretty tableware out and get yourselves to safety." His tone appeared cool compared to yesterday.

When she merely nodded, he turned around and went back to telling people to sit down.

"Henrik?"

He looked over his shoulder. A brief flicker of hope danced in his eyes.

But there were others around her, and the apology she wanted to make to him died on her tongue. The heart of the matter was that she wanted to say something to him, but she didn't believe being angry about Wim wrongfully accused of poisoning was bad. She might apologise for shouting at him, but she would never apologise for that.

So they each went their own ways. Henrik towards the dais and Nellie into the foyer.

A little dream inside her died in the time she took to walk into the foyer. The dream that she had as a girl, that she could have a tall and handsome husband who would go every day to his position in the palace while wearing a uniform with shiny buttons. That he would come home and she would have cooked for him, and he would read from the Book of Verses for her and the bevy of children they would have.

Wake up, Nellie, you're far too old for that kind of daydream.

Even out in the foyer, the noise coming from the hall was deafening.

Casper was also in the foyer, seated on a couch. He was alone. It looked like the partying had caught up with him, because he rested his head against the side, and his eyes were half-closed.

The baroness Hestia was nowhere to be seen.

Nellie delivered the dirty plates in the scullery where it

was still reasonably tidy. Els and Maartje were heating water, ready to wash plates.

She went back upstairs with the empty trolley. One of the Regent's upstairs servants had discovered Casper in the hall and was trying to wake him up. Casper sat with his elbows leaning on his knees, his hands over his ears. Neither he nor the servant paid Nellie any attention when she walked past.

A big group of local merchants had gathered in one corner of the hall, talking in angry voices.

"He's a foreigner," a well-dressed nobleman said as Nellie pushed the trolley past where they stood. "Surely if we are to have a royal family, we can find someone in our city."

"Yes, someone like yourself?" another noble said.

The men laughed.

And that, ultimately, had been the problem.

When the royal family was killed, none of the local noble families agreed to their rivals taking up the position of Regent. Many of them of them could claim relationship to any of the royal families who were also related to all the guests here. They could all claim rights to the throne.

More and more local nobles arrived in the foyer to ascertain for themselves that the news was true.

At the dais, several people stood around Shepherd Wilfridus, who was still wearing his cloak. His cheeks were red from the cold. Nellie couldn't hear any of the vigorous discussion that went on, with much waving of hands, between the shepherd and the Regent.

People around her watched.

She overheard a lot of comments.

Many of the guests thought Regent Bernard should be king because it was his right.

A local merchant said if he became king, Saarland

might as well become part of Burovia, and that Estland and Gelre would never agree to that.

An old man Nellie recognised as an army commander argued that if Saarland wanted to be at war with any of the surrounding countries, making Regent Bernard king was the way to go.

"No ruler, no house in any of the lowlands or beyond, wants control of the only port city with access to all mainland rivers to be in the hands of their rivals. If control of the city is given to any powerful family except them, they'll come and seize control of the city. Do we want another siege and occupation by some foreign power? I say we depose the Regent and we give control of the city to a council. No royal families, no church."

Even the workers in the kitchen were talking about the Regent's plans to have himself crowned king.

"If he plans to have more guests than there are in the palace now, we must buy more plates," Dora was saying, always seeing the practical side of things.

"There is only one problem with all this," said Wim, who evidently felt better, because he had been doing odd jobs around the kitchen, and had just come in from feeding the pigs.

"Only one?" Dora laughed.

"Well. The most important one. The shepherd is the only person who can make anyone king. And he will not do it."

"Someone will hold a knife to his throat," Dora said, holding up a knife.

"They'll have to use a sharper one than that," Corrie said from the bench where she sat with her foot in a bucket of cold water.

Wim said, "Regent Bernard can just reopen the Belaman Church, invite a priest and let him do it. He's got feet in both camps."

"Yeah. He's a foreigner."

And that was the ultimate verdict. Regent Bernard was a foreigner, and none of the locals wanted a foreigner on the throne, but they wanted their rivals on the throne even less than they wanted a foreigner.

When Nellie went back upstairs, some people had started leaving. They were mostly locals, and Nellie did not miss the anger in their discussions as they made their way through the hall saying that the shepherd should not allow it, and that they should put this self-important man in his place. There were comments about Casper, too.

"I'd die before I'd see that misbehaving brat on the throne," one woman said.

It was quiet in here, and sounds echoed in the foyer, so Nellie would not be surprised if Casper heard it.

Meanwhile, cheers came from the hall.

What a load of selfish pigs.

Here they all were, eating the Regent's food and enjoying his hospitality.

They still only thought about themselves, as rich people often did. *One does not become rich by being generous to others*—that was a conclusion to a story in the Book of Parables. That story showed what she had seen the last few days: the nobles would come here and smile to the Regent when they thought there was an influence to be gained, only to complain if they didn't get their way.

Rich people were disgusting. They gorged themselves while common people slept in the streets, they started wars that common people didn't want, about things that common people didn't understand, just so they could keep the common people busy while they raided the coffers for their own good. And they made rules that people got angry about. If all magic was banned from the city, then who would bake nice bread, who would make the best clothes and who would know about herbs and about the weather?

And so Nellie's angry thoughts kept going around while she cleared the tables and helped serve tea to whoever still wanted it—and there were plenty of rich, disgusting people who did.

Those people spoke of *sticking by the Regent* who had *done so much good for the city* and yet didn't mention a single good thing he had done.

That man deserved no support.

"I told you about my father's book last visit. I know that the dragon box is no longer in the church."

His face cleared, and his expression darkened. "I also told you to forget about that."

"So it did get stolen? And Shepherd Wilfridus is trying to get it back?"

"I don't know how you know about all these things, but I can only plead that you not probe too far and not get involved."

"It is already too late for that." Nellie dug in the folds of her satchel and set the box on the table, the lid still securely tied to it.

The shepherd's eyes widened. He took a couple of shallow breaths. "What—where did you—you must take this thing out of here immediately. You'll be killed if they find it in your possession."

"I didn't ask for this thing, but I took it from someone who has no right to have it. I took it, stole it, if you want, for the good of the people of Saardam. My father wrote about it. My father believed the safest place for it was the church. I want to return it to you. Take it back to the crypt where it belongs."

"No." He leaned back from the table as if he was afraid of the box.

"Doesn't this box belong to the church? Didn't they buy it fairly?"

He blew out a breath through his nose. "I don't know what you would call fairly, but I've been told that it came to us via the Guentherite order. I don't know how it came to be in their possession. They may have been offered it in exchange for a meal by a weary traveller who had picked up it by the side of the road, for all I know. But the order realised the value of what they had and they knew that the Church of the Triune had paid top coin for a magical book, so they offered the box for sale."

Nellie was tempted to ask whether the Guentherite order needed any more money, because they seemed to have plenty already.

"When the box arrived in the church, it sat in the middle of a table in the crypt. At the time, I used the library a fair bit, and saw it there every day. Then one day, it was gone. There were rumours that two deacons who were curious had tried to open it and had been attacked by a creature from within."

"Did they make it angry? Did they tease it or poke it?" When Nellie opened the box, the fire dragon had plenty of opportunity to attack her, but hadn't done so.

"They said, in their words, that as soon as they opened the lid, the magic spilled from within and the evil soared out. The shepherd locked the box in a cupboard after that. It sat there for a long time, but recently it was stolen."

"People all over the palace are looking for it. They turn over every room until they have it. They even kill each other for it."

"I can well believe that. A dragon box is said to lend the owner amazing powers, especially to those who already have abilities. But much of this might only be a rumour, child. This is why I often pay no heed to stories."

"Except when parts of it are true."

He gave her an intense look.

"I want to give the box back. I think it's better for you to have it, because you can return it to the crypt where no one can get their hands on it."

"I can't accept it. Take it from me, the church is the least safe place for it. Child, child, please. Do not get involved. Don't leave this thing here. I don't want it. I didn't hear you say you have it. Please, put it back in your bag before someone sees it. I can't guarantee its safety. I have none of the influence you're seeking."

"But what am I supposed to do with it?"

"I would burn it in the hottest fire, together with your father's book that speaks ill of people in the church."

"Was my father wrong?"

"Worse. Everything he says is right. There are people in our church whose evil knows no boundaries. Take that thing out of here and don't come back. Better still, leave the city while you're still free. Bad times are coming."

Nellie was shocked. She certainly hadn't come for this kind of advice. "But what—"

"No, don't tell me any more about it. You're a good woman, and ultimate victory will always come to those who are honest. But for now, this is not the place for you to be."

He would hear no more, so she took her satchel with the box, and put her coat back on, all in silence. She wanted to say so many things:

That if you never said what was right, then wrong would prevail.

That obeying was good until it became evil.

But he was the shepherd, and he knew best, even if he sometimes preached those same things during the service. He would have reasons for telling her this, and if she lived long enough, she would learn those reasons.

Nellie left the room.

The shepherd watched her with a sad expression on his face.

CHAPTER 21

OUT ON THE STEPS of the shepherd's house, Nellie stopped to gather her frayed thoughts.

What in all the heavens was she going to do now?

Well—go back to the palace, because there was always one more meal to be cooked—but she couldn't hide that dragon in her cupboard forever.

A brief flicker of an idea went through her mind: what if, instead of trying to destroy it or hide it, she tried to use it? If the dragon had wanted to attack her, it had plenty of opportunity when it escaped from the box. It hadn't scratched her like it had scratched Madame Sabine or Lord Verdonck. More than that, *the kitten* had been trying to play with it. Nellie believed trust without ulterior motive only existed in animals. If a dog could smell evil on another creature, it would bark and growl. If a cat was spooked, it would arch its back and bush up its tail. The kitten had done none of that. The kitten had tried to play with the dragon. The kitten trusted it, so maybe she should trust the dragon, too.

Nellie saw herself standing in the middle of the great

dining hall, ordering a big dragon around. She'd tell it to *Go and find this thing that was stolen from this noble's room*, or *Chase those rude young people to their rooms*, or *Make sure that boy doesn't misbehave again*. But then again why should she use her dragon to help the nobles? They could help themselves. She should tell it to *Burn all the porcelain to cinders so we don't have to do any washing up*.

That would be funny.

But quick as the thought came, she dismissed it. Who was she to think that once she opened that box, she could get the dragon back in? She knew nothing about its magic. She had seen the fire demons burn the city. A dragon might do the same, and then it would be all her fault.

No way. She would not finish her life in prison.

And she had better get back to the kitchen.

Nellie was not yet across the courtyard outside the shepherd's house when a great tumult broke out in the church.

There was a bang of a door being flung open and hitting a wall. A man yelled out, and others replied. Then a woman started screaming.

By the Triune, what was happening?

Nellie ran to the side entrance and peeked in.

Several men in dark clothing had entered the church through the main entrance. She counted at least five. They were dragging people out through the main doors, picking up their meagre belongings and tossing them into the street. A woman hung onto a man's arm.

She yelled, "What have we done to deserve this? Tell us, what have we done?"

The man ignored her, batting her hands off his arm and continuing on his way out of the church carrying a blanket by the corners, filled with pillows and bedding.

Two of his fellows were searching the makeshift beds, upending homemade mattresses and ripping blankets.

A man held a bag upside down and the contents—bronze candleholders and a few mismatched plates and cups—clattered to the floor with a shattering of porcelain.

"Look, that one is a thief!" one man shouted.

"I stole nothing!" a woman yelled. "Those things are mine. I need to sell them to feed the children!"

The man kicked the broken pieces of the plates aside and pocketed the candleholders.

"Those are mine!" the woman screamed. She pulled the man's jacket, but he stepped away, as if she were some dirty thing.

A young boy called for his mother.

Two other men were dragging a crippled man between them.

"My wife and I have nowhere to go," he shouted. "I'm a cripple. I can't work. What do you expect us to do?"

A deep cold fear clamped a hand around Nellie's heart.

She knew none of the men, but they worked efficiently like mercenaries. They had swords, but they didn't even use those.

A door closed behind her and when she turned, Shepherd Adrianus came walking across the yard.

Nellie scooted into the darkness of a niche—he'd told her to leave after all. He walked past Nellie into the church, meeting a tall man inside.

Shepherd Adrianus said, "By the Triune, this is a church, what in all of heaven's name is going on?"

The other man said, "They have to be gone."

His voice was hard and definite and so aggressive that Nellie shivered. The sound of it was familiar, but it was too dark in the church to see anything except the man's silhouette. She held her breath and listened.

"I will not be the one to put them on the street," Shepherd Adrianus said.

"Aren't you lucky then, that I thought you might react

that way? I have brought people who can do this on your behalf."

"These are your mercenaries? You cannot be serious."

"The church belongs to the Triune. It is not a poor house."

"I will *not* let you do this."

"You have no say over this. It's my decision. They will leave. Peacefully or by force. We are dedicated to serving the Triune. We are not an inn for all and sundry who needs a roof over their heads."

"But we *are* serving the Triune."

"Exactly. I've heard worshipers are afraid to come to your services, because this building has become a refuge for peddlers of magic and other evil trades. I've heard stories of honest faithful citizens being accosted by people with magic trinkets for sale. In our church. It has to stop."

Nellie realised with horror that the second man was Shepherd Wilfridus.

"Then what should I do, just toss these people out onto the street? Is it going to be on my soul when any of them die?"

"This is why there is a poor house."

"It is full. People cannot find beds anywhere; people do not have the money to pay the rent. Men are being picked up willy-nilly off the street and their families are left with no way to support themselves. There are children here. Would you put children in the poor house with the sick and the destitute and the madmen?"

"I want no more people complaining about the smell of piss in this church. I want our congregation to come in here without fearing for their lives."

"Their lives! In these hard times, we should look after the downtrodden and protect them from those who think money can buy everything."

"You know, sometimes I wonder how someone with

such a naïve outlook has ever made it as far as you have. If you'd open your eyes, you'd see that those are not innocent people, because if they were, they'd have no trouble finding work, like that obedient little kitchen wench who was just visiting you."

Blood rushed to Nellie's cheeks. She clutched the box against her chest, desperately glad that Shepherd Adrianus hadn't accepted it, and beginning to understand why.

Shepherd Wilfridus was still ranting. "These people are hidden magicians, doomsayers, heretics, deniers. They cannot pay the rent because they have never done a single day of honest work in their lives."

"I know a lot of these people, and I know that is not true. They are people who have fallen to misfortune, illness, deaths in the family, accidents."

"So that heretic who continues to preach against the good of the Triune has left?" He was talking about Bert.

"Well, no, but there are many others who—"

"That woman whose husband sold magic has left?"

"She has six children. Do you want me to just throw this whole family onto the street?"

"Not the street, dear friend, the poor house. While we clean up the church and check the rubbish they have collected for things they have stolen."

"Oh. I see. It's still about that, isn't it? You haven't found it."

From the darkness of the church, over the shouts of the people came the sound of a slap of skin hitting skin. Like a hand on someone's cheek.

"How dare you mock me? Our pride is at stake. It was *stolen* from the crypts, and we still don't know by whom or the exact day. We *have* to find it, and if you're going to stand in the church's way, you may well find yourself in the poor house with all this rabble you profess to stand up for. Then you get to see what sort of people they really are.

I'm done here. You're warned. The next time I have to come here to discipline you will be the last."

Shepherd Wilfridus strode out of the door and down the steps, his robes flying.

He didn't see Nellie at all, but he strode across the little courtyard and into the alley. He disappeared from sight.

Shepherd Adrianus came towards the door more slowly, wiping his face.

Nellie understood the bandage around his hand. A feeling of utter horror filled her.

She whispered, "Shepherd."

He gasped.

"It's me, Nellie."

"What are you still doing here?"

"Let me take you inside the house. I'll help you."

"No, please. You must leave. Go back to the palace. Burn that thing before anyone finds it. Forget about all of this."

"And let those poor people in the church be tossed into the street?"

"I'm sorry. There is nothing I can do."

"You can tell him it's wrong and that the church should look after poor people. Show him the parable in the book of—"

"No. He has his reasons."

"But he's *wrong*. These people are not thieves. You know that! You have to stop this. The people have nowhere else to go—"

"No. Please, child, go now."

That was when Nellie understood. Despite knowing she was right, Shepherd Adrianus still defended the leader of the church.

All her adult life, she had adored and respected him, listened to his sermons and accepted his views as truth.

In the end, he was just a coward.

She faced him wordlessly for a moment. She couldn't bring herself to tell him this, and wouldn't have found the right words even if she wanted to.

She figured, half-hoped, that he could feel he understood what she felt anyway and that no words were necessary. Because the sense of betrayal for her was too great to put into language.

Her whole life she had spent doing the right thing in the name of the church, and being obedient was a lie.

This was, finally, what her father had tried to express in his book.

Do not place trust in others to act in good faith because they will not.

Without saying another word, she turned away from the shepherd. She crossed the courtyard, past the open church door, where most of the noise had now moved to the street outside the main entrance.

She strode into the street, turned left towards the palace, and didn't stop running until she could no longer hear the voices.

There were few people in the street, and she avoided looking at those people who came the other way. Her cheeks were wet with tears—they might think she had fought with a husband.

But this was much worse than a fight with a family member could be.

Her whole life was a lie. If the men she respected wouldn't do respectable things, then why should she respect the institution that housed them and had been the centrepiece of her life?

But where did that leave her?

She didn't respect Regent Bernard. He was only interested in eating and drinking as much as possible and grabbing the power of a position that wasn't his to take.

Shepherd Wilfridus was purely, utterly evil. She had never liked him, but she now knew why. He was obsessed with the church's influence. Of course he'd never let the Regent become king, because if he did, then he ceded power to someone else.

And all the people she knew, and ones she respected, were too cowardly to even express an opinion about the power struggle.

Everyone except her father.

While Nellie walked, and the dragon box bumped against her leg, she pulled out the pins that kept her bonnet in place. She took off the bonnet. It was *ridiculous,* but it was more than that: it was a symbol of her unquestioning obedience.

Well, no more.

She was fifty years of age, too old to be told to be a nice little girl.

Not just that, but, unlike Jantien, she didn't need to protect her children; unlike Henrik, she had no partner; unlike Shepherd Adrianus, she had no position she cared about that she wanted to keep.

She had nothing left to lose.

Everything she loved, mistress Johanna, the little prince and princess, the loveable oaf King Roald, had been taken from her already. And now the final blow had shaken her awake. The church would not care about her. The church cared for itself. So it was time she should care for herself, too.

She flung the bonnet into the stall of a surprised apple seller at the markets.

He called after her, "Hey, miss, you're forgetting your—"

"Keep it."

Keep the blasted thing and the life it represented.

And something else.

She stopped in an alley between two of the houses of rich merchants on the other side of the marketplace. In the dark, she fumbled in her bag and pulled out the dragon box.

If the dragon wanted to be free of the box, let it be free.

If the kitten wanted to play with it, then let them play.

If the dragon clawed at people who had ulterior motives for wanting to control it, let it claw their hearts out.

If the dragon belonged to Prince Bruno, and its master was still alive, let them be reunited.

She had no use for the box and no evil plan for the dragon.

She took the lid off.

The dragon must have been waiting because it burst out of the box with a giant whoosh and a blast of fire. Nellie jumped back, hit the wall behind her, and almost dropped the box. Whoa.

The dragon soared past the roofs of the merchant's houses, leaving a trail of magical sparks, and disappeared into the night.

Nellie listened for inevitable shouts, but all remained quiet, except for the thudding of her heart.

Phew.

Well, if things were that easy, maybe she should have done this earlier. She shut the box and slipped it back into her satchel. A pretty box like that was much better for storing jewellery anyway.

But being all angry and rebellious got much harder when she entered the palace grounds.

For one, the kitchen rules said hair needed to be tucked away or covered.

So she stood in the dark, running her fingers through her knotted hair, attempting to plait it, like Els' hair.

Clearly, the first things she would need for her new box was a nice comb and some hair clips.

There was dinner to be prepared and served and Nellie was quite late already, so she ran to her room, dumped her coat and satchel on the bed and returned to the kitchen.

"What happened to you? Where is your bonnet?" asked Corrie as they passed each other, Nellie on the way up and Corrie on the way down.

"I thought I'd try something different."

Nellie knew that this reply puzzled Corrie as much as the absence of her bonnet. In all her years of working in the palace, Nellie had never tried something different. Even when she lived and worked upstairs, she had barely ever taken off her regular work clothes and her bonnet.

Being *different* was quite frightening.

And of course Nellie ran into Henrik at the top of the stairs. He did not raise his eyebrows, but his eyes widened, and from his post at the door, his gaze followed her into the hall where she went to start setting the table for the evening meal.

Breakfast, midday, evening—was there any time of day that these people didn't stuff their faces?

CHAPTER 22

NELLIE KNEW HENRIK watched her all the way until she reached the hall. A coach was arriving at the palace steps, and he would be required to assist its noble owners up the narrow steps, but he remained at the door to watch her.

She pretended not to notice and took brisk steps so that her plait swayed over her back.

When she was young, Mistress Johanna used to be sassy, and Nellie had watched her often enough to be able to imitate her. It was quite childish, but fun.

Nobody owned her.

Two kings and queens and an evil magician had been her masters. Nothing was new to her.

She had just solved the dragon problem by releasing the creature so it could go home.

Nothing would guide her except what was wrong or right. Her father had known what was best for his family, and she was proud to be his daughter.

But as she set out clean plates in the hall, the sound of angry voices drifted in from the foyer. A woman said, "It's your fault, and nothing you can say will convince me otherwise."

That sounded like Madame Sabine.

A group of guards crossed the foyer, carrying something between them: a stretcher with, on it, a person covered by a sheet.

By the Triune.

She sped to the main entrance.

The icy wind hit her in the face. Flurries of snow drifted from the leaden sky.

The guards carried their load to the coach. Lord Verdonck's coachman held open the door, and the guards lifted the stretcher inside.

Nellie lifted her hand to her mouth. "Is that. . . ?"

She spoke to no one in particular, but a female voice next to her replied. "It's murder, nothing less."

Madame Sabine.

"I don't agree with you on many fronts, but I agree with you there." That was Adalbert Verdonck. His face was hard with anger. He wore his travel cloak, a hat and gloves.

"Old men have weak hearts," Regent Bernard said. "None of us, none of my staff in my palace did any such thing as you suggest."

"Murder," Adalbert Verdonck said again. "At the hands of someone in this palace, someone you allowed under your roof. I swear I will not rest until I know who did this."

"Adalbert, please," Madame Sabine said. "This is a time of mourning and respect."

"Respect? I have none for you or you." He pointed at the Regent and Madame Sabine. "You won't be getting any more of your loans. In fact, I will insist that you pay them back. And you, harlot." He pointed at Madame Sabine. "Don't you dare set foot in our house ever again."

He turned around, bounded down the steps, and shut the door to the cabin. Then he climbed up onto the coach driver's seat. He grabbed the reins, and the horses started moving.

As the coach pulled away, Adalbert Verdonck shouted, "I'll find out who did this, even if it takes me the rest of my life. There will be no more money until you tell me who did this. I'll be back. You won't get away with this!"

Nobody moved until the coach had gone through the palace gates.

Nellie glanced aside at Madame Sabine.

She still wore her man's outfit, and if she felt any grief over the death of her lover, she didn't show it. Her face carried a hard expression that made Nellie wonder what else this strange woman had done with her life.

"Harlot," the Regent said.

He turned on his heel and walked back into the foyer.

Madame Sabine turned as well and strode after him in huge steps. "Watch what you're saying, doormat."

"Don't you dare insult me."

"Then don't insult me, either."

"You're still a harlot. I don't even understand how you could ever get close enough to that disgusting man to share a bed with him."

"I had practice. I got close enough to you to give you two children."

"Harlot."

Madame Sabine swung her hand, but Regent Bernard was quick and grabbed her wrist in an iron grip.

"Don't you dare try that on me." His voice was soft and menacing.

Madame Sabine tried to wrench her arm free while glaring at him, but she couldn't.

He let her worm and squirm, not breaking eye contact.

After she had tried to twist and pull for a while, Madame Sabine said, "Let me go, fat pig."

The Regent's face was red.

For a moment, Nellie feared that he would hit her, but Shepherd Wilfridus had come into the hall, and the Regent had enough sense to realise that hitting his wife in front of the shepherd was probably not a good idea.

With a jerk, he let go of Madame Sabine's wrist. She stumbled backwards and glared at him, nostrils flaring. Then she whirled around and stormed up the stairs.

Casper and Frederick had seen everything from the gallery.

Neither the Regent nor Madame Sabine came to the hall for the evening meal. Casper and Frederick sat at the dais instead, joined by all the noble sons and daughters who were still at the palace.

Whenever Nellie walked past, she overheard Casper boast about what he would do when he became crown prince. Every time, her disgust with this family grew.

The Regent ate himself stupid while people in the city had trouble feeding themselves. Madame Sabine took lovers under her husband's roof, those two boys grew up while the adults around them behaved abominably. If there was any goodness in their hearts—and Nellie believed all people were born good—it had long since been corrupted by their parents.

She prayed with all her might that Casper would never sit on the throne because Saarland would be well and truly lost.

When dinner was done, and none of the young nobles had made off with a girl to the laundry, none of the nobles had attacked anyone else in the hall with a piece of cutlery, and no one had been insulted or—heaven forbid— poisoned, Nellie joined the other kitchen servants around the table sharing leftover pastries and tea.

She felt exhausted. Most of the guests had gone home and life would return to normal, yet this was only the beginning of further trouble.

"That ended quite well," Dora said, smiling at Wim.

Nellie said, "Depends on what you call well. Lord Verdonck is dead. His son has sworn revenge on the Regent and will probably call for his loans to be paid back. You call that good?"

"Those are noble's troubles. Not my troubles."

"Yes, we'll be the King's servants again," Corrie said. She had also worked for King Roald.

How could they be so indifferent? Didn't they see the Regent was a disgusting man with no morals? Didn't they see that Shepherd Wilfridus only thought of himself?

"Tell us what really happened to your bonnet, Nellie," Dora said. "You've never done anything different for as long as I've known you."

"It's never too late to start," Nellie said.

"No, Nellie, that answer won't make me happy. I've been your friend all this time. We've worked here when it's been cold and hot, when we've both been sick."

Yes, Nellie remembered that day.

She blew out a breath.

"Sometimes you feel old and useless," Nellie said.

"Tell me about it."

"And when you feel old and useless, you think about it, and you know a lot of things you think matter when you're young don't matter at all. You toil away in the kitchen every day and you might think if you dropped dead, people would struggle. But they find someone else to cook and carry on, and before long everybody has forgotten you."

"Yes?"

Dora was a practical woman, and Nellie wondered when her *spare me the sermon* comment would come.

"But what really matters is when something bad

happens, you tell everyone it's not acceptable and that we should all do something about it. I thought I understood, because I'd seen mistress Johanna do it all the time, but what I didn't see was that often it's not the people we call enemies who we need to fear. It's the people to whom we have given our unquestioned trust."

"Yes, and? What is all that supposed to mean? What *did* actually happen today?"

"I went to talk to Shepherd Adrianus and while I was at his house, mercenaries came in to forcefully remove the poor people from the church."

"You mean the ones who sleep at the back, who are homeless? The ones that you sneak out leftovers to?"

"Yes, those."

"That's . . . really harsh. It's winter. Those people don't have a home to go back to. Did the shepherd say why?"

"Because . . . do you remember how they all came to shepherd Adrianus' church after they got booted out of the main church?"

"Wasn't that because someone stole something?"

"Someone did steal something, but it had nothing to do with the poor people. Those poor people were just made scapegoats because Shepherd Wilfridus wanted them out of the church and he needed an excuse to get rid of them."

Dora frowned. "Isn't the church all about helping the poor?"

"It is. It's in almost every story of the Book of Verses. I've gone through all of it and checked what it says."

"So why did he want to get rid of them?"

"Because he's an evil man."

Dora gasped, bringing her hand to her mouth. "Nellie! He's the shepherd. I don't go to church as often as you do, but you can't say that about the shepherd. He's the reason that there is peace in Saardam. He has kept away the kings and barons who would have claimed us as part of their land and he kept the bad magicians away."

"That doesn't make him less evil. He is so obsessed with his quest against magic, he will hurt innocent people because of it. Don't tell me you're not afraid of the day when guards will tell you to leave because of magic."

"But that's not the same. It's a flair I have for cooking. It's not magic. I can't use it for anything else."

"It's artisan magic, and to the shepherd, it's absolutely the same as the conjuring of fire demons. I have seen things . . ." She shuddered when thinking about the books in the crypt. ". . . That would make your blood run cold."

"How do you know all these things? Is it from that book your father gave you? I thought he worked for the church."

"He did, but he saw all the church's involvements: the good ones and the not-so-good ones. The people in the church are just that: people. Not all of them have our best interests at heart, certainly not right now."

Dora grabbed Nellie's wrist. Her hand was warm and fleshy and exuded a smell of cooking fat. "Please, Nellie. I still don't understand what has gotten into you, but please stop saying these things. You're my friend. I don't want anything to happen to you."

"If it does, you'll find someone else to do my work and carry on. I don't have a family who needs me."

"We need you here in the kitchen. You have a good job, enough to eat and good friends. You have a dry place to sleep. Why make a fuss and throw it all away?"

"I'm not throwing anything away."

"Most of us would to disagree. You even have a handsome guard chasing after you."

Nellie gave a hollow laugh. "Henrik? He lived a few houses down from me that's why I know him. But he's married and has two daughters. He's not chasing after me."

"You haven't heard that his wife died three years ago?"

Nellie met Dora's eyes, feeling heat creep up in her cheeks.

No, she hadn't known.

Why hadn't he said anything about that when she told him he was trying to flatter her?

Because he thought she knew.

By the Triune, could she have acted any more ignorant?

While they spoke, Corrie had pushed herself up from the table and hobbled into the pantry with her sore foot. She came back a moment later. "Has anyone seen that bag of carrots we got this morning? I wanted to wash them, but the bag's not there."

Dora frowned. "It should be. I saw it there this afternoon."

She set her cup down and went into the pantry. "Well I never . . . It's gone. Wonderful. Not only is there a poisoner in the palace, now we have a thief as well. I'll have to report that to the guards. Wonder what someone wants with just a bag of carrots."

"Make soup?" Corrie said. "Many people out there are desperate and poor."

CHAPTER 23

NELLIE RETURNED to her room, feeling uneasy and impatient. She didn't belong in the servants' quarters of the palace anymore. She knew too much, had seen too many things and asked too many questions.

The dragon might have gone, but she would be surprised if they had seen the last of it.

Winter had barely begun. There would be discontent amongst the people if the Regent kept holding banquets like these. Deep inside her, she wanted no part in it. Sure, she would be comfortable in the palace, but didn't that just make her part of the problem, too?

"So it's just you and me now," she said to the kitten, who was much more interested in the bowl of cream than in anything she had to say.

Nellie picked up the dragon box from her bed.

Her hairbrush was too long to fit inside its silk-lined interior, but her mother's old brooch and a couple of pearl buttons would do. And a half-cent coin from Florisheim, reminding her of her travels.

While she sat there, the kitten clawed its way up the

bedspread and onto the bed. It stuck its head inside the dragon box and nosed the corners.

"It's gone," Nellie said.

The room felt empty and cold.

Nellie opened the drawer in her little table and read a story from the Book of Verses, but she found it hard to concentrate because she kept seeing Shepherd Wilfridus in the church, justifying the violence against those poor people. Where were Mina and Jantien and her children? Where was Bert? What had happened to Shepherd Adrianus? Would he continue to obey a man who condoned cruelty in the name of the church?

She didn't even finish reading the story about her favourite character Rose. It had been easy for Rose to say what she thought because everyone always knew she was right and accepted it easily. Real life wasn't like that at all.

In real life, if you said something the rulers didn't like, they made it so that no one believed you, and they forced you to flee, so it was better just to keep your mouth shut, like her father had done.

Nellie sat with the Book of Verses in her lap, feeling aimless and empty.

Now that it was gone, she wanted the dragon to come back. She wanted it to teach all these people a lesson, especially Shepherd Wilfridus. But she had no idea where to look for it.

She set the box, with the lid open, on the table next to her Book of Verses. The kitten meowed until she picked it up and let it sniff the box. But the only things inside were her brooch and other items she'd put there, which she took back out because they didn't belong in this box. It was a dragon box and needed to have a dragon inside, not little trinkets.

Eventually Nellie must have dozed because she woke suddenly through some kind of noise.

By the Triune that sounded like someone was calling out.

Nellie went back into the dark corridor. A glow of light came from the kitchen, but when she got there, the room was empty.

A single pot stood bubbling on the stove. The hearty smell of vegetable soup spread through the kitchen. Loaves of bread lay on the table, two of them cut into slices. A large ham sat on a tray, covered with a thin layer of glazing, and with brush still in the jar of glazing. People had just walked away from their work. It was not late enough for the bakers to have arrived yet, so maybe Dora and Wim had been in here, and Dora made sure that no one was ever idle in the kitchen.

"Anyone here?" Nellie said.

There was no reply except the popping of the fire.

That was strange. Really strange.

Nellie strode through the kitchen into the corridor—which was empty, too. The sound of a man's voice calling out instructions came from upstairs.

A group of people stood on the top steps.

Most of them were servants. Dora was there, wearing her apron and carrying a ladle.

One guard—not Henrik—was talking. "When my colleague says it's your turn, go into the audience room. Only one person at a time."

By the Triune, what was going on? At this time of the day, too.

Even when she stood on her toes, the heads of people blocked her view of the happenings in the foyer. Most of it seemed to be empty and dark. The doors to the hall were shut.

Just as Nellie was going to ask a man what was going on, the guard near the door beckoned and someone from the front of the group went to the hall. A guard opened the door, giving Nellie a small glimpse of the dining hall, which had been returned to its regular formation, with all the tables back in storage and the chairs stacked around the perimeter of the hall.

What was going on in there?

"Oh, there you are." Henrik touched Nellie on the shoulder. "I'm glad you're here."

He was, too, she could see that in his face.

And she was just being stupid. "Look, I'm sorry for what I said. I didn't know—"

"It's fine, don't worry about it."

But she did worry about it. She had been silly. "What's going on?"

"The Regent is combing the palace for who may have poisoned Lord Verdonck."

"So he has decided it wasn't old age after all?"

"Whether it was or not, he needs someone to blame. Adalbert Verdonck demands that a culprit be found or he will withdraw his financial support. The younger Verdonck has never liked the Regent, but now he has the final word over what happens to the loans his father granted the palace. He seems to be looking for reasons to demand his money back."

Nellie's heart jumped. It was just as she feared.

"He's now interrogating everyone in the palace as to whether they've seen anything."

By the Triune. Did that mean she would have to go in there alone and talk about what she had seen in Lord Verdonck's room? Did Madame Sabine know she had the dragon box? Was Madame Sabine in that room, too?

The man who had gone in came back out and the next person, a servant for the audience room and the Regent's office, went in.

The people on the stairs waited.

Nellie wanted to go back downstairs, but a guard stood behind her.

"I have a pot on the stove!" Dora said.

"Everyone has to see the Regent," the guard said.

"Does the Regent want burnt soup?"

"I'll see what I can do."

Dora was the next one to go in.

Nellie watched Henrik. He stood in the line of guards that went from the stairs to the door into the audience room.

The door opened and Dora came out. That was quick.

She grinned and gestured at Nellie. "Your turn."

The threat of burnt soup worked well, evidently.

Nellie climbed the last few steps into the foyer and walked between the lines of guards.

The guard opened the door.

The hall had been returned to its normal setup, with the carpet down the centre of the hall leading to the dais where the Regent sat on an elaborate chair in front of the throne.

In the years since the King's death, no one had touched the throne. The cleaners dusted it, but it sat there as a memory of the good times and a promise that those good times would return. These days it made a mockery of the Regent's court, and taunted him that he could not use it; and if it was up to the church, he never would.

It was a testament to the church's power that no one had yet removed it.

Nellie walked along the carpet, feeling very small. She could feel the eyes of the people in the room on her. To be sure, there weren't that many people in the room, but each of them was important.

It looked like the Regent was conducting the investigations himself.

He sat on the chair in the middle of a row, which

included Madame Sabine and a couple of the minor court advisors. There was no one from the church.

Nellie bowed when she got close. Servants in the palace were told to keep their heads bowed when facing the Regent, so she only saw the bottom of his gold-coloured robes and his shoes with big silver buckles that stuck out from under the hem. They were blue. Ridiculous. Who ever wore blue shoes?

The black stockings he wore bulged at the ankles, where the flesh was constricted by the top of the shoes and kind of spilled over, turning his legs above those elegant shoes into shapeless sausages.

She waited for him to speak.

He began, "State your full name."

Nelly cringed. Full names were for times when there was trouble. "Cornelia Dreessen."

"I'm sure you are well aware that a man was poisoned and has sadly died. You served at the banquet, and I understand that you visited Lord Verdonck's room after he became ill. Did you at any time see anything unusual, or do you have any knowledge of who might have poisoned him?"

"I do not, my lord." Nellie spoke into the carpet. It was uncomfortable standing like this and not looking into a person's eye.

Nellie risked a glance at Madame Sabine. Clearly, she knew Nellie visited the lord's room, and she had told him about it.

Madame sat a little sideways on the chair, oh, so slightly turned away from her husband. She wore a green dress with lots of frills and held her dainty feet crossed at the ankles. He shoes were plain, without much of a heel, green to match her dress and decorated only with little rosettes of glass beads.

"I understand my wife called you as herb woman.

When you visited our sad departed friend's room, you did not bring any concoctions?"

"A kitchen girl brought some juniper berry tea, but by that time the lord was already gravely ill. He was ill the first time I saw him."

"What was the last time you saw him healthy?"

Nellie had to think about that. "I think it was when I served the afternoon meal and he was meeting with business associates." He had argued with a deacon from the church. "Or maybe it was in the hall."

"Who was he talking to in the hall?"

"Your son, my lord." It was so awkward, this talking into the carpet!

"Did he talk about anything other than my son's exuberant behaviour?"

"I don't think so, my lord." Depending on what he classified as exuberant behaviour.

"You don't think so, or you're sure?"

"I'm sure. He was telling the young people to go to their rooms."

The Regent snorted. "He's always been a killjoy, that one. Can't say the son is any better. But you saw nothing unusual?"

"No, my lord."

Except she had seen a monk talking to Els, a monk who was really a girl. She knew not all the wine served at the banquet was tested because the palace trusted the Guentherite order. But there was no reason to distrust the wine and she truly had no idea about what might have been the poisoned item. But that still didn't mean the poison couldn't have been in the wine.

She knew Lord Verdonck had obtained the dragon box illegally through someone with a key to the crypt that the church was unaware existed or had lost track of. Her father's key was one of those, but it had probably not been her father's key—or had it? How long had Lord Verdonck been in possession of the box?

Did the church know he had stolen it? Nellie didn't think so. He might have used a monk to steal it, someone with a secret key.

All those things Nellie knew, and Madame Sabine, who sat next to her husband looking prim in her green dress, knew a good lot of those things, too, and either the Regent would already know or he would know as soon as his wife told him.

All of which made Nellie wonder: will she say anything? Is she going to talk about the box? Is this just a game?

Sweat broke out all over her body. Her neck was getting sore from keeping her head bent.

Just one word by Madame Sabine, and things would end badly for Nellie.

But Madame Sabine continued to say nothing. She held her hands—with painted fingernails—in her lap, and the fingers of those hands worried at each other.

The Regent asked a few more questions to back up Dora's replies that nothing strange had happened in the kitchens, and then Nellie could leave.

Nellie bowed again, and turned around, finally releasing herself from that uncomfortable position. She walked across the carpet to the door as fast as her wobbling knees would allow.

By the Triune, she had to get out of here.

And she had to do so without raising suspicion. If they were looking for someone who had poisoned a noble guest, and one of the servants disappeared, it was clear this person knew something they weren't willing to share.

And how—*how*—had Nellie got herself into this situation?

What a terrible, terrible, tangled mess.

CHAPTER 24

NELLIE ARRIVED AT the door to the hall as if it were a portal to freedom.

Under the eyes of the servants still waiting to go in, she crossed the foyer and walked around the group to go down the stairs.

"Nellie!" Henrik came after her. "Nellie, are you all right?"

"I'm fine."

"You don't look fine. You look like you've seen a ghost."

"I don't get questioned every day. You may be used to it, but I'm not. Really, I'm fine. A bit shaken, but fine."

But then she noticed Maartje who came running out of the corridor to the bottom of the stairs, her eyes wide.

"Nellie! Your room!" She pointed. "There's a . . . a . . ."

By the Triune, no. The dragon.

Nellie jumped down the stairs and turned into the corridor. She ran into the kitchen to grab a lamp and turned back towards her room. Maartje stood on the stairs, her hands over her mouth, but Henrik followed her. He held his hand on the hilt of his sword. Nellie gestured for him to stay behind her.

She was only halfway to her room before a waft of warm air hit her.

The dragon was already in her room.

Nellie crept along the corridor.

The cupboard door stood open. Towels and aprons lay in a mess on the floor. A hollow atop them was flecked with black cat hairs. That darned kitten had gotten in. Many of the cats in the palace could open doors. This one had learned quickly.

Nellie held up the lamp to light the room.

The dragon lay curled up on the bed.

It had assumed a solid form, and oh my, it had grown so much.

Its head lay along its sinuous body and its tail curled around it. Nellie had never seen its powerful wings as clearly as this, folded up against its body. Previously, the dragon seemed to be able to fly purely through magic.

Its eyes were closed. Its skin colour had deepened to dark red, overlaid with a satin sheen. The nostrils, the bearded protuberances along its chin, its ears and paws and tip of its tail were all much lighter in colour. The nails on its paws were black, curved and needle sharp. Those were the nails that had left scars on Madame Sabine's back and Lord Verdonk's leg.

The kitten lay in the curve of the dragon's neck, fast asleep.

There was a soft sound behind her, and Nellie found herself pushed aside by Henrik's hands. He drew his bow.

"No, no, don't do that! It's a magical creature, you can't kill it like that." If was possible to kill the dragon at all, which she doubted. At least not with an ordinary weapon.

Henrik lowered the bow, but the dragon had woken up and opened an orange eye.

It uncurled itself from the bed.

First it set one forepaw, with its fearsome nails, on the mat next to Nellie's bed, and then the other. The paws were bigger than dinner plates.

Then it added the hind paws. The tail pushed against the far wall, threatening to swipe the books and oil lamp off Nellie's bookshelf.

It moved towards the door. Henrik stepped back into the corridor.

"Look at the cat," Henrik said.

The little kitten sat on the dragon's back, between the folded wings. It showed no signs of panic.

The dragon lowered its head, letting out a low hiss.

"Stand back!" Henrik raised the bow again.

"Don't!" Nellie said. Did he really think a puny weapon like that would make an impression on a dragon?

The dragon turned its head to her. Both orange eyes met hers. It blew out, and Nellie could feel the warmth of its breath.

The dragon looked at her, and she looked at the dragon. It had grown far too large to go back into the box, and there was no way she could subdue it by covering it with an apron.

But why was it here? She had given it freedom.

It *wanted* to come back.

No, *she* wished it to come back. Ultimately, it wasn't her dragon. It belonged in the box, and the box belonged to Prince Bruno. But Prince Bruno had been dead ten years and the poor dragon didn't have a master.

The kitten still sat in princely fashion between the dragon's shoulder blades. It was looking at Nellie, too.

Once, when King Roald was still alive, a wild boar wandered into the palace garden. The guards were all atizz and telling the king not to go outside until they caught and shot it.

But the king said, "I saw it run across the lawn with some of our dogs. Animals know when something is evil and won't go near it. The boar is lost. If we leave it alone, it will eat some dogs' food and then go back to where it came from."

And that was exactly what had happened.

The kitten was not afraid of the dragon. In fact, it seemed to like it. The dragon was also happy being in Nellie's room.

For whatever reason, the dragon had ended up with her. It had taken swipes at the church deacons, Lord Verdonck and Madame Sabine. It had not attacked her even if she had been forceful in getting it back into the box.

Nellie wanted no one else to have it. Not Adalbert Verdonck, the witch Julianna, Madame Sabine, or the Regent. She didn't want the Guentherite monks to have it, or the church. Not while Shepherd Wilfridus ruled the main church.

Nellie had no magic and knew little about it, but this dragon was hers. If Prince Bruno was still alive, she would keep it in custody until she could deliver it to him.

She stepped into the doorway to the room and held out her hand.

"No, come away from the door," Henrik said.

"You don't understand. I have to do this, because so many people want this dragon, and they all want to do ill with it. It has accepted my custody. It's my responsibility to make sure it doesn't fall into the wrong hands."

"Nellie, I don't want anything to happen to you. You're the only reason that a little light shines in the darkness of my life. I never thought I'd find it again after Martha died."

Nellie stared at him, dumbstruck.

He was—what?—two or three years older than her. She wanted to laugh and ask if he didn't think he was too old for declarations of eternal love.

But he was not joking about any of this—that was clear in his expression.

And she was utterly taken by surprise. Yes, he had shown more interest in her recently. She'd had no idea that his wife had died until this afternoon. She had no idea he had even remembered her from back when they lived in the same street. She had no idea that the thing that had stopped them getting together back then was the same thing that ruled the rest of her life: her father.

"Just come away from the door," Henrik said, his voice kind. The lamp lit his face from below.

Nellie took his hand, which was warm and dry. He still held the bow with his other hand, but the dragon didn't seem interested in violent action. If anything, it looked curious. Like mistress Johanna's tree, it was not good or evil until instructed to perform acts of good or evil.

Henrik pulled her out of the room and pulled the door shut before the dragon's snout. "You must run. People will find the dragon here. They will know you were the last servant of the palace to see Lord Verdonck alive. They know you brought him herb tea."

"I had nothing to do with his death. He was already ill."

"I know, but they'll readily believe otherwise. They might even know whose daughter you are and they might draw any kind of conclusions from any of those things. They might think you stole the dragon from the church. Or that you tried to infiltrate the church with evil."

"I did none of that." And what was this about *whose daughter you are?* Her father had been nothing more than a bookkeeper and the only sign of his discontent had been in his "book of thoughts", right? Just what sort of rumours circulated about him?

"You're not at fault, but once they find this creature, they'll recall whatever rumours others tell about your father's knowledge. They'll know they are right and you are wrong about everything. Once people see this dragon, no one will believe you, or think you should be alive."

It was true, and she realised the horror in his words. What could she do? Her home was in the palace. She had nowhere else to go.

"There is an empty warehouse at the east end of the harbour. You can find shelter there."

"I don't want to run. I have nowhere else to go."

"They'll put you in jail. They're looking for excuses not to have to jail monks. You make a much better criminal. They'll tell the Regent you were upset that Lord Verdonck refused to pay you for services and so you poisoned him."

"I did no such thing!"

"Shhh. I know, but that's what they'll say. I've seen this before. When something bad happens, people want someone to blame. They can't blame those in power without endangering themselves, so they'll jump on rumours about ordinary citizens. It happened during the reign of the Fire Wizard, too."

"But . . ."

"Go. I want to see you safe." And as she stared into his face, he bent over and brushed his lips over her forehead. "Go. I'm serious."

"I need to get my warm clothes."

"Be quick."

Her clothes were in the room and there was still a dragon in the room. If she were to leave the palace, she didn't want to leave it behind. People would try to kill it, and they would kill themselves trying. She went into the room, almost hitting the dragon in the nose with the door.

She touched its neck—it was warm and dry—and it made a kind of purring noise.

"Did you teach it to do that?" she asked the kitten.

It only responded with a *meeeeeeww*.

Nellie took her satchel and stuffed handfuls of clothes inside, including her warm knitted jumpers and her jacket and woollen socks. Then the box and her mother's few treasures. The Book of Verses went in as well.

"There she is!" a voice yelled at the bottom of the stairs.

By the Triune, had Maartje warned the other guards?

Nellie tied up the satchel, hung it over her shoulder and went into the corridor. A couple of palace guards had come down the stairs.

"It's all under control!" Henrik yelled at them, but he whispered to her, "Run, Nellie!"

Nellie hurried towards the dark end of the corridor. It led to the laundry and there was a little door that—when it wasn't stuck—gave access to the courtyard, but she had barely entered the laundry when people came in from that direction, too.

"Wait." Henrik caught up with her, holding the lamp in one hand and his bow in the other.

Behind them were the guards who had come down the stairs. In front of them were a couple of stable hands who had come in through the laundry.

The guards exchanged surprised looks with Henrik. "We have to arrest her. She has killed Lord Verdonck. She has the dragon."

"She has not killed the lord, and she deserves a fair hearing."

"I have done nothing!" Nellie called over the top of them. "I looked after Lord Verdonck when he fell ill."

One of the guards said, "That's just old women's ramblings. We have never found anyone who could have slipped him poison. Are you sure you haven't borrowed some of the lord's wine?"

"You're just making that up!" She looked at Henrik. "Tell them the truth. I did nothing."

"Fine, we'll arrest you for contradicting the guard."

The man lunged for Nellie's arm but only got a handful of her sleeve because she quickly withdrew her arm.

She protested. "I want to be heard by the Regent!"

They laughed.

And Nellie couldn't win because Madame Sabine only needed to say one word about stealing Lord Verdonck's possessions.

Another man was now grabbing her arms from behind.

And Henrik . . . he did nothing. He stared, his mouth open in horror, as his colleagues restrained Nellie and dragged her to the stairs.

"Nellie," he mouthed. "No."

"Help me! I've done nothing. Help me!"

He mouthed, "I can't. They'd kill me."

At that moment, there was an almighty crash down the corridor, like the splintering of wood and a hiss of fire. The door to Nellie's room burst into fire and flew outward in pieces.

A clawed paw came out, and then a snout and a head with two fierce orange eyes. A set of pointed ears.

The dragon blew out a breath of smoke.

Several of the guards turned around and drew weapons. But if they didn't burn up in the dragon's breath, their arrows merely glanced off the dragon's head.

The creature came into the corridor. It seemed as if it had grown again as it barely fitted through the door. Its wings trailed on the ground. The kitten still sat between its shoulder blades.

A guard yelled, "Shoot all at the same time. Now!"

A volley of arrows flew through the hallway. The

dragon shook its head as they all glanced off and fell to the floor.

The dragon came closer. A guard threw a dagger which also glanced off. The dragon stepped on it on its way forward. It hissed.

"Run!" a man called.

A few people ran up the stairs. Someone yelled, "Get out of the way, it's down here!"

The guards closed around Nellie. The smell of their sweat drifted on the air.

"Am I dreaming or is there a kitten sitting on its back?" one said.

"It's a black cat. It's evil."

The guard at the front yelled, "After three we charge. One . . . two . . ."

He didn't get to three.

The dragon jumped forwards and pushed the guards aside. They fell and screamed and scrambled up the stairs calling for reinforcements.

The dragon grabbed the collar of Nellie's coat. She couldn't help let out a squeal. "Hey, what are you doing?"

It dragged her through the corridor while the guards were scrambling out of the way. The dragon's feet crunched over bows and arrows they dropped, breaking them as if they were mere sticks.

Then it galloped to the far end, past the stairs, past the door to the kitchen. All Nellie could do was pull her legs out of the way of its claws.

It was going way too fast and the door at the end was shut—

The dragon jumped against the door with both front paws and pushed the door right off its hinges. As a blast of cold air hit Nellie in the face, the dragon jumped out into the night—and never hit the ground in the yard. The giant wings unfolded. It flew right over the back wall of the palace yard, with Nellie holding on for dear life.

The screams of the guards faded in the distance.

Thanks for Reading

Thank you for reading *The Bastard Prince*. Book 2 in the Dragonspeaker Chronicles is called *The Wizard Priest*. Find out more about this book on my website.

ABOUT THE AUTHOR

Patty Jansen lives in Sydney, Australia, where she spends most of her time writing Science Fiction and Fantasy.

Her story *This Peaceful State of War* placed first in the second quarter of the Writers of the Future contest and was published in their 27th anthology. She has also sold fiction to genre magazines such as Analog Science Fiction and Fact, Redstone SF and Aurealis.

Patty has written over twenty novels in both Science Fiction and Fantasy, including the *Icefire Trilogy* and the *Ambassador* series.

pattyjansen.com

BOOKS BY PATTY JANSEN

MORE INFORMATION:
PATTYJANSEN.COM